The Point Between

A Metaphysical Mystery

by M. A. Demers

Egghead
Books

Egghead Books, Canada

Cover photography and design by Michelle A. Demers

Library and Archives Canada Cataloguing in Publication

Demers, M. A., 1964-, author
   The point between : a metaphysical mystery / M.A. Demers.

Issued in print and electronic formats.

ISBN 978-0-9916776-4-1 (paperback).--ISBN 978-0-9916776-5-8 (kindle).--ISBN 978-0-9916776-6-5 (epub)

   I. Title.

PS8605.E562P65 2015   C813'.6   C2015-906137-7
                                      C2015-906138-5

I wish to thank all those who helped me on this project: members of the Whatcom County Sheriff's Office; members of the Investigative Assistance Division, Washington State Patrol; forensic pathologists Dr. Gary Goldfogel and Dr. Charles Lee; Staff Sergeant Lindsey Houghton, Organized Crime Agency of BC; John Aveline for the Latin translation; Warren Tsang for his computer help (both for book details and my aging laptop); and my beta readers Joyce, Evan, Megan, David, Lorraine, Sheila, and Bruce for their excellent feedback and suggestions. Much appreciated.

THIS IS THE STORY OF A MURDER. Sort of. Not the murder part—
that's definitive—just the story part.

You see, at the moment the details are rather sketchy because
Lily Harrington didn't actually witness who killed her, which is
an awkward situation to be in when you were an award-winning,
bestselling crime novelist: Lily always knew before she wrote the first
word who the culprit was. Thus you can imagine her embarrassment
that she should be as baffled as the deputies staring up at her, their
faces awash with that quizzical look one gets when you think you have
seen it all only to find yourself in the presence of an immaculately
dressed and stylishly coiffed middle-aged woman dangling at the
end of a rope, with what can only be described as a perfectly formed
yellow icicle hanging off the tip of her nose.

And, believe me, Lily was just as curious as you are as to what that
peculiar thing was.

"What the hell *is* that?" the taller of the two deputies asked a
middle-aged man who had joined them at Lily's feet, a man she
assumed was the medical examiner for he had the pasty complexion
of one who rarely sees the sun, and the hunched shoulders and deep
facial lines of a man who squints at things most of the day.

"It's her brains," Pasty Man declared.

You're kidding me? Lily thought, horrified.

"Get ouuuuuut," the shorter deputy drawled with a grin.

"Her internal organs have started to decompose and gravity has
drawn brain tissue down through her nasal passages," Pasty Man

explained. "When it hit the air it crystallized. Hence the brain icicle."

"Cool," the two deputies chimed together.

Yeah? Speak for yourself.

"Detective Paul Greene," a man introduced himself to the tall deputy who had remained behind while the other had gone off on a clearly less interesting call: the two men had flipped a coin as to who had to respond and who got to remain with Lily's corpse. The detective had traveled over from Bellingham, a fact Lily deduced from the deputy's earlier phone call and from her knowledge as a long-time resident of Point Roberts. With only two deputies to police this little-known American oddity on the southern tip of the otherwise Canadian peninsula of Tsawwassen, detectives from the Whatcom County Sheriff's Office are called upon to deal with all major crimes in "The Point," such as there are in this sleepy hamlet of sixteen hundred escapists from mainland Washington State.

The detective was altogether unremarkable, forgettable in a crowd of one, not at all like the handsome, virile men of Lily's imagination. He was in his early fifties, Lily guessed, dark haired but balding, with the bulbous nose and florid face of an alcoholic. His average height was diminished by his rotund frame, and his suit was clearly purchased about ten pounds ago. With chubby fingers he fished a handkerchief out of his tight trouser pocket and wiped his nose. If Lily's face were not frozen by rigor he would have seen creases of dismay creep stealthily across her forehead, and her lips purse with disapproval: Lily thought Greene might be no better a detective than his name suggested.

"Deputy David Thornfield," said the lucky one who had stayed behind, firmly shaking Greene's hand. "Thanks for making the trip."

Lily eyed them both. Thornfield had the muscular body and confident stance of a military man, yet he had bent over slightly to grasp his elder colleague's hand. Was this an act of subtle deference to the senior officer's age and rank, or the opposite, that Thornfield had exaggerated their minimal height difference to compensate for his relative youth and lesser status? Lily decided the latter, for the deputy quickly tucked his fingers beneath his armpits as if he were afraid his hands would give him away should they be left unattended. Greene, however, did not seem to notice, or perhaps did not care, an underling's discomfort the least of his concerns.

The detective sniffled loudly and swallowed the results. "Why the hell is it so cold in here? It's seventy degrees outside." His voice was as gruff as his manner, and Lily quickly soured to the sound.

"It's the air-conditioning," Thornfield explained, jutting out his chiseled chin in the direction of the air vents. "Was on full blast when I arrived. I figure she put it on to maintain her dignity."

"Come again?"

Yes, Lily thought, *come again?* She did not feel the cold, but if it *were* freezing in here she felt some comfort that this likely meant she was not in hell.

"You know, keep her body pristine for whoever finds it. As a mystery writer she must know what happens to a dead body in the June heat."

"Hmmh," Greene grunted and wiped his nose again. His handkerchief was made of smooth white cotton and monogrammed in one corner in navy blue thread, the typeface ornamental. The incongruity suggested a gift, likely from a mother who sought to elevate his station, a futile attempt to match his exterior to her romanticized interior image of him.

Thornfield was unable to interpret the grunt, whether it meant the detective agreed or not. The ambiguity was disconcerting. Thornfield was a man who needed to know where he stood at all times; uncertainty threatened his center. He straightened his back and hooked his thumbs over his equipment belt, a gesture meant both to detract from his insecurity and to compensate for it, and which seemed to confirm Lily's earlier assumption. "Anyhow," he added, hopeful he sounded confident, "I thought it best to leave it as is until everyone arrived."

"Good call." Greene stuffed his handkerchief back in his trouser pocket, briefly sucking in his abdomen to make room for his hand. He looked up at Lily, his face curious. "So, this is the mighty Lily Harrington," he declared with feigned admiration, leaning back on worn heels as he looked up. "My wife reads her stuff. Loves all that romantic mystery nonsense."

The man has a wife? Lily thought, incredulous. *Dear God, no wonder she reads my books.*

"The one and only," Thornfield confirmed with a wave of his hand, like a magician introducing his pretty assistant just before he proposes to cut her in half. "Point Roberts' resident celebrity. There's going to be a media frenzy. Thank the Lord we only have the one small inn down here; the press will all have to stay up in Canada." He laughed at the thought.

"Don't kid yourself," Greene snorted. "You watch, people will be renting out rooms in their homes faster than you can say 'cash under the table.' And there's also the RV park. That'll sell out quick."

Thornfield nervously scratched his arm, his mistake eating away at him like psoriasis or a rash of tiny insect bites. "Damn, this is going to be a nightmare."

"Which is why we're going to get her out of here as fast as possible," Greene assured his colleague. And Greene meant it. He was only here because Lily Harrington was famous. Normal procedure would be to treat the death as the obvious suicide it is until and unless the medical examiner concluded otherwise, but by then the cops would be days behind in their investigation and evidence compromised. Those were unfortunate facts best kept from public scrutiny, and the death of someone famous always invited scrutiny. Thus, and only so as to avoid any potential embarrassment for the Sheriff's Office, Harrington would get special treatment. This irritated Greene, but he was a team player and would take this one for the department.

Changing track he asked, "Who found her?"

"The housekeeper, Runa Jonsdottir," Thornfield answered, grateful to be certain of at least that fact. "Comes every Thursday morning at nine to clean and do laundry. Let herself in, saw the missus and ran back out. Called me from her cellphone. Said she was too scared to stay inside to use the house phone."

Well that explains the shout I heard earlier, Lily concluded, wrongly: it would be another two days before she would learn the truth behind the raised voice that awoke her to her new reality.

"Where is she now?"

"At home beside the RV park just up the road. I told her to wait there until you come to question her."

Greene nodded his approval then tilted his head toward Lily. "Any idea why she killed herself?"

Lily's head shot up in alarm. *Killed myself?! I didn't kill myself. What on earth would make you think that? Look at me, Detective. I'm wearing Armani. I had my roots done day before last. And my nails. Who goes to the salon then kills herself?*

"*If* she killed herself," Pasty Man chimed in, pushing his thick John Lennon eyeglasses up his nose. "She seems a bit dressed up for a suicide."

Exactly! How was this not obvious to Greene? Who sent him here? One would assume the Sheriff's Office would have assigned their best detective to Lily, but it seemed they had sent their failure—you know the kind: long in the tooth but so close to retirement that nobody has the heart to fire him. Lily was both insulted by this and fearful of the consequences. She had a mind to call the governor and complain. She glanced over at the phone on the kitchen counter, then up at the rope she was hanging from. *Huh,* was her next thought when she realized that phoning the governor, or anyone else for that matter, was currently not an option.

"Of course, we won't know for certain until the autopsy is complete," Pasty Man continued.

"Fred," Greene said with barely concealed irritation, "why are you in here? You know you're supposed to wait outside until we release the body to you." Fred lowered his head and skulked off. A moment later the slam of the front door was heard.

"Isn't he the medical examiner?" Thornfield asked, scowling.

"Nah," Greene shook his head dismissively. "That's Bag and Dash. Real name's Fred Helder. He's on contract to pick up bodies for the medical examiner if he's too busy to attend in person."

Damn, thought Lily, *Fred had seemed so promising.* That Greene might actually be the best man in the room was a sobering thought.

"Ah, my bad then," Thornfield apologized and ran a hand over his dark crew cut. "When he showed up in the transport van I assumed he was the M.E. and invited him in." He hoped he sounded nonchalant but inwardly he cringed. His errors were adding up; any minute now Greene might dismiss him, which was the *last* thing Thornfield wanted.

"Don't sweat it."

"Couldn't anyway," Thornfield chuckled awkwardly. Greene responded with a blank look. "The air-conditioning," the deputy said, pointing his finger in the air. "Probably explains the brain icicle."

"Brain icicle?"

He pointed to the icicle on Lily's nose. "Fred said it was decomposing brain tissue." Thornfield grimaced, suddenly remembering Fred's true position. "*Are* those her brains?"

Greene scrutinized Lily's face. The same peculiar look she had seen earlier on Thornfield's face now fell across the detective's. "Hell if I know," he shrugged, "but it's definitely a first."

2

GREENE AND THORNFIELD HEARD THE SOUND of footsteps behind them. They turned to see two crime scene investigators, dressed in white forensic "bunny" suits and their arms laden with metal suitcases, walking into the great room. The CSIs glanced up at Lily, hanging from one of the thick cedar trusses that spanned the width of the space. She stared back, and the first thought that came to her mind was how inarguably unflattering their outfits were, especially the puffy surgical hats. It took her back to the time she'd had surgery to fix a deviated septum, broken in a skiing accident the winter before; how her then-teenaged self had refused to put on that silly hat until the very moment she was out of sight of everyone except her medical team, and even then had cringed when her handsome plastic surgeon came in and greeted her. That he was twenty years her senior, married and off market, had done nothing to alleviate her embarrassment.

"Hey, Paul," one of the Forensics officers greeted Greene, interrupting Lily's thoughts. The CSI was taller than the detective, slimmer and better looking even with the bunny suit. If it were not for that humiliating brain icicle—and the inconvenient fact that Lily was currently strung up like a possum—she would probably offer him her phone number.

"Hey, Mick, Kerry," Greene welcomed his colleagues. "This is Deputy David Thornfield, first attending."

"Mick Sheraton," Sheraton introduced himself as he put his cases down.

Thornfield reached out to shake the man's hand. The gesture was not returned. The deputy's hand hung awkwardly in the air for a few seconds before he realized Sheraton's was already gloved and sealed and touching anyone meant contamination. Thornfield felt like a leper, and quickly pulled his hand back to his side.

"And this is Kerry Reeds," Sheraton introduced his partner next, charitably glossing over the deputy's mistake.

"Do you?" Thornfield asked Reeds, a twinkle in his eye.

Reeds' face puckered. Was this doofus seriously flirting with her at a crime scene? She turned the question back on the deputy. "Do I what?"

"Read," Thornfield soldiered on despite the poor reception.

"Ha, ha," Reeds replied with a forced smile. "Why?"

"It might come in handy on this one." Thornfield smiled anxiously: somehow he could not stop putting his foot in it.

Reeds stared blankly at the men. "Vic's a novelist," Greene explained. He paused to let Thornfield's lame joke sink in then returned to business. "Okay, here's the warrant," he announced, pulling out a folded document from his breast pocket. "Colby signed off on it."

"It's freezing in here," Reeds observed, perplexed. "How long has it been like this?"

"Don't know," Thornfield responded. "The air-conditioning was on when I got here."

"Damn," Sheraton complained. "That's going to make time of death difficult."

"I know," Greene lamented, shaking his head wearily and wiping his nose again, the linen's monogrammed corner crushed in his fist. "We're going to have to retrace her movements to the minute."

"I don't understand," Thornfield said. "I thought the cold preserves evidence." He shivered as he spoke, the frigid air finally piercing his thick biceps to reach the bone.

So did I, Lily thought and immediately regretted it: that she might be as clueless as this Thornfield was proving to be was cause for reflection.

"Well, yes," Reeds explained, pouncing on the opportunity to show up the deputy, "but rapid cooling brings the body down to ambient temperature faster. Once that happens, time of death based on body temp is no longer an option. The cold then slows normal insect activity and bacterial decomp, which would have been our fallback data. Bugger us."

Bugger you? Lily thought, staring down at her dangling feet. *I'm the one who's dead.*

"Yes, indeed," Greene said, nodding his head in agreement, "bugger us." He turned to Reeds and Sheraton. "Okay, room's yours to start. I'm going to take Thornfield on a walk through the rest of the house, see if anything looks unusual from a local's perspective. Check in with you later."

The CSIs nodded, opened their cases and got to work. Sheraton found and turned off the air-conditioning while Reeds took out a digital camera and began photographing Lily. The intrusion made her uncomfortable. She was used to being photographed—there had been numerous headshots over her career, photos taken by journalists to complement their coverage, and of course the multitude of selfies taken by fans at public signings—but this was different: not only did Lily look ghastly, but she couldn't control the angle, couldn't put her best side forward, couldn't tilt her head just so to make her eyes the focal point. The lack of command was unnerving. And then there was that wretched icicle. How would she ever live that down? Oh wait, she was dead. Damn.

Annoyance turned into anxiety when Lily saw Greene and Thornfield climbing the stairs to the second floor, headed, she knew, for her private quarters. To her surprise she found she was able to leave her body, briefly glancing at it hanging there before racing up the stairs after the men.

She spied on them as they entered her bedroom, pulled on latex gloves and began opening drawers and closets, invading her privacy as if it no longer mattered to her. She felt the heat rise in her cheeks when Greene opened the goodie drawer in her bedside table and lifted out her vibrator. "Hey, check this out," he smirked as he flipped the switch, "the queen of romantic suspense needs a mechanical boyfriend."

His words filled her with fury. "Well of course I need one," she snapped at him. "Have you *seen* the men my age? Either they're in my social class, in which case they're pompous bores, or they're fellow writers, in which case they're pompous bores who look like *you*." She tried to snatch the device from Greene's hand only to watch her own swipe uselessly through the air. Her impotence was exasperating.

Greene did not respond to her anger, just looked right through Lily as if she were not there. Her invisibility made his disrespect all the more infuriating. To Thornfield's merit he merely smiled awkwardly at the intrusion then quickly averted his gaze, and Lily felt a surge of gratitude for the man whom she had passed on the road on several occasions but, she was now ashamed to admit, had never bothered to address or even to remember his name.

The men found nothing of significance in her bedroom and moved on to the large en suite. Their eyes swept over the bathroom, looking for anomalies. Lily walked around them and sat on the edge of her tub overlooking the sea, and pondered the many wonderful moments she had spent in this porcelain cocoon. It was especially magical at night when she would watch the lights from the ferries as they left the Tsawwassen terminal less than two nautical miles from her window. She would sometimes imagine passengers on board and create stories about them in her head, stories that often became plots in her novels. She did her best writing in the bath.

On the gray marble countertop Greene found Lily's estrogen gel and the antidepressant paroxetine, both prescribed by a doctor in Bellingham but filled at a pharmacy in Blaine. Lily watched as Greene pulled out his cellphone and snapped photos of the medications, then the three moved on to the guest rooms. The bedrooms were clean and showed no signs of any recent use, and the officers quickly abandoned them for the open media room.

The cozy space was dominated by a high-end but modestly sized flatscreen television in front of a large sectional littered with throw cushions and quilted blankets that invited you to put up your feet and find a ball game. Greene briefly gave in to temptation on the pretext of checking the DVD player and PVR for any recent activity; both came up empty. He rifled through the few magazines that sat atop the glass coffee table, before reluctantly rising once again to his feet.

The three moved back down to the main floor and entered Lily's office. It was an expansive room facing west to the strait, its rolling waves visible between two tall trees rising from the cliff side. Late morning sunlight poured in through the large window and bounced off a lower bank of white custom-built storage units. Greene glanced up at a huge panoramic painting of a field of flowers that hung above the built-ins, and smiled unintentionally: something about the relaxed ambition of the flowers, the way they reached for the sky yet bent willingly in the breeze, moved him, though he was not the type to articulate such thoughts.

In the middle of the room sat a reading sofa and lamp. When her eyes fell on the couch, Lily stopped dead. She suddenly had the sensation of falling, the soft give of the red cushions bending beneath her weight. But why the creepy feeling? Lily did not know, and she wasn't certain she wanted to.

She looked over at Thornfield. He was standing in front of the south wall, its floor-to-ceiling bookcase (also white, custom built, with an antique brass ladder to reach the higher shelves) packed with tomes of every kind, his eyes scanning the titles. At eye level, in pride of place, were first-edition hardback copies of Lily's forty-nine novels, arranged in chronological order: *Bitter Revenge, The Haunting of Elside Manor, Mantova's Secret, Mystery at Castle Rock, Rendezvous Under the Moon* …

Thornfield's voice broke the silence. "When you see them all in a row like this, they look kind of …" He paused, searching for the right word.

"Formulaic?" Greene suggested.

"Yeah, that's it. Formulaic."

Lily bristled at the allegation. Sure there was a formula to the genre, but each book, each character and plot, was original, born of her mind and nursed at her bosom. These were her *babies*, each with its own personality. To suggest they were formulaic was like insisting identical twins were incapable of their own uniqueness. She was really starting to dislike this Greene.

"They serve a purpose," he shrugged. "Just like James Bond and Jason Bourne do for us, I suppose."

"Never thought of it that way." Then, failing to censor himself yet again, Thornfield added, "You said your wife reads Harrington's books. What purpose do they serve for her?"

Greene glanced over but did not answer, and the deputy realized he had touched a sore spot. He had done it again, another foot in the mouth. He could almost taste the dusty leather of his combat boot, the dirt on his sole gritty against his teeth. The sensation made him crave a drink, but his canteen was in his cruiser; leaving the scene to retrieve his water bottle would only draw yet more attention to his ineptitude. He was beginning to think he would have been better off responding to the other call and leaving Collins to this.

To Thornfield's relief Greene ignored the impertinent question and instead opted for diversion. "What was Harrington like?"

"I dunno," Thornfield replied truthfully. "This is the first time I've met her, so to speak. I'm told she hobnobbed a bit with the yacht crowd that come in off the islands, played golf with the club's richer members. She'd do a reading at the library whenever she had a new book out, but I haven't been here long enough to attend one. She was known to frequent our few local businesses, and they all have a photo of them with Harrington on display. I saw her once in a while at the Marketplace or getting gas, but like most folks around here that was it: groceries, gas, and golf. She crossed into Canada or went to the mainland for just about everything else."

"What about fans? Paparazzi?"

"Not many. Most of the time outsiders just got a chance encounter if Harrington was out and about, and if they recognized her. We'd get a few drive-bys, but as you can see the property is set well back from the road and shielded by trees. The gate keeps vehicles out. There's a staircase down the cliff to the water but it's too shallow to get a large boat near; you'd have to row in on something smaller like a dingy, or walk across the flats during low tide. I heard a few fans made the trek here when Harrington first bought the property, but quickly realized it was difficult and pointless. And people here look out for each other. If anyone sees someone skulking about, they call it in. There's no record of any previous calls to this address. I've never had a reason to attend in the short time I've been here."

"Which is exactly why I chose this place," Lily confessed as she looked out her office window at an eagle swooping low over the strait. The Point's isolation was often inconvenient but the upside was limited access by strangers: one needed a boat to get here by water, a small plane if by air, and if by land then a passport or an enhanced driver's license to pass through Canada first. And the Canadians, well, they didn't give a damn that Lily was famous. She could walk freely among the aliens and be left alone.

That last part was particularly important to her. The hustle and bustle of New York had been fun in her younger years, but as she aged she began to resent the constant intrusion of the city: the traffic beneath her bedroom window that often kept her awake later than she intended, the constant social invitations that cut into her writing time, the fans who loitered outside her Park Avenue apartment, hoping to meet her. Then the towers had fallen, and Lily traded the lights of the Big Apple for the starry sky and small town life of Point Roberts.

"Good thing I didn't bring the wife, then," Greene said, bringing Lily's thoughts crashing back to the present. "When Harrington first moved to The Point, Ellie begged me to drive her here for a look at the house; I said that was stalking and it wasn't going to happen."

"And I suppose a selfie's out of the question now," Thornfield joked, and laughed. His earlier apprehension had begun to wane: he was connecting again with the detective.

Greene walked over to Lily's desk, a plain but finely crafted double-pedestal mahogany piece that Greene rightly assumed was from the Victorian era, though this was less an educated guess than a fluke: every antique looked Victorian to him. The desk had previously belonged to Lily's father, and she paused to finger the spot on the green leather inlay where the cufflink from his left sleeve had scratched its history into the desk, a hieroglyph that only the Harrington sisters could decipher.

Greene opened the lid of Lily's laptop. To his surprise the computer was on, an open Word document on the screen. He leaned down for a closer look. "Looks like a novel," he said after a moment. "That's odd."

Odd? Lily thought, dismissing the man for yet another perceived inadequacy. *How is that odd? I'm a novelist. Seriously, this is not funny. Somebody get me the governor.*

"Why is that odd?" Thornfield asked. "She was a novelist."

Exactly! Twit.

"Who works on her novel, gets dressed up like she's going out, then hangs herself?"

"A vain but frustrated writer?" Thornfield suggested, chuckling.

Okay, now I'm starting to hate you both.

Greene clicked on Lily's email program. It was opened on a message dated six p.m. Tuesday, sent by Donald Martin at Creative Minds Agency and copied to Jarod Ross at Sellinger Press. It read:

> Lily, darling, are you crazy? You mustn't do this to
> them, to you, to us. I beg you to reconsider. I'm coming
> there. Don't do anything foolish until we talk.

Harrington had not answered the email, but she had read it—or somebody had—and there were later messages, also read, followed by several unopened ones. Greene opened the last read email and checked its file properties. It had been received at 5:03 p.m. on Wednesday and "modified" at 8:38 p.m., indicating this was when the email had been read. Harrington had likely been alive until at least then.

"Hey, Dave," Greene called over to Thornfield, "there's an email here from someone named Donald Martin. Says he was coming out to see Harrington. Did the housekeeper say anything about a guest?"

"No."

"Hmmm," Greene murmured. He stared at the text, his brow furrowed. Had Harrington threatened to kill herself? And who was "them"?

He closed the laptop but left it and the program running; this way CSI would not need to crack her passwords. Beside Lily's laptop sat her cellphone; Greene turned it on but it was password locked. Forensics would have to open it. The detective put the phone back exactly where he found it—Reeds would need to photograph the scene before any evidence was removed—then began looking through the papers on the desk. Within easy reach was a thin red folder; Greene opened it and began perusing its contents.

"What the hell?" he said, thinking aloud.

Curious, Thornfield walked over to the desk to see for himself what Greene was looking at. It was a notebook with pages of Lily's nearly indecipherable handwriting, printed Internet pages on various knot configurations, information on types and widths of sailing rope and their maximum loads, another sheet on the sedative effects of paroxetine, and a Wikipedia entry on hanging. "Jesus," Thornfield said, shocked. "She was researching her suicide."

"No, no, no," Lily insisted aloud as if they could hear her. "It wasn't like that at all."

"That's what it looks like," Greene surmised as he snapped photos of each page.

"Should make this easy then," Thornfield concluded, looking relieved.

The detective shook his head. "It's never easy. Just some are harder than others." He tucked his phone away in his breast pocket then left the office, Thornfield and Lily in tow.

"No, no, no, you have it all wrong," she persisted as she followed the men back into the living room. "You need to listen to me. I did *not* kill myself." She stopped short when she saw Sheraton helping Fred load her tiny frame into a long white bag. It was a truly unsettling image.

Sheraton closed the zipper and the two men lifted Lily up. "She's a wisp of a thing, isn't she?" Fred remarked as they lifted the body onto a stretcher. "I've bagged twelve-year-olds bigger than this." It was the kind of backhanded "compliment" Lily had heard her entire life, and what she whispered next about Bag and Dash was too defamatory to print.

Fred said his goodbyes and wheeled Lily's corpse toward the west patio doors. "You need to follow the body through Canada and down to Bellingham, maintain chain of custody," Greene instructed Thornfield.

"What do I need for the Canadians?"

"Nothing. They know the drill." The deputy headed for the front door. "Hurry back," Greene called out after him. "I'll need you to help with the canvass." Thornfield nodded then disappeared from the house.

Anxious to keep watch over her dignity, Lily followed Fred out the patio doors. As her body was wheeled down the path toward the waiting white transport van, Lily caught sight of a man loitering about her back lawn, the sparkling waters of the strait framing him with light. His broad shoulders were evident beneath a black trench coat, cinched at the waist despite the June heat. Wisps of silky dark hair peeked out beneath an equally unseasonable black wool fedora. His hat was down, shielding his face, but she could feel his eyes on her. Had the media intrusion already begun?

Lily strode over to the man, believing that somehow she could pierce the veil between worlds and give him a piece of her mind. As she approached he looked up at her, his dark-brown bedroom eyes smoldering under the shade of his hat. *Could it be? No, that's impossible!*

"Marcus?" Lily asked, disbelieving her eyes.

"Lily, darling, I came as soon as I heard," the man cooed in a velvety voice. "What compelled you to do such a terrible thing?"

"First of all, I didn't *do* anything," Lily replied, her voice shrill. "I was *murdered*. Secondly, you are a product of my imagination, so clearly I'm imagining this too. And now I'm leaving before this gets any weirder."

She turned to follow her body to the morgue. Fred had already disappeared around the side of the house; he would be leaving any minute now.

"On the contrary, Lily, I'm very real," Marcus called out after her, and she heard in his voice a hint of mockery. "I always have been. That's what imagination is; it's a portal to the other side."

She stopped at the corner of the path and turned back around. "What are you talking about?"

"You didn't create me, Lily. You only gave me form in your world, the words on the page. And now I'm here and I can help you. If you were truly murdered, who better to help you get to the bottom of it than your most successful detective?"

"This is crazy. In fact, I bet this whole 'I'm dead thing' is just me hallucinating. I just need to see Dr. Nelson to get my antidepressants adjusted. I haven't been sleeping well again." She was babbling now, a rising panic inching through her body.

"I can assure you, Lily, I'm not an hallucination. And you are very much dead."

The panic reached her throat. It was all starting to sink in. Her initial anger at the discovery of her death was giving way to despair.

She looked over at the transport van. The bag containing her remains had already been loaded and Fred was shutting the doors.

He got in the driver's seat and started the engine. And now Lily could hear Thornfield starting his. If she really was dead she needed to follow her body, needed to ensure no further insults were heaped upon it, but if she left would she be able to find her way back to the house and to Marcus, to the mystery he had just dumped at her feet?

She looked at Marcus then over at Fred, torn. "Okay," she said, giving in. "I believe you. But if we're going to solve this case together, we'd better get going."

Marcus nodded and the two ran for the van, jumping inside just as Fred started down the gravel drive to the road beyond.

LILY STARED DOWN AT HER BODY BAG. Despair had given way to disappointment. Death was wreaking havoc on her emotions, even more so than menopause. She wondered if they would let her take her estrogen and paroxetine in the afterlife. "This wasn't how I imagined my death," she sighed. "I imagined myself a fabulous, eccentric eighty-year-old in the arms of a much younger man. I wanted the certificate to read 'Death due to orgasm.' But now look at me. It's going to be all over the news that I hanged myself when I absolutely did not. It's not right."

"Don't worry, Lily," Marcus assured her with a kindly squeeze of her hand, "we'll get to the bottom of this. We'll save your reputation."

She looked over at Fred. He was drinking a cola and singing along to country music. So far the journey to the morgue had all the reverence of a barbecue. It was humiliating.

Lily reached out one hand to touch her body bag but found she could not. Not exactly, anyway. She could place her fingers on the plastic, could presume what it felt like from recollections past, but it was as if her hand had overdosed on Novocain. She imagined this was what it was like to be a paraplegic: your legs are there but you could stick a fork in them with impunity.

The sensation was disorientating. Lily surreptitiously touched the skirt of Marcus's trench coat; that she could feel. She wondered if it would be like this forever now, or if there would come a time when she would feel both worlds, would be able to cross back and forth at whim, and sadly thought it unlikely.

They traveled down the two-lane road that ran along the verdant properties of Marine Drive, the lots becoming smaller, more densely populated, and overtly less opulent as one moved south. The trees gave away at the intersection with Gulf Road, creating a vista to the sea. Lily looked out the window and silently cursed: a semi-trailer delivering boxes of alcohol to Kiniski's Reef Tavern was blocking her view.

Fred turned left onto Gulf Road, headed east. Lily said a silent, sad farewell to the yellow-sided Caffé Capanna with its summer patio overlooking the strait. She waved goodbye to the Blue Heron Gallery where she would often buy handcrafted ornaments for her garden, and locally made gifts for friends or family. A few yards later she whispered "ciao" to Brewster's Fine Foods where she would sometimes pick up a whole pan of their roasted vegetable lasagna and eat it for the week along with fresh salad from her garden. They passed the town's beloved tiny library to which Lily had donated a signed copy of every one of her books, not to mention a sizable sum to their fundraising campaign. Another tenth of a mile east and it was a fond adieu to Auntie Pam's Country Store with its popular blue Kool Off Spray that served double duty for Lily: it helped with the hot flashes *and* kept the mosquitoes at bay. She wondered if there were mosquitoes here in the afterlife. And Kool Off Spray.

They came upon the town's tiny post office—which Lily would *not* miss—then Fred reached the intersection with Tyee Drive and turned left again. Lily glanced to her right. The grocery was busy, the two banks less so. With a wistful glance she wished them all well as Fred headed north for the border a mere mile away.

Thornfield followed close behind, careful not to lose sight of the van. If he did so he would mess up the investigation—and with it his own career. He gripped the steering wheel tightly, his nerves wound like a spring that threatened to catapult his body through the roof of his cruiser and into the cloudless sky. He could not—he must not—screw this up. So much depended on it, so much more than anyone realized.

They arrived at the border, such as it was. All that separated the two nations was a narrow ditch along the 49th parallel, a straight line that had been drawn without foresight to conclude the Oregon

Treaty of 1886. That it left the peninsula isolated from the mainland was an unfortunate oversight; and while the British later brought the error to the attention of the Americans, somebody clearly didn't get the memo: Point Roberts remained in U.S. hands and later officially joined the Union as part of Washington State.

Necessity had thus dictated that the border remain an invisible line, the trench treated as nothing more than an extension of Tsawwassen homeowners' backyards. Hedges and fences formed a de facto wall, but in years past, before the war on terror began, gates were practically mandatory, the ditch dotted with small footbridges to facilitate quick trips across to visit friends.

The bridges were gone now, replaced by hidden sensors. There was still no formal fence, just an invisible one created by rulers from on high, and long-time residents on both sides mourned the loss of their once unified community. Everyone still laughed, though, when recalling the post-9/11 gaffe when overzealous federal agents erected new signs warning would-be border jumpers they were illegally entering the United States, but accidentally faced the signs into The Point.

Fred pulled over to the side of the road and waited while Thornfield stopped to lock his gun in the steel box in the trunk of his cruiser. The necessity complete, they crossed Roosevelt Way into Canada. Only two of the four lanes through the tiny Boundary Bay border post were open; Fred went through the expedited NEXUS lane and was waved over to secondary. The deputy followed and parked his cruiser beside the van.

A tall, turbaned man walked out of the Canada Border Services Agency station and joined them. His nametag read "Jaipal."

"Hey, Fred," Jaipal greeted them in a friendly tone, "who you got this time?"

"Lily Harrington," Fred replied, handing Jaipal a form. "Apparent suicide. Doc's waiting for us at the morgue."

"Suicide, huh?" Jaipal said with a wry grin as he scanned the paperwork. "I thought people in The Point only died of old age or boredom."

"No, that's you Canadians," Thornfield tossed back, leaning casually against the side of his cruiser.

Jaipal let out a laugh. "You're new," he said to Thornfield and handed Fred back his form.

"Yeah. Came in three months ago. Name's David Thornfield." He leaned forward to shake the border guard's hand. "Thought I'd met all of you guys, though."

"I was on loan to the Abbotsford crossing for four months. Just got back last week." Jaipal paused, then added, "So, break or ball bust?"

"I don't follow," Thornfield lied, standing straight again.

"The deputies who work down here do so either because they need a break or they're being punished," Jaipal explained, grinning.

Thornfield's face went blank. "Neither. Just wanted the free housing," he replied with a tense smile, and his body language said he was done.

"Okaaaaay," Jaipal said, raising his eyebrows. Then, switching to a more formal tone, he asked, "You carrying, Deputy?"

"Nope," Thornfield said with a deliberate shake of his head. "Locked in the trunk, as required."

"Okay, gentlemen, you're free to go. Have a safe trip."

Fred and Thornfield got back into their respective vehicles and headed out. Jaipal waved at Fred as the convoy drove off, then headed back inside.

"Who died?" another CBSA officer asked.

"Woman named Lily Harrington."

"*Lily Harrington?*"

Jaipal looked nonplussed. "Should I know her?"

"She's the writer, dude. And she's *huge*. What happened to her?"

"Suicide, apparently."

"No shit?" the other officer responded, the wheels in his head turning. He excused himself to go to the bathroom, his cellphone tucked discreetly in his pocket: overtime was not the only way to earn a little extra cash.

The convoy left the border crossing and headed north along 56th Street in Tsawwassen. Lily looked out the window and was struck, as she always was when she drove through here, by the feeling that she had passed not just into a different country but into a different world. The Point was like a national park: five square miles of mostly forested land with a sparse population and even smaller business community; Tsawwassen was densely inhabited suburbia, dotted with strip malls and restaurant chains, schools and recreation centers, tennis clubs and arts centers, an upscale neighborhood with five churches to bless the private academies and family pools. That she was now viewing it from the afterlife made the sensation all the more intense, and somewhat ironic.

Marcus stuck his head through the back door of the van and cast a wary eye on Thornfield behind them. "He didn't take that question well, did he?" Marcus said when Lily joined him.

"No, he did not," she agreed, shaking her head with curiosity and suspicion. What was Thornfield hiding?

"What do you know about this guy?" Marcus asked when they sat back down again inside the van.

Lily glanced out the windshield as Fred merged onto the highway, leaving suburbia behind for the flat farmlands of the district's remains. "Nothing, really. Every time there's a new deputy it's announced on the radio and in the *Bulletin*, but I never met him. He came to the property once, dropped Runa off for work." Lily was sincerely regretting her earlier indifference.

"He dropped Runa off?" Marcus asked. Lily could have sworn she detected a hint of jealousy in his voice but quickly shook it off as her imagination. But then what was it he had said earlier about imagination?

"Well, yes, but that wasn't unusual. Runa has a car but prefers to walk; keeps her costs down that way. It's only a mile to my place, and neighbors regularly offer her a lift if they see her walking on the road, especially during inclement weather."

"Ah, nothing there then," Marcus decided, sounding relieved. "Still, we mustn't rule anything out. We'll need to investigate further."

"Speaking of which, how *do* we investigate? We're dead. Or at least I am. I mean, I'm dead to that world. So how are we supposed to influence something going on there?" Lily frowned: it was all so complicated.

"You have to pierce the veil," Marcus explained, adjusting his fedora as if he were standing in front of a mirror. "How well you manage to do so depends on how determined you are. There are the poltergeists who manage to literally move stuff about, but they're a rare breed. Most of us have to settle for inserting ourselves into people's thoughts. How successful you are at *that* depends not only on your own efforts but on the personality of the recipient. You creative types are among the most susceptible because you tend to have open minds. Children are the easiest to contact but completely unreliable as agents. And no one believes them anyway."

"Is that what you've been doing these past twenty years?" Lily asked. "Inserting yourself into my thoughts?" She suddenly felt invaded, used.

"You sound angry," Marcus replied in a tone that suggested her feelings were inappropriate. "I don't see why. I made you."

Lily's eyes narrowed and her fists clenched involuntarily. "You *made* me?"

Marcus shrugged. "I made you rich. I made you famous. And what did I ever ask for in return? Just another great case to solve and the love of a good woman at the end. Well, maybe not love but at least good sex." He laughed and nudged Lily in the ribs, hoping to lighten the mood. It didn't work.

"You *made* me?" she repeated.

"Lily, please, don't take it so personally. I agree you worked very hard at writing down my stories, and your marketing efforts were excellent, but you have to admit it all starts with a good idea and great characters, and I had both in spades. I *am* both in spades."

"*Your* stories?" she hissed. Lily was starting to feel homicidal, which only confirmed her earlier decision, the one she had made before she was so impolitely interrupted by her killer. "What does that make me? Your *stenographer*?"

"Calm down, woman. You're letting your emotions get the better of you. It's probably just the menopause again."

"That's it!" Lily shrieked and lunged for Marcus's throat. "I'm going to kill you!"

Marcus grabbed her wrists and held her at bay, her tiny frame no match for his strong arms, the strong arms *she gave him*. At least she thought she had.

"For God's sake, Lily, I said calm down. You're missing the big picture. If I can infiltrate your thoughts, you can sneak into Greene's. Don't you see? That's how we'll investigate. We can see stuff he can't.

So we work with him, on him, and hopefully we'll figure out who did this horrible deed. You need to stay focused. Who killed you is far more important now than your books."

Lily crouched back down in the van, subdued. Marcus was right. Finding her killer was more important than arguing the metaphysics of creativity. But when this was all over …

She straightened her dress and repositioned the bra strap that had fallen when she attacked the detective, then left his side to sulk in the passenger seat beside Fred. He was still slurping his cola but the music had changed to Bob Dylan's "Knockin' on Heaven's Door." *How ironic,* Lily thought as she gazed out at a field of blueberry bushes. So far there was nothing heavenly about any of this.

Their arrival in Bellingham was uneventful. The van pulled in at the rear dock, away from public view, and Lily's corpse was unloaded and carted inside like a pallet of produce at the grocer's. She looked to Marcus for emotional support but he was preoccupied, checking his teeth in the van's side mirror.

The medical examiner's office signed for the body, preserving chain of custody. Bag and Dash was thanked for his services and sent on his way. Lily watched with consternation as her body was transferred onto a rolling stainless steel cart and wheeled into the morgue. The M.E. removed a fat black sharpie from his pocket and wrote Lily's name, date of birth and death, and case number on the outside of the body bag. She was expecting the infamous toe tag but apparently that would come later, after she had been sliced and diced.

Dr. Clive Anderson unzipped the body bag and looked down his silver-framed spectacles at Lily's corpse. He was a tall, gangly man whose lab coat hung unevenly off his bony shoulders, sprinkled with flecks of dandruff barely visible against the bleached white fabric. "Hmmm," he murmured more to himself than Thornfield, then added, "Found her hanging, I see."

"Well, technically the housekeeper did, but yeah."

Anderson rolled his eyes at the deputy's semantics. "Was the room where you found her cold?"

"Yeah. Air-conditioning was on full blast."

"Explains the icicle," Anderson murmured again, absentmindedly scratching his white head with the end of the sharpie.

"Oh, hey, yeah," Thornfield said eagerly, "I wanted to ask you about that. Fred said it's her brains."

"It's not her brains," Anderson snorted with another dismissive roll of his eyes. "It's mucus and liquefied fat from the nasal cavity."

"It's a *snotsicle*?" Thornfield's jaw dropped in awe.

"If you must."

God help me, Lily thought, aghast. *I died with a snotsicle hanging off my nose?* Her hand instinctively went to her nostril, and she was relieved to find no snotsicle there.

"Does it tell you anything?" Thornfield asked.

The M.E. looked over the top of his spectacles, his face expressionless. "Yes. She's dead."

"No kidding," Thornfield retorted churlishly, folding his arms across his wide chest.

Anderson straightened his back and looked down his nose at the deputy again, then reluctantly added, "It tells me she died in an upright position and remained that way during initial decomposition. But then that's no surprise seeing as you found her hanging." Anderson zipped up Lily's body bag. "I'll have more for you in a day or two. Won't get to her until tomorrow." He gestured to the partially autopsied corpse lying on a nearby cart. "Tom over there got here first." Anderson wheeled Lily's body over to a large steel door, opened it, and pushed her into the walk-in fridge. Once again she was expecting something different—the individual cold chambers most often seen on television—and realized her research had not kept up with the times. She scowled at the thought.

Thornfield left the morgue and walked across the quiet North State Street to a tavern. "Didn't Greene tell him to hurry back?" Marcus asked, finally breaking the silence that had developed between him and Lily.

"Yes, he did," Lily replied slowly. This Thornfield was either lazy, insubordinate, or keen to delay the investigation. Or maybe just hungry.

As they sprinted across the street behind the deputy, Lily glanced up at Marcus. "You're not six feet tall," she said as if accusing him of a lie. It was payback for the menopause comment.

He shrugged, nonchalant. "I am with my hat on."

"But in my books you're six feet tall in your birthday suit. I *made* you six feet tall," she declared with a self-satisfied smile.

"No," Marcus insisted, "*I* made myself six feet tall. And so what if I did? You're what? Five feet at most? You're practically a dwarf."

"I'm five three and a half," Lily declared, straightening up.

Marcus glanced down at her wedge sandals. "Only with those shoes on," he said dismissively.

Lily tried to think of a snappy comeback but came up empty-handed. Truth is, she disliked being tiny. In elementary school, when her class was lined up from shortest to tallest for the annual pictures, she was always embarrassed to be first. It annoyed her that every piece of adult clothing she bought had to be altered. She was thirty years old before liquor stores stopped carding her. She almost slapped the pimply faced worker at the Coney Island Cyclone who made her stand in front of the "you have to be this tall to ride" sign when she had attended the roller coaster's 70th birthday celebrations. And don't get her started on crowds: as a teenager Lily avoided the mosh pit at rock concerts after nearly suffocating in front of The Clash when they played the Bond Casino in Times Square the summer of her nineteenth birthday, and the phobia remained.

They entered the tavern. It was large but quiet, sparsely occupied despite the arrival of the lunch hour. Thornfield sat away from the others, in a corner booth normally reserved for larger groups. He flirted for a moment with the young waitress before ordering a beef au jus sandwich and fries. Ten minutes later the platter arrived, and as Lily watched the deputy eat she suddenly became aware she did not feel hunger anymore. Curiously, though, what did persist was the memory of food: the taste, the longing food could create, and the satisfaction that often accompanied the first bite. Sitting in a tavern watching Thornfield eat was creating a hole in Lily's stomach that she longed to fill with a handful of fries au jus, but he never offered her any, remained blissfully unaware of his table companions as he chomped on his beef sandwich and washed it down with a nonalcoholic beer.

"Tell me more about this thought invasion process," Lily requested, momentarily looking over at Marcus before turning a hopeful eye back on Thornfield's fries.

"Well," Marcus explained, "you start by concentrating on the thought itself. What do you want the person to think or feel? Then you focus on the person while simultaneously concentrating on the thought. If done right, your thoughts will enter your subject's mind."

"Okay, but how do I know it was really my thought? Take Thornfield here. I think he should order more fries. But if I do as you say and he doesn't order more fries, then my failure is easily documented. But if he does order more fries, how can I be certain that he didn't just have his own independent thought to order more fries?"

"You don't."

"So then how can you be so certain that what you thought were your stories were not mine?"

"Are we back there *again*?" Marcus asked, raising his hands in a gesture of futility.

"It's a legitimate question," Lily argued.

"I am *not* here to debate metaphysics with you," Marcus replied, his voice rising. "I am here to help you find your killer. If you insist on dragging my efforts down with your hurt pride, then I might as well go help someone else."

"Fine. But how do I *know* I am the cause of Thornfield ordering more fries, that it isn't just a happy coincidence?"

"Repetition," Marcus explained, exasperated. "Once or twice is a happy coincidence, more than that and you get to claim some credit."

"Humph," Lily grunted and stared down Thornfield again. "Okay, should I try it?"

"No."

"Why not?"

"Because he doesn't need more fries," Marcus replied in a tone that suggested the answer was obvious. "He needs to get back to Point Roberts and help with the canvass. And he's already overweight."

"Now you're just being unkind."

A few minutes later Thornfield paid the bill and left the tavern. Lily eyed the small paunch he carried on his otherwise muscular body, how the cut and color of his drab green, jumpsuit-style uniform, cinched at the waist by his belt, drew attention to the developing bulge and enhanced it a bit, and concluded that Marcus had been right: Thornfield did not need more fries. Still, the comment *had* been unkind. Lily wondered if she was at all responsible for that, or if the detective's surliness was all his own.

They piled into the cruiser again. As the trio drove back to The Point, Lily leaned forward and eyed Thornfield intently, wondering what it was that had brought him to Point Roberts for reasons other than free housing. She had only been staring for a few moments when the deputy began twitching in his seat and rubbing the back of his neck. He looked nervously in the rearview mirror but saw nothing. Lily sat back, amazed. She had only meant to scrutinize him, had not intentionally tried to pierce the veil, and yet Thornfield had definitely felt her presence. This happy discovery resulted in the first bit of elation Lily had felt all day—had felt in a long time, actually, now that she thought about it. When had writing stopped giving her the same joy?

Greene sat in Lily's great room, in one of a pair of brass-studded leather chairs the color of chestnuts, and looked up at the raw cedar beam she had been hanging from. The detective was perplexed. So far there was nothing found to indicate foul play: no forced entry anywhere, no signs of a struggle. The place was immaculate. The bank of windows to the west was as pristine as the million-dollar view. Not a mark blemished the white walls that reflected the light and provided a neutral backdrop to a triptych of large red paintings that graced the north wall. At his feet, a plush wool area carpet, beige in color, sat undisturbed atop the unmarked hardwood floors and beneath a large cream sectional that lay directly opposite the leather chair Greene sat in, his body at a right angle to a massive fireplace on the south wall. His eyes wandered in that direction. Both the large Inuit stone carving that graced the mantle, and the abstract metal artwork that hung above it, failed to elicit any emotion from him. He liked the red paintings, though, even if they were too abstract for his usual taste.

In the kitchen behind him an empty bottle of red wine in the recycling bin and a single used glass in the dishwasher seemed innocuous enough, as were the contents of the victim's garbage: a Calorie-Wise chicken and broccoli fettuccine box sat atop an empty packet of pre-made balsamic vinaigrette, and in the attached organics waste bin the shriveled rind of a Chinese mandarin orange stuck to the remnants of pasta long since dried. Beneath that were carrot peelings, the skin of an avocado, bits of green onion, and lettuce clippings.

A walk around the Harrington property had also brought up nothing of consequence. The cedar gazebo that looked out over the water lay empty of debris or anything else to suggest there had been any recent visitors. A walk down the staircase through the scrub and fir trees of the cliff side served up nothing more than a handful of wild blackberries. Back up top, a hybrid car sat recharging in an otherwise empty double garage; nothing seemed amiss in the large gardening shed. The vast lawn had been freshly cut, the flowers on the patio watered. The small vegetable garden had been meticulously weeded. It was likely Harrington also employed a gardener; Greene had made a note to look into this.

He glanced down at his watch, the second hand moving interminably slow, as if time were partially suspended in The Point. What the hell was taking Thornfield so long? Greene hoped to God the deputy hadn't screwed up following the body. How hard could it be to follow a van? On the mainland it was Greene's habit to maintain chain of custody himself, believed in the maxim that if you want something done right you should do it yourself. But out here on this spit of land that would float out to sea if it weren't attached to Canada, one's options were limited. He had no choice but to utilize local law enforcement, even if it meant dealing with the likes of David Thornfield. The man had been jumpy from the onset, his hand clammy when he had greeted the detective. No doubt uncomfortable with a dead body. Lots of cops were; most were just better at hiding it.

Greene was just about to call Thornfield when the deputy returned, Marcus and Lily in tow. "Why the delay?" Greene asked. "Was there a problem at the border?"

"No. Just my blood sugar. Had to get a bit of lunch."

Greene looked annoyed but did not berate the deputy. *Probably just whine to the union*, Greene thought as he strained to pull himself up and out of the chair.

"Besides," Thornfield added, his hands resting defensively on his hips, "it looks pretty open and shut to me. Lady committed suicide. Hardly the first writer to do that. These creative types, they all live on the edge."

Greene scowled. "I'm not so sure. It's all so normal, so unremarkable. This doesn't strike me as the home of a woman depressed enough to kill herself."

"Why, thank you," Lily said, truly appreciative. She stood a bit taller and straightened her dress.

"You know he can't hear you, right?" Marcus said sarcastically, his hands buried in his coat pockets.

Lily ignored him, choosing instead to relish the compliment even if it had been unintended and not consciously directed at her. She was dead now, she reckoned, and future compliments were probably going to be few and far between.

"What about the paroxetine?" Thornfield argued. He did not like being wrong. "Obviously she was depressed or she wouldn't have been taking it."

"I was *not* depressed," Lily said indignantly. "It was just for night sweats."

Greene dismissed the idea with a shake of his head. "The dose is only ten milligrams and a quick count of her pills suggests she wasn't abusing her medication." He paused, his forehead wrinkled. "But you know what's really bugging me? The lack of a suicide note. What writer fails to have the last word?"

Marcus swallowed a laugh but not well enough to evade Lily's attention. "I do *not* always have to have the last word," she insisted, crossing her arms.

"Maybe she typed it out but didn't print it. It could be on her computer," Thornfield suggested, subconsciously scratching his chest.

"Hmmm," Greene replied. "Possible. But in the meantime we need to talk to this Runa woman and then canvass the neighbors. Sheraton and Reeds should be done soon."

"I agree," Lily concluded as they all headed out. This time Marcus didn't bother to stifle his laugh. "What?" she confronted him in the second before the irony struck her. "Oh, shut up."

"I didn't say anything."

"But you were thinking it."

"So now you're clairvoyant?"

"No need: your face is an open b—"

Suddenly the front door burst open and in rushed a short and slightly built older man. Thornfield reacted first, grabbing the man and pushing him back out the door. "You can't come in here," the deputy barked, "it's a crime scene."

The man flailed frantically against Thornfield's grasp and wailed in falsetto, "Liiiiilllllyyyyyy. Let me see her. Liiiiilllllyyyyyy." He managed to squirm free but only for a second before Thornfield recovered, pinning the hysteric against the railing. "Stop it! Now! Or I'll arrest you for disobeying a peace officer."

The man slumped over the railing and began to cry. "Why, Lily, why?"

Lily stood in the doorway and watched Donald Martin sobbing like a baby on her porch. His anguish was making her uncomfortable, and the fact that she felt discomfort rather than empathy was doubly unnerving. She squirmed in her skin, trying to ascertain what it was exactly that was making her feel this way, when Marcus interrupted her thoughts. "Who's this?" he asked.

"My agent," Lily answered matter-of-factly. And then she understood her discomfort: she was not sure if she should be touched by Donald's anguish—or suspicious of it.

"WHAT HAPPENED?" DONALD MARTIN PLEADED with the police officers staring intently down at him. He was seated in the cushioned wicker settee on Lily's porch and sipping a glass of cold water Greene had fetched from her kitchen. The veins on Martin's temples pulsed behind wisps of wiry gray hair, and his prominent Adam's apple bobbed erratically in his thin neck. "She's hurt, isn't she?" he demanded in a nasal voice, its repellant sound exacerbated by the whiny tone of his queries. "I know, I can feel it. We were so close. We were like family."

"Oh please," Lily scoffed, "you were a necessary evil, a parasite. I was your host."

The accusation was not entirely fair. Donald Martin had been with Lily since her first book, had adroitly navigated her through the treacherous waters of publishing, had protected her interests when no one else would. He had guided her to success, and for that she would always be grateful. But his mentorship and protection had come at a cost, and not just the fifteen percent of Lily's income she paid him. No, it had come at a creative cost: he had helped shape the Lily Harrington brand, and when the brand became wildly successful Donald Martin became more interested in maintaining the brand than in helping Lily grow as a writer. And she hated him for it. Hated him for subtly steering her back to Marcus Mantova whenever she talked of retiring the detective, hated Martin for discouraging her from working on something more substantial, more literary. While she hid her jealousy of the great novelists of her generation and secretly coveted a Pulitzer, Donald Martin secretly coveted a second vacation property. And so he had feigned approval and encouragement of her literary efforts only until the new work threatened the delay of the next Mantova mystery. Fearful a late delivery would jeopardize the down payment on the townhouse in the Bahamas, Martin had turned on the psychological manipulation. When that failed he got on a plane.

"Who are you?" Greene asked, sizing up the little man. "And why are you here?"

"I'm Donald Martin, Lily's agent," he answered indignantly, as if that fact should be obvious or the agent as famous as his client. His indignation made him momentarily forget his concerns and reminded him of his irritation that Lily was refusing to answer when summoned. "We had a meeting scheduled for this morning but she didn't show up and she isn't answering her phone. So I took a taxi here. He let me out at the gate."

"When did you last see Harrington?"

"Yesterday. Now tell me what's happened," Martin insisted, gripping the water glass. His fingers were taut around the tumbler, partly due to anxiety and partly because the glass was now covered in condensation and he feared he would drop it. He nervously wiped one hand on his dress pants, thin streaks briefly dulling the sheen. "Where's Lily? Is she in hospital? Who hurt her? You must tell me. We were like—"

"Family," Thornfield interjected. "Yeah, we got that."

Lily let out a chortle but Greene was not amused. He flashed a warning look at Thornfield then turned back to the agent. "She's in a safe place, Mr. Martin," Greene said, his words deliberately opaque, "but there was some trouble here last night. Can you please tell me about your movements yesterday."

Martin's shoulders relaxed with a sigh. "Oh, I'm so glad she's all right. You had me worried there for a moment. I feel so foolish now for the way I acted." He looked at Thornfield. "My apologies."

"No problem," he replied then went quiet, not wishing to incur Greene's wrath again.

Martin took another anxious sip of water and looked to the detective for validation, but he merely smiled weakly and looked expectant. "Your movements, sir?" Greene reiterated, taking out his notebook.

"Yes, yes, of course." Martin wiped his other hand on his pants. "I took an early flight from La Guardia, flew into Vancouver via Toronto. I arrived about noon. Lily met me for lunch at the airport hotel—"

"What time?" Greene interjected.

"One o'clock. We parted company at about four. I then took meetings with two aspiring writers at the hotel bar."

"I'll need their names and contact information."

"Cynthia Christenson lives in Vancouver and writes romance. Randy Markham lives in Seattle and writes noir. Very talented writers," Martin said, smiling awkwardly. He knew any display of pride was inappropriate at the moment and yet he could not help himself: he did not become one of New York's premier literary agents by being modest. He fished out his cellphone to get the writers' contact information. "They've been hounding me for months," he smiled again as he scrolled through his phone. "And I figured since I flew all the way here I might as well kill two birds with one stone and meet with them."

"And did you kill two birds with one stone," Lily asked suspiciously, "or just me?" She subconsciously folded her arms protectively across her torso and glared at her agent.

"Where and when were you supposed to meet Harrington today?" Greene continued, unimpressed.

"I was supposed to take the red-eye back to New York last night, but we weren't able to conclude our business yesterday so I changed my plans. We agreed to meet for breakfast at my hotel at nine o'clock. When Lily didn't show I started calling her but there hasn't been any answer. So I've come here to see what's going on."

"Why do you think she's avoiding you?" Greene asked, hoping to bait the man.

"She isn't *avoiding* me," Martin retorted, straightening his back. "Lily doesn't *avoid* me. I am an integral part of her team." He took a sip of water and pouted.

Greene made a mental note of Martin's churlishness: indignation was often a sign of guilt. "And what was your business with Harrington yesterday?"

"Just the usual agent–client stuff. Lily's behind schedule and needs the personal touch. That's often my job, gentlemen. Writers can be very insecure; they often need some fatherly guidance and encouragement," Martin declared with a self-satisfied smile.

"Why you arrogant little worm," Lily spit at him, "that was *not* what our meeting was about!"

"Then what was it about?" Marcus asked.

"None of your business. What I discuss with my agent is confidential."

"How long have you represented Lily Harrington?" Greene asked.

"Over twenty years," Martin beamed, his pride seeping through again. "Been with her since the beginning. This next book will be our fiftieth together."

A look of curiosity crossed the detective's face. The comment had sparked a memory, something his wife had said about Harrington. "There's something planned for that, yes? Something big?"

Martin's face lit up and he waved his free hand in the air like an excited schoolgirl. "Oh God yes. It's going to be huge. *Huge.* The fiftieth book in the Mantova mystery series will be a significant milestone. There are compendiums being released this year, another TV movie for this Christmas, big press tour, the works. A lot of money and energy has been spent. It's very important that Lily deliver. Please tell me again she's all right."

"See what I mean?" Lily seethed and took a menacing step toward Martin. "You only care if I'm able to deliver. I trusted you to look out for my interests and instead you're just looking out for yours. And you're nothing like my father!" Indeed, Lily's father had been a quiet, unassuming man, a well-respected chartered accountant who worked long hours in his darkly paneled office at the rear of the family's stately Connecticut home, the only sounds the crackle of the fire and the chugging of his Sharp calculator. He allowed his daughters access to his inner sanctum so long as they were quiet, rewarding them later with an inspired reading of *Wind in the Willows* or perhaps a spirited game of Monopoly. He had died young, only 54, from an aneurism no one saw coming, least of all him: slumped over his desk, the fingers of his right hand still on the calculator, his eyes frozen wide with surprise. Lily had been the one to find him, and for days afterwards she wondered if the surprise was from his death or what he saw beyond it. And then she couldn't determine if it had been a look of joy or horror: the shock of discovering nothing, or something worse than nothing. And now she was here, and she wondered what, if anything, people would find in her eyes, and if they would see her killer reflected there.

"Is that why you're here?" Greene continued quizzing Martin. "Is that why you sent that email to her day before last? Is Harrington failing to deliver?"

Martin looked taken aback by the revelation that Greene had read Lily's email, but quickly recovered. "Not failing, Detective, *refusing*."

"Come again?"

Martin shook his head sadly and loosened the knot on his silk tie. "Lily is holding her publisher hostage. She's written another book, a literary novel, and wants it published. They've agreed to do so but only under a pseudonym; they don't want to risk damage to her reputation if the book bombs. But Lily wants it published under her own name and she won't back down."

"Damn straight I do! I worked hard to earn my reputation; it's *mine* to risk, not yours, not Sellinger's."

"So what happened?" Thornfield butted in, more interested in this new development than he was in continuing to observe protocol. Greene flashed him a dirty look that said *Stay out of my interview.*

"Lily gave Sellinger and Sentient Media—that's Sellinger's parent company—two options," Martin explained, shifting his weight from one buttock to the other. "One, publish her new book under her real name and she will finish the Mantova book, do the press junkets, promote the movie, and all with a smile on her face; or two, refuse to publish her book and she will kill off the detective."

Marcus's jaw dropped. He turned an accusing eye on Lily. "You were going to *kill* me? You witch!"

"Oh shut up, Marcus," Lily retorted, raising her hands in supplication. "Do you have any idea how *boring* you've become? Fifty books. Fifty! How many do you need? How insatiable is your ego?"

"But if Harrington wants to write a different kind of book," Greene continued, oblivious to the argument taking place on the other side of the divide, "it seems to me that either way she's done with the Mantova series. Right?"

Marcus's eyes bored into Lily's. "Is he right?"

"Yes!" she exclaimed. "I admit it. Yes, yes, yes. I'm sick to death of these books. I was done with you thirty books ago. It was fun at first, the affirmation was intoxicating, but it stopped being fun when you stopped being a character and became a brand. When *I* became a brand. I'm an *artist*, not a cola."

"An artist?" Marcus scoffed with a long roll of his eyes. "You're not an artist, Lily, you're a hack. And you were willing to lose it all over the delusion you could write literary fiction? Maybe you *are* insane. Maybe you really *did* kill yourself. What happened? Did Donald tell you your book stinks? Did the truth send you over the edge?"

The color drained from Lily's face until she looked as white as her corpse in the fridge back in Bellingham. "I ... I ...," she struggled to reply. She burst into tears, turned on her cork wedge heels and fled into the house.

Marcus did not follow her. He remained where he stood, angry and eager to hear the rest of Lily's diabolical plot to kill him off.

"Yes," Donald Martin answered solemnly. "She said fifty is enough, and it's a nice round number to end the series on. She believes she still has enough writing years left in her to build a new career as a literary novelist. She certainly has the money to."

"But does she have the talent?" Greene asked.

Martin sighed and shook his head, his eyes downcast. He set the water glass aside and said, "That one's harder to answer. The book is good. She's not Harper Lee but it's good for a first crack at something more complex. Maybe with a bit more work it could be great."

"So why not just give her what she wants? Why all the drama?"

Martin sighed again and waved his hands in a gesture of futility. "Because, Detective, it's not as simple as that. Consumers have expectations, and literary critics hate genre writers. Her existing fan base will not likely move with her; she'll have to start all over again, earning the loyalty of a new demographic. Meanwhile the critics will be chomping at the bit to tear her down, to let her know that a writer who got rich off romance and mystery isn't welcome in their rarefied world. And she'll have to change publishers—not leave Sentient Media, but they will have to send her to a different imprint of theirs, and a different editor. It's like starting from scratch. It makes sense to publish under a pseudonym; that way, if the book fails, Lily can go back to writing mysteries and no harm done. But if she damages her name she risks losing the respect and loyalty of her readers, devaluing her entire catalog. But she just won't listen. She's making demands and holding everyone hostage, people who have already spent a great deal of money promoting this fiftieth book."

The agent's claims brought Greene some welcome relief, and renewed his hope this was indeed the suicide it appeared to be. Harrington had clearly been unbalanced, had taken her life over artistic frustrations. There was a noticeable lift in Greene's voice when next he asked, "Did anything specific happen on Tuesday to make you send that email?"

Martin nodded. "We argued. Lily said the publisher's time was up, that she'd had enough of their stalling. She had the manner of Mantova's death all worked out in her head, even recited it to me over the phone. It wasn't just a threat anymore; she was going to do it."

"How?"

"He was going to hang himself with sailing rope."

Greene's eyes widened and he began to smile—but only for a second. He quickly recovered to hide his surprise and keep his voice neutral. "Who knew these details?"

"Me, of course. I told Jarod Ross, Lily's editor. He may have told his bosses; I don't know."

"Anyone else?"

"Not that I'm aware of. Lily keeps works-in-progress very quiet: leaks infuriate her."

"What happens if she's unable to finish the book. Not unwilling, unable?"

"I knew it!" Martin exclaimed, his words laced with accusation. "Something terrible has happened to Lily. Tell me. I have a right to know." His anxiety had raised his already unpleasant voice an octave, and Greene decided he would rather tell the man the unfortunate truth than listen to him any longer.

"Okay, but you have to understand that nothing can be made public until we notify next of kin." Martin's face went white: he knew what was coming next. "Lily Harrington was found deceased in her home this morning. I can't go into the details of her death, but suffice it to say that we're only here because of her status in the community, not because foul play is suspected."

Donald Martin's hands began to tremble. He grasped his legs to steady his tremors. He looked down, his eyes darting to and fro as he tried to comprehend how this could have happened. Greene gave the man a minute to grasp the situation then reiterated the question: "What happens if Harrington is unable to finish the book?"

His hands still shaking, Martin removed his gold-rimmed glasses—designer, ten karat, naturally—and wiped the sweat from his eyelids. He took another moment to collect himself, then quietly answered, "Under the terms of Lily's contract, the publisher has the right to hire a ghostwriter to finish any manuscript for which Lily has received an advance."

Ah crap, Greene thought, and his recent optimism sank as quickly as it had arisen. "So they have an invested interest in seeing her dead?"

Martin's head shot up. "No! Lily is the golden goose. Her sales pay the salaries of at least half a dozen employees. Her death will be like losing one of their own limbs." He cast an accusing eye on Greene. "Besides, I thought you said foul play is not suspected."

"It isn't. But we have to proceed as if it is until we know otherwise," Greene explained, then carried on with his questioning. "So, back to business. Harrington was retiring the goose. And risking sales. Seems to me her publisher has more to gain if they finish the book their way. And don't a writer's books become more popular when she dies?"

Martin reluctantly nodded. "Everything you say is true, but I can't imagine anyone at Sellinger doing anything to hurt Lily. These are people who love books, who love writers."

"Maybe not Sellinger. But what about Sentient? They're a mega-corporation. I doubt they care at all about Harrington as a person. She's probably just a line in their shareholders' report."

Martin pondered this for a moment. "I can't answer that. I have no idea. They can be ruthless businessmen, that's for certain, but murder? Would they go that far? I don't know."

"And what about you?" Greene pressed on. "If Harrington didn't deliver, she had to return the advance, correct?"

"Not exactly. She only had to return the advance if she *refused* to deliver, but not if she was unable to because of illness or death." Martin's face paled. He knew exactly how that sounded and he now wished to God he had never said a word. His eyes darted to the road as if he were plotting his escape.

"But what happens now that she's dead? What happens if the publisher finishes the book themselves? Do you get paid?"

"Well, y-yes," Martin stammered. "But I wouldn't kill her over it."

"But you stood to gain financially if she died. Am I right?" Greene persisted.

"Well, y-yes," Martin stammered again.

"And what about future sales?"

"Lily's heirs will own her copyright for the next seventy years. They'll receive the income."

"And will you continue to receive a percentage?"

"Yes."

"So your interests are aligned with the publisher's." Greene's aggravation was building: all he was getting from Donald Martin was motive and more suspects, and the detective wanted neither.

"I don't think that's a fair interpretation," Martin whined.

"Why's that?"

"My job is to protect Lily, to protect her career. Sometimes writers need to be protected from themselves. They like to think it's all about art when it's a business. If you want to write for ten people then vanity publish." He raised his chin as he said this, his contempt obvious.

Greene's tone turned authoritative. "Donald Martin, can you account for your whereabouts last evening and through the night?"

Martin understood the change in tone. "I finished my meetings with the writers at seven o'clock," he huffed. "I ate dinner in the hotel restaurant and then went to my room. You can check with them. I'm certain they have security cameras all over the place. And I don't like what you're insinuating. I would never harm Lily. I loved Lily. We were like—"

"Family," Greene interjected. "So you keep saying. Do you know most murders are committed by a close relative or loved one?"

The agent stood up, his expression hostile. "I'm done answering your questions," he announced. "I'm going back to New York. You can contact my attorney if you want to know anything more. His name is Syd Leventhal of Leventhal, King and Associates."

Martin stomped off but only got a few steps down the drive when he turned back around. "Um, do you know how I might get a taxi around here?"

The two officers gave Martin sour looks and shrugs. Point Roberts did indeed have a small taxi service, but he would have to figure it out for himself. "Fine," he pouted, "I'll ask at the golf course." And with that Donald Martin headed down Lily's driveway, his designer loafers kicking up dust behind him.

WITH NOTHING MORE TO LEARN OUTSIDE, Marcus went in the house to check on Lily. He found her on the sofa, weeping in the arms of a woman. She was in her midthirties, tall, with shoulder-length blonde hair framing an attractive face unfettered by makeup. Her Amazon figure was quietly clothed in flat-panel black trousers and a crisp long-sleeved white shirt buttoned all the way up save for the top, revealing a triangle of flawless flesh at the base of her long neck. She was a perfect specimen of female beauty—except for the half-inch hole right in the middle of her forehead.

The woman looked up when Marcus entered the room, and their eyes hardened at the sight of each other. "Penelope? What the hell are you doing here?" he demanded, not bothering to hide his contempt. Or what he hoped looked like contempt. He was not fooling anyone, least of all Penelope Winters, his great love, the one who got away and took a sizeable chunk of Marcus's heart with her.

"You snake," she sneered as she rose to confront him. "Is there no depth to how low you will sink just to maintain the upper hand?"

Marcus straightened his back in an attempt to meet Penelope eye to eye. It was pointless: he was still three inches shy of her five-eleven frame, *and* she was wearing one-inch-heeled boots. That was not playing fair. But when did Penelope Winters ever play fair with Marcus Mantova? "I have no idea what you're talking about," he lied. He raised his chin to add more height, and was grateful he still had his hat on.

"A *hack? Delusional? Your* stories? You were *nothing* before Lily took you in, Joe. And right now you'd better apologize to her—or else!" Penelope crossed her arms and tapped one foot on the floor, counting down the seconds.

"Joe?" a voice said from behind Penelope. They both looked over. Lily's tears had dried and she was sitting up straight, listening, her face riddled with confusion. "Why are you calling him Joe?"

Penelope smirked and jerked a thumb in Marcus's direction. "Lily Harrington, meet Joseph Esposito, unemployed actor and all-around asshole. At least until you took him in. Well, the unemployed part anyway. He's still an asshole."

"I-I don't understand," Lily said, bewildered.

"There's nothing *to* understand," Marcus insisted. "You needed a detective and I rose to the challenge. I had the credentials—"

"Credentials?!" Penelope interjected. "You played a detective for one season on cable TV. That hardly made you qualified."

The hackles on Marcus's neck stood up. "You're just jealous that I was able to achieve in Lily's books what you couldn't in real life," he retorted and tightened the belt on his trench coat.

"For your information I had an eighty percent closure rate," Penelope argued back. "I would hardly call that a failure. *And* I was headed for promotion. I would have been the first female head of Homicide if this"—she pointed to the hole in her head—"hadn't happened."

"What did happen?" Lily asked, choosing to remain on the couch, out of the line of direct fire.

"Got caught in an ambush," Penelope answered matter-of-factly, momentarily forgetting her anger. "Never even had a chance to draw my weapon. Just—pow!—and next thing I knew I was here."

"How do you two know each other?"

"Yes, Penelope, tell Lily how we know each other," Marcus said in a snarky tone. "Then tell *me* who's the asshole."

A thin veil of guilt clouded Penelope's face. "I … well, you see, Lily, it was like this. When I got here I was really confused, and Joe … he was there, you know what I mean? He knew the ropes and he was handsome, so I did him. But I caught on quickly enough and the sex wasn't that great, so I moved on."

"Not that great?!" Marcus spit at Penelope. "I was—*I am*— amazing in bed. You're the frigid witch who lay there like a limp slab of warm cheese."

"Okay, now you're just mixing your metaphors," Lily said.

"I wasn't frigid," Penelope struck back. "I was *bored!*"

"What *is* it with you two calling me boring?!" Marcus exclaimed, his open hands furiously jabbing at the air. "I am *never* boring. I am *exciting.* Millions of women around the world fantasize about me every day. Women do not fantasize about boring men."

"You are not exciting," Penelope said, a look of incredulity on her face. "You are a womanizing narcissist who appeals to Harrington's readers for reasons it would take a whole psychology degree to unravel." She looked over at Lily. "Never date an actor."

"I appealed to *you*," Marcus said smugly. "What was your excuse, if I'm such a narcissist?"

"A trauma-induced critical lapse in judgment," Penelope shot back.

"Recant, you witch, or else I'll—"

"You'll what?" Penelope mocked him. "Kill me? Newsflash"—she pointed again to the hole in her forehead—"somebody beat you to it."

Lily quietly rose from the couch in search of respite. Listening to ex-lovers bicker was more than she could bear. It was *all* more than she could bear. In less than a day she had been murdered, found with a snotsicle hanging off her nose, driven by a social misfit to the morgue, slandered by her agent, and now the great Marcus Mantova, detective *extraordinaire*, a man she had thought a product of her wonderful imagination, was actually a manipulative actor who existed in this strange place she now found herself in.

And what is this place, anyway? It certainly is not heaven, and it too closely resembles ordinary life to be hell. Or is that the message? That ordinary life *is* hell? No, Lily thought next, life is too full of wonderful moments and surprises to be hell. Life is not easy, but it is not hell. So then what is this place? And how do you get out of here?

She went into her office. Reeds was dusting the laptop for prints. Sheraton was cutting a hole out of the carpet beneath the desk. The sight of the CSI taking a sharp knife to a hand-knotted Persian silk left Lily needing a drink, and she headed for the kitchen in the hope of a glass of wine.

In the pantry she found a 2010 bottle of French Merlot, only to realize she had no way to open it and, even if she could, probably could not drink it. The thought made her doubly melancholic, so she moved to the window and gazed despondently out at her beloved garden.

Point Roberts' only other resident deputy, the one Lily had seen earlier in the day with Thornfield, had returned bearing coffee and was chatting with him and Greene. Lily couldn't hear them over the noise of Penelope and Marcus still lobbing barbs at each other. She glanced over her shoulder at them, then walked through the window and onto the porch.

Collins had been summoned to stand guard at the base of the stairs: no one could afford another blunder like the entrance of Donald Martin. "Your relief should be here soon enough," Greene was instructing the deputy. "I've asked for two men, round the clock, at least until we notify the sister and she arranges for private security. We can't risk anything being pilfered from the home by fans or opportunists. That happens and the press will crucify us."

"Where you headed now?" Collins asked.

"To interview the housekeeper," Greene answered, then he and Thornfield headed for his cruiser. "And thanks again for the coffee," the detective added, raising his cup in salute.

Lily looked over her shoulder at the house, wondering if she should get Marcus, then decided she did not want his company. "You two stay here and keep squabbling," she said as if he and Penelope could hear her. "Me, I'm going with them."

She jumped into Thornfield's cruiser as he started the engine. The men did not look back as they left, and neither did Lily.

RUNA JONSDOTTIR WIPED HER TEARS AWAY with an unsteady hand. "I-I," she stuttered and sniffled, "came to the house at nine o'clock as usual. It was f-freezin'. I went to the livin' room t-to turn off the air-conditionin' 'n—" Runa burst into tears, unable to finish.

"And that's when you saw her?" Greene asked sympathetically and pushed a box of Kleenex across the table. Runa nodded and covered her face with a tissue.

The two were seated at the small pine table in her rented single-wide mobile home on Park Lane just west of Sunny Side RV Park, south of Lily's Marine Drive house. Their respective abodes were only about a mile apart yet the two women lived in completely different worlds: Lily's home was large and expensively decorated; Runa's was tiny and haphazardly furnished with bits and pieces collected from other people's bins or bought at thrift shops. Not that she cared. Runa was not one to covet material goods, or anything else for that matter.

The tiny table did not suit her, though. Runa was a tall, big-boned young woman who could trace her family back to the nineteenth-century Icelandic settlers of The Point. Over the generations her family had scattered to the four corners of the country, but Runa had returned, had sought to reclaim some peace in the safest "gated" community in America. The price of tranquility had been cleaning rich people's houses here and in Blaine, but Runa didn't mind so much. She was a loner, and the solitude suited her fine.

"There you are!" a man's voice said from behind Lily. She turned around and groaned. It was Marcus and Penelope.

"How did you find me?"

"We just focused our thoughts on you until we picked up your energy trail," Penelope explained, as if this made perfect sense to a newbie like Lily.

It was all so confounding. "But how did you get here? We took the car."

"We just willed our way here. You don't need to hitch a ride with the living, Lily; you just have to know where you want to be."

How Lily was supposed to pick up someone's energy trail, or relocate by will alone, was not clear in the least, and confusion crept across her face. "Don't worry," Marcus assured her, "you'll get the hang of this place soon enough. Just stick with me and I'll teach you everything you need to know."

"I'm not sleeping with you," Lily mocked. "I'm not *that* confused."

Penelope snickered. Marcus glared at them both.

"Anyhow, it's best not to take off like that," Penelope cautioned, resting a reassuring hand on Lily's shoulder. "Right now you need help and people you can trust." Penelope cast an accusing eye in Marcus's direction—at least, that is how he interpreted her look— and it made him squirm a little in his Italian black leather loafers. "Let me help you, Lily," Penelope continued. "At least you'll have *one* real detective to work on this."

Marcus's eyes hardened but he kept his voice upbeat. "She's right, Lily. We have to get to the bottom of this. That's why *I* came to investigate, and I'm not going to abandon you. I may not have been a trained detective before we met, but I now have twenty years' experience, which is fifteen more than *some* people I know."

Penelope opened her mouth to reply but there was no time to argue further because Runa had finally stopped sobbing and was able to speak again. Penelope and Marcus sat down on the sofa to listen, and when Lily failed to get the hint and sit, too, the pair reached up and yanked the novelist down between them, their bodies weightless against the sofa's failing springs.

"How long have you worked for Ms. Harrington?" Greene resumed his interrogation now that Runa had regained her composure.

She absentmindedly pushed a stray lock of her shoulder-length blond hair back behind her ear. "'Bout two years now."

"And how long have you lived in Point Roberts?"

"'Bout the same." Runa kept her head down, only glancing up briefly to answer the detective's questions.

"Where were you before that?"

"Here 'n there," she answered vaguely.

Greene sighed audibly, unable to disguise his impatience. There was something seriously off about this woman. He wondered how people could trust her in their homes. "Could you be more specific, please?"

Runa shrugged in resignation. "Was a farm worker for a while. Followed the crops, ya know? Spent some time in Napa Valley 'fore comin' up here." She looked down and scratched the head of a serpent tattooed on her left inner forearm, then licked her thumb and began rubbing the creature's eyes as if cleaning them.

"Ms. Jonsdottir," Greene said, "stay with me, please." Seriously, questioning the woman was like pulling teeth. Which reminded him he needed to see the dentist. When he got home he would have to ask Ellie to make him an appointment.

Runa raised her head briefly to look at Greene. "Sorry."

He soldiered on. "How would you describe your working relationship with Ms. Harrington?"

"It was fine," Lily responded from her spot between her captors. "We got on very well and—"

"Lily," Marcus interjected angrily. "Could you be quiet, please? We need to hear what Runa has to say, not you."

Lily slumped back into the sofa, duly chastised.

Runa shrugged again. "S'okay. Gave me a job when I needed one. Helped me get a few more 'round here, too, so I wouldn't have to travel to Blaine so much."

"Why did you move here, to Point Roberts?" Greene asked.

"Just wanted to call someplace home, I guess." Runa turned her face away and looked out the small kitchen window at the bank of trees that cradled her trailer. She felt their closeness and their strength and wanted to crawl back into their cocoon, but the detective was pestering her with more questions.

"Where were you last night?"

She turned her face back and answered, "Here."

"Were you with anybody?"

"No," she responded blankly, unaware of the negative consequences her solitude might have on an alibi. Runa did not think about an alibi, did not think she would need one.

"Did anyone see you here?"

"I dunno," she said and began rubbing the serpent again.

"What were you doing last night?"

"Readin."

"Reading what?"

She gestured to a paperback lying on the kitchen counter. Greene looked over and read the title: *Love and Secrets*. "That's one of Harrington's," he said.

Indeed it is, Lily confirmed in her head, mindful not to interrupt again. *Not my best work, though. Was a bit rushed, that one.*

Runa nodded. "She let me borrow from her library. I wasn't allowed to touch the hardcovers but she said I could read the paperbacks. That's my favorite." She fell into her own thoughts again, gazing wistfully at the cover image of Marcus in his signature black trench coat and fedora, laid over an image of him in a steamy embrace with an attractive blond woman.

A look of mild irritation crossed Greene's face. Lily smirked. She had always liked Runa despite her odd personality, and at the moment she was liking her because of it.

"What was her state of mind lately?" Greene continued, waving a hand in front of Runa's face to get her attention back.

"Norm—" She stopped short, as if someone had ordered her to be quiet. Then she said, "She was different. Distant. Well, she was always distant with me but more so lately. She seemed depressed."

"Wha-what?" Lily stammered, her mood suddenly turning sour. "That is *not* true," she declared indignantly, sitting up straight. "I was always welcoming. I gave you produce from my garden. And I *tipped* you. You ungrateful wench." She looked to Penelope for validation but she merely shrugged. Lily tried Marcus next but he ignored her completely, his brown eyes focused intently on Runa. "And I was *not* depressed," Lily added before slumping down in the couch again to sulk, her arms and legs crossed in resentment.

"I thought you said she was nice to you?" Greene said, and Lily wondered if she had put that thought into his head or if the credit was all his.

Runa fidgeted a bit in her seat. "Well, yeah, nice but, you know, it's not like we was friends."

"Anything else out of the ordinary?"

"She was drinkin' more. There was more empty wine bottles to take to the depot than before."

"*I was not!*" Lily jumped up in defiance. "Runa, why are you lying? I was *nice* to you. I *liked* you."

Penelope reached up and pulled Lily down into the sofa again. "You're blocking my view."

"Any idea why?" Greene asked, hopeful for anything that would confirm a suicide and make his life easier. "Was she having any difficulties with anyone here or elsewhere?"

"Was mad at Mr. Owen."

"Mr. Owen?"

"Richard Owen, Harrington's neighbor to the south," Thornfield stepped in to help. He was standing, aloof but observant, leaning against the wall behind Runa. "Weird guy. Moved here the summer of '08 after his mother died. He's a recluse. Has everything he needs delivered and always pays online. Rumor is he made a fortune in the stock market just before the crash, but no one really knows."

"So what was the problem between Owen and Harrington?" Greene asked Runa.

"He was spyin' on her. Last Thursday she caught him sittin' at his bedroom window watchin' her through binoculars while she was gardenin'. She was really mad. Said gardenin' was her sanctuary, her Zen moment she called it, 'n he was takin' that away from her. She went over to talk to him but he wouldn't answer the door. So she threw garden manure at his window."

"He deserved it, the creep," Lily sneered. She had just stood up from weeding the vegetable garden when she saw him at his second-story window, his binoculars focused on her, or so it seemed, and when she stared back he showed no sign of embarrassment at being discovered, didn't even move an inch, as if challenging her to retaliate: give him the finger or moon him maybe. The first option had struck her as banal and ineffective, the second likely to be more appreciated than resented; then she saw the bag of fertilizer she had been spreading among the tomatoes and it seemed the most fitting response: manure for a pig. When he wouldn't answer the door, wouldn't answer to *her*, she stood beneath his bedroom and aimed the pungent mixture squarely at his head.

"Then what happened?" Greene asked, his balloon deflating: he might now have a viable suspect for murder.

Runa shrugged. "Next day he paid me to clean it off."

Greene looked over at Thornfield. "You guys know about this?"

The deputy shook his head. "Nope." Lily caught what she was certain was a flicker of confusion in Runa's eyes, but it was gone as quickly as it came. Lily glanced at her companions; both were too focused on Runa to return eye contact.

Greene turned his attention back to Runa. "I assume you have a gate pass or the code?"

She nodded. "I have a code."

"What is it?"

"Seven-nine-four-eight."

Remind me to delete that, Lily thought angrily.

Greene scribbled the number down in his notebook. Penelope did the same, and Lily wondered where she got the notebook, and how.

"And the security code to Harrington's home, yes?" Green pressed on.

Runa nodded again. "The same."

"Did anyone else besides you and Harrington have the code to the house?"

"Her sister in Santa Clara. She's the emergency contact."

Oh no, Amanda! The thought of her sister filled Lily's heart with dread, pushing aside her anger. She had been so wrapped up in the day's events she had completely failed to consider the effect of her death on others, in particular Amanda, Lily's elder and only sibling, her best friend. Lily lowered her head and bit her lip, fearful she would start crying in front of her otherworldly companions.

"Do you have a name and number by any chance?" Greene asked, doggedly scratching away for information.

"Amanda Clarins. Her number's on the cork board in the kitchen."

"Was the alarm on when you arrived this morning?"

"No."

"Was that unusual?"

"No," Runa replied with a shrug and a shake of her head. "Ms. Harrington was an early riser 'n she turned the alarm off soon as she got out of the bath in the mornin'. Said she hated the chime every time she came in 'n outdoors."

"You said Harrington liked to garden. Did she have any help?"

"Arni in the corner cuts the grass on Wednesdays."

"In the corner?"

"Next door in the park," Thornfield answered for Runa. "Name's Arni Heimirsson. Lives in a trailer at Sunny Side. We can pay him a visit next."

"Okay," Greene sighed in defeat and closed his notebook. "That's all for now. If I need anything more I'll call you." He had taken down Runa's cellphone number along with her date of birth when they had first begun the interview, and now he would be checking both when he got back to Bellingham. He pulled out his card from his pocket. "And if you remember anything else that you think might be relevant, please call me. These are my direct numbers." He rose to leave. "Do you mind if I use your bathroom? Nature's calling."

Runa shook her head and gestured to the back of the trailer. "First door past the kitchen."

Thornfield waited until Greene left the room, then asked, "You doing okay, Runa?"

Her eyes welled up again. "No," she whispered and hung her head to hide her tears. "I-I never s-saw a dead b-body before."

Thornfield walked over to place a comforting hand on her shoulder. "I know it's been a shock. But you'll get through this. We all will. That's what makes The Point so special, right? We all watch out for each other."

Runa nodded her head, but was it in agreement or obedience? Lily could not tell.

"If you need anything, you just ask."

Runa nodded again. The sound of Greene blowing his nose was heard, followed by the toilet flushing. A moment later he alighted from the bathroom and headed for the door. Thornfield opened it for the detective. "Thank you, Ms. Jonsdottir. We'll be in touch," Greene said then disappeared down the stairs.

The three spirits joined Thornfield at the door. He glanced over at Runa and quietly said, "You take care, now."

She looked up in acknowledgement. "Tell me you love me," she implored, her pale blue eyes sad and unfocused. Runa's words seemed to make both men uncomfortable.

"Not now, Runa. I'll call you later," Thornfield replied, letting the door shut behind him with a bang.

Marcus strode toward the cruiser, Lily nipping at his heels. "What was up with you staring at her like that?" she asked him.

"The key to good detective work, Lily, is observation," Marcus pontificated. "I was scrutinizing every movement in her face and body for clues. You would do well to do the same if you want to find your killer."

I was, Lily thought indignantly. *More than you know.* Out loud she added, "And what was up with the way she was staring at my book like some lovesick teenager?"

"What can I say?" Marcus smirked triumphantly. "I have that effect on women. I've got it all: charm, good looks, hot body"—he nudged Lily in the side—"hotter mouth. Also intelligence and a perfect track record in solving cases. What woman wouldn't want me?"

Lily rolled her eyes. "I created a monster."

Marcus's smile melted into a thin hard line. "For the last time, you did *not* make me. I existed before you and I will exist after you are gone. I made myself *available* to you. And those women who buy your books, they *love* me. *Me.* Not *you. Me.*"

Lily left his side, not wanting to quarrel any further. She marched to the cruiser. Thornfield was leaning against the hood and watching Greene walking around Runa's mobile home, checking out its visibility to its neighbors. The trailer was on the north side of the lane, set well back from the road and bordered by a large forested area that terminated at Marine Drive about three hundred yards west. Trees nestled her home on three sides, but the front was visible by at least one other home. Runa's white 1990 Toyota Corolla was parked in the dirt-and-gravel drive that led to her door. Greene and Penelope scribbled the license number down in their notebooks.

Penelope was talking, seemingly to Greene, but Lily could not hear what was being said, nor could she determine if Greene could hear Penelope or if she was merely thinking out loud. Either way, it was making Lily nervous.

Greene walked over to the cruiser. "Do people know about her mental health issues?" he asked Thornfield.

"Oh for the love of God, I do *not* have mental health issues!" Lily protested with the stomp of one foot. "The paroxetine was just for night sweats, I *swear*." She cast a wary look at Penelope, wondering if she had put that idea into Greene's head.

Thornfield looked puzzled. Greene smiled. "I didn't need the bathroom. She seemed a little off. I was checking for meds. I found paliperidone."

Oh, he's talking about Runa, Lily thought, relieved, and a little embarrassed by her outburst.

Greene waved his smartphone. "I checked online. It's used to treat schizophrenia and schizoaffective disorders."

"What's the difference?" Thornfield asked, genuinely curious.

"Have no idea, but I'll look into it further. She's on the lowest adult dose, three milligrams. But it looks like she may have stopped taking it: the prescription was filled three months ago for sixty tablets but there's still pills in the bottle."

Greene looked over to the house with a view of Runa's. "Do you know who lives there?"

"No. But let me call Collins; he might know." As Thornfield pulled out his cellphone and dialed, Greene walked across the road to the tiny cottage and rang the bell. No one answered, the metal screen door locked tight beneath his inquiring hand. He walked back across to Thornfield, who put his phone aside and said, "Belongs to a family from Everson. They come down for the month of August but that's it."

"Ask him about the house next door to the west."

Thornfield did as requested. "That's Mrs. Gudmussen," he said after a moment. "Says she's quite elderly but we can ask."

Lily followed the men as they walked next door. Greene looked a little less portly from behind, his extra weight carried predominantly in his belly. His buttocks were flattened from sitting long hours, his walk reluctant, hips stiffening with age. Back bent slightly forward, shoulders rounded: a man carrying heavy burdens. Guilt crept stealthily up Lily's spine, her initial assessment of the detective feeling harsh and premature. She blamed her earlier haste on posthumous shock. The trick worked: a mental sleight of hand meant to thwart distracting introspection.

They found Mrs. Gudmussen sitting in a rocker in the shade of her porch, knitting a white baby blanket and looking very much the part of everyone's grandmother: polyester-blend dress, support hose, sensible flat leather sandals, thin white hair permed to add volume. She looked up over the rim of her trifocal glasses, surprised but not concerned as the men approached. "Afternoon, ma'am," Thornfield said.

Lily did not recognize Mrs. Gudmussen but did recognize her knitting: she always used the same pattern, engraved on her memory, and sold the soft wool treasures at the Blue Heron Gallery. Lily had bought a yellow one for a colleague's baby shower two years ago.

"Afternoon. You must be the new deputy I read about in the *Bulletin*," Mrs. Gudmussen greeted the men with a purl and two knits.

"Yes indeed, ma'am, Deputy David Thornfield," he respectfully replied. "And this here is Detective Greene from Bellingham." Greene tipped his head hello.

"Detective?" Mrs. Gudmussen said, surprised, her interest piqued. She set her knitting down in her lap. "How can I help you?"

"By any chance did you see your neighbor Runa Jonsdottir at home last evening?" Greene asked, wiping his nose with his handkerchief.

"No, but I'm in bed by eight so I don't see much around here anymore. Why? Is Runa in trouble?" Mrs. Gudmussen turned an expectant eye on Thornfield.

"No, ma'am," he answered, shaking his head. "There was some trouble at the Harrington property last night and we're just checking on everyone who works there, that's all."

Mrs. Gudmussen now looked equal parts worried and intrigued: everybody in The Point knew about the famous Lily Harrington. "What kind of trouble?"

"I'm not at liberty to say."

The deputy's cryptic answer sounded ominous, and the elderly woman's worry visibly increased. "Are we in any danger?"

"I don't believe so," Thornfield assured her. "It looks like an isolated incident."

Mrs. Gudmussen shook her head sadly. "My, my, things have certainly changed around here. Ever since New York and those silly men got all fickle about the border. And then the Californians came and bought up all the empty lots. Used to be we could leave our doors unlocked. They say they are keeping us safer but I lock my doors now." She shook her head again and picked up her knitting.

"Well, thank you for your time," Greene said.

She raised her head in farewell. "Saline rinse and magnesium," she suggested, pointing the end of one knitting needle toward Greene.

"I beg your pardon, ma'am?"

"For your nose. Saline rinse twice a day and magnesium in the morning."

"Um, thank you," he said, embarrassed to be discussing his nasal issues with a stranger, and in front of Thornfield no less. The deputy wisely pretended not to notice, saying nothing as the men walked back to the cruiser.

Marcus was using the window of the rear passenger door as a mirror, adjusting his fedora in minute increments while he waited for everyone to return. "Anything useful?" he queried Lily.

"No. Nobody saw Runa come or go last night."

Marcus nodded. "I don't think she was involved in this. She's too flaky to kill anyone in such a calculated way, in my opinion."

"Perhaps. But you're not a psychiatrist, so what do you really know?"

Marcus scowled. "There's no need to be insulting, Lily. And if you keep it up, maybe I'll decide you can do this on your own. Or worse, leave you to Penelope."

Lily pursed her lips but said nothing. She was not sure how, exactly, either Marcus or Penelope was helping her, but they were all she had in this world. The thought filled her with sorrow.

She suddenly noticed Penelope's absence. "Speaking of whom, where *is* your ex?"

Marcus snorted. "Who knows? Saw her snooping around toward the backyard then she disappeared."

Lily was about to go in search of Penelope when she came through Runa's trailer door. "What were you doing back in there?" Marcus demanded, suspicious.

"Something's weird about the woman. Wanted to check a few things."

"Greene said the same thing," Lily offered, trying to be useful. "He found paliperidone in her bathroom. It's used—"

"To treat mental disorders, I know. There's also a man's shirt and birth control pills in her bedroom."

Marcus raised an eyebrow. "Runa is on the pill?"

"What do you care?" Penelope replied. "You couldn't get a woman pregnant even if you agreed to be reborn."

"And you couldn't get laid even if you paid the guy."

"You were free. And also cheap, as I recall."

Lily sighed and slid into the cruiser. She had no idea what to make of those two. Marcus was a pain in the butt but he was a great detective—or so she had thought until Penelope arrived and blew his cover. At first Lily had been irate at Marcus's declaration of authorship of her books, but then she realized that if indeed he were a real detective he might actually be able to help her find her killer. The thought had tempered her initial anger. But now Lily was in a quandary: if Marcus was really an actor, then he had been acting out *her* character, *her* stories, the thought of which should bring her joy and a sense of vindication; on the other hand, if Marcus was not a real detective, who could help her now? Penelope?

And who *was* this Penelope, besides Marcus's ex-lover? And why had she come to Point Roberts? She had appeared uninvited, like some of the characters in Lily's novels who seemed to write themselves into the narrative, leaving her wondering where they had come from, what far recess of her mind had conjured up the apparition. Or the way a minor character, written in to bridge a gap or maybe create a red herring, would then take on a life of their own and become central to the plot. It was always a spooky feeling when such events occurred, and each time they did Lily would assign responsibility to her muse, yet this muse never had a name or even a face, was nothing more than a mechanism to explain the inexplicable.

Which brought Lily back to Marcus. Was Joseph Esposito her unnamed muse? (*Please, God, no!*) Or was he just an actor as Penelope claimed, a mouthpiece for Lily's creation, a leech taking credit for someone else's efforts? Marcus Mantova had arrived in her imagination fully formed: it was not that his personality had changed over the fifty novels so much as it had been revealed. Or so she had believed. But had she been fooling herself all these years? Where did her Marcus Mantova end and Joseph's begin? Could one even make such a distinction? It was a testament to their shared identity that even now Lily still called him Marcus, still thought of him *as* Marcus, as if Joe were the alter ego and not the charlatan.

So what did this mean? Did it mean that Lily *was* nothing more than a stenographer? And, if so, why her? She must have had *some* aptitude for the job or her muse would not have chosen her: you certainly don't hire a mechanic to perform brain surgery, or vice versa. Maybe the relationship is more interdependent than Marcus, or Joe, or whoever he is, is willing to admit. And whatever the truth is, could Lily now write herself out of this mess?

Her ruminations came to an end when the two live officers joined her in the car. As Greene buckled himself into the passenger seat, he reiterated his first question: "Did you know about Jonsdottir's mental health issues?"

Thornfield's jaw tightened as he started the engine. He kept his eyes on the road, avoiding Greene's. "I heard she had some trouble down in California, but what kind of trouble has all been rumor and speculation. She's never been arrested, that much I know. And she's never been a problem here."

Never was a problem with me, either, Lily thought, *at least not until today.*

THEY HEADED EAST TOWARD THE TRAILER PARK. Seconds later Penelope and Marcus realized they had been left behind and transported themselves into the back seat of the deputy's cruiser. They sat silently seething on opposite sides of Lily, and she wondered how long she would be stuck in the middle like this.

Their resentment reminded Lily of her own failed relationships. She had never married, had never felt the desire to. She enjoyed the company of men, enjoyed bedding them between fine Egyptian cotton sheets and sharing a glass of wine afterwards, but soon it was time to start her next novel and then the conflict would begin. With each man it was the same thing: she asking to be left alone while she wrote, he agreeing to it then pestering her with emails, texts, and phone calls. She never understood such neediness: she was attracted to ambitious men with consuming careers of their own, and naively assumed they could busy themselves while she was unavailable. When she emerged each evening from her office she would meet her lover for dinner or some cultural event, her attention on him lavish and undivided, and once the book was finished it was time for a lengthy holiday, usually Europe in summer and somewhere hot in winter. What was there to complain about?

And yet when each man left her, usually for someone far less intelligent but evidently more available, Lily was never entirely surprised. She would occasionally Google an ex-lover and find he had married his secretary or hairdresser, who was invariably expecting their first child. Years later would come the divorce, and

Lily guessed rightly that the woman had signed a prenup despite the earlier public show of undying trust and devotion.

Lily had thus given up on the idea of love, and when she moved to The Point had transferred her affections to her garden, though there were days she had considered adopting a dog, a miniature poodle she could cuddle on the couch with but who wouldn't shed as much as the chocolate labs Lily was most fond of. Perhaps it was not too late for that, seeing as all dogs go to heaven, or so saith United Artists and Pope Francis.

Thornfield turned off Julius Drive and into Sunny Side RV park. He drove along the dirt road that ran through a mishmash of motor homes, mobile homes on permanent foundations, and towable trailers, all nestled among dozens of tall trees. Most of the units were vacation properties owned by Canadians from British Columbia and Alberta, a few by visiting Americans, and others were rentals for the likes of Arni Heimirsson. In the woods to the north there was a large children's summer camp that provided additional playmates for the smattering of kids heard yelling their way through a game of soccer on the small plot of grass in the middle of the park.

The deputy made his way to the far northeastern corner of Sunny Side and parked in front of a midsized trailer, the kind that could be towed but which had been secured to a heavy wooden post. As Greene alighted from the cruiser, the smell of hamburgers on the barbecue wafted across the muggy air, the scent reminding him he had not eaten since breakfast.

Heimirsson's trailer was about eighteen feet long with a frayed retractable canvas awning, under which they found him sitting in a lawn chair and drawing on a small sketchpad, an open beer resting on a round plastic table beside him. He was in his midtwenties, well built and tanned, with a shock of blond hair that fell down over soulful blue eyes. "Hey, Dave, what's up?" Arni said in welcome. His voice was soft, and when he spoke he kept his head slightly bowed as if apologizing for his existence.

"Arni, this is Detective Greene from Bellingham. There's been some trouble up at the Harrington property and we need to ask you a few questions." His tone was confident, that sweet spot between authoritative and relaxed. Greene noticed the deputy was more comfortable here, back out in the open air, away from Lily's corpse and the stench that even the cold had not entirely masked. You couldn't blame the man, Greene thought: it had taken him awhile, too, to get used to the odor and the finality of death.

"What kind of trouble? Did somebody break in?" Arni asked, his azure eyes sparking with worry.

"Why do you ask that?" Greene joined the conversation. He scrutinized the young man, noted the way his fingers pressed anxiously into his sketchpad when he asked about the trouble. Greene's antenna went up: most people in Arni's situation would be curious about a break-in at a client's home, not worried. The three spirits also noticed it, each for different reasons.

Arni frowned. "She's a rich lady, in a big house." His eyes fell back to his sketchpad and he nervously began to draw a caricature of Greene.

"I understand you work for her," the detective said lightly, keeping his suspicions hidden. "When were you there last?"

"Yesterday." Arni drew in Greene's thinning hairline.

"What time?"

"I got there at nine, left about six forty-five." He added the rumpled chin and bulbous nose.

Penelope and Greene opened their notebooks and wrote down Arni's answer. Marcus glanced over at Penelope then instinctively shoved his hands into the pockets of his trench coat: he didn't have a notebook to write down observations, didn't have any props at all to occupy his hands and make him appear more professional. It made her presence all the more irritating. *At least I have my trench coat and fedora,* he consoled himself. *Beats those generic black pants and white shirt. You could be anybody in black pants and a white shirt. Even a waitress.* He imagined himself in a greasy diner, some hole in the wall where he was meeting a snitch or maybe the girlfriend of the killer, and Penelope would serve him coffee and maybe a slice of apple pie. *Yeah, yeah, that's good.* But he'd ask for the pie only after she brought him his coffee, make her work twice as hard.

If Penelope's notebook was causing Marcus distress, Greene's was causing Arni equal discomfort: he squirmed noticeably in his seat then quickly glanced away.

"And what did you do there?" Greene continued.

"I mowed the lawn and weeded the south flower beds." The questions confused Arni. He looked over at Thornfield for an explanation. "What's this about, Dave? You know I don't steal from my clients."

"I know, Arni," Thornfield assured him, "I know. But we have to ask these questions. It's just routine."

"And where was Ms. Harrington?" Greene asked.

"She was home at first but left around noon. Got back just as I was finishing up." Arni's shoulders tensed. Routine or not, he did not like being grilled like this, as if they already suspected him of the crime. He nervously returned to his sketch, adding in Greene's heavy eyebrows.

"When was that?"

"About five." Arni eyed Greene as he scribbled the answer down in his notebook. The more he wrote the faster Arni sketched, as if it were a race and whoever finished first won the prize.

Lily walked over to see what he was drawing, and laughed. "Don't forget the hair in his ears," she suggested with a grin. Marcus and Penelope took in Lily's body language, noticed the way she leaned toward the boy.

Greene made a mental note of the gardener's apprehension. "You finished at about five but you didn't leave until almost seven. What happened between five and the time you left?"

Lily's smile evaporated. Her eyes flickered with surprise, and Penelope noticed the almost imperceptible tightening of her jaw. "Something wrong, Lily?"

"No," she answered a little too abruptly. "Why would anything be wrong?"

"She gave me a glass of lemonade," Arni replied. "We talked about writing for a bit and then she paid me and I left." He shifted again in his seat, raising the detectives' suspicions further.

"Do you have the security code to the house?" Greene asked.

"No. Just a gate code and a key to the garden shed."

"What is the gate code?"

"Three-seven-two-zero." Arni's eyes fell on Greene's notebook again as he wrote down the number. "Am I a suspect?"

"Relax, son, no one suspects you of stealing anything," Greene said, choosing his words carefully. He sniffled: a drop of mucus was slowly descending through his right nostril, distracting him from the task at hand. He fought the drip—thanks to Mrs. Gudmussen's comment—for as long as he could before giving in to fate and fishing out his handkerchief. "Did you notice anything unusual yesterday, either about the property or Ms. Harrington?"

"She seemed mad about something," Arni said. He paused as if giving Greene time to write down the answer. "Didn't say what. She doesn't tell me stuff like that." He looked down again at his caricature and with a few strokes added the wattle beneath Greene's chin.

The detective noticed the use of the present tense: Arni did not seem to know Harrington is dead. The subconscious submission cast the young man in a more favorable light, and Greene wondered if this soft-spoken kid with his sketchbook could have been involved in a murder. Still, it was too early to rule anyone out. "And what did you do the rest of last night, after you left the Harrington property?"

Arni jutted his chin in the direction of the trailer next door. "Me and Jimmy watched the Mariners. We lost to the Blue Jays."

"Can anyone vouch for that?"

"Um, the MLB?" Arni suggested.

Lily let out an involuntary laugh.

"Don't be a smartass, son," Greene warned, thrusting his handkerchief into his pocket for emphasis.

Arni looked blankly at the detective, and suddenly Greene could not tell if the boy was messing with him or just literal minded. Thornfield seemed to think the latter, for he clarified the question: "Arni, what Detective Greene meant was, can anyone vouch for you being with Jimmy last night?"

Arni swept one hand in an arc, indicating his neighbors. "I guess you could ask them. I'm sure they all heard Jimmy swearing at the TV."

Greene changed tactics. "Do you know Harrington's housekeeper, Runa Jonsdottir?"

"Just to say hello," Arni replied, and began drawing in Greene's plump body.

"So you don't have any kind of relationship with her?"

"Well, we're neighbors," Arni answered, then realized that was not exactly the case. "Sort of."

"But nothing romantic?"

"No," Arni said, particularly perplexed by that last question. He briefly looked up at Thornfield, who crossed his muscular arms and stared down in return.

Everyone cast a sideways glance at Thornfield, including Greene, who kept his thoughts to himself and his expression neutral. "Did you notice if Jonsdottir was home last night?"

"No," Arni frowned, shaking his head. "I can't see her trailer from mine. She's on the other side." He pointed his pen west.

Greene thought a moment then chose yet another approach. He gestured toward Arni's sketchpad. "What are you working on there?"

Arni's face brightened. "Characters for my graphic novel."

"Mind if I take a look?"

Arni glanced down at the caricature. "Um, I'd prefer you didn't," he answered, pulling the pad cover down. "It's not finished yet."

"I didn't know you were a writer," Thornfield said, surprised.

"I wasn't, not really anyway," Arni replied modestly. "But I showed some of my stuff to Lily and she's been encouraging me. She says I have talent. Promised me she will show it to her agent once she feels it's ready."

"Did you mean it?" Marcus asked her, thinking the truth was likely the opposite.

"Why wouldn't I?" she answered sharply and crossed her arms.

"He called you Lily," Penelope said. "How intimate was your relationship with the boy?"

Lily was taken aback by the question, but before she could answer, Greene asked Arni, "You called her Lily. How intimate is your relationship with Ms. Harrington?"

"Did you just direct him to ask that?" Lily angrily demanded.

"No," Penelope smiled. "Great minds think alike, that's all."

Lily's eyes narrowed in suspicion. Arni scowled. "She's my boss, my mentor, and my friend," he answered.

"In that order?"

"I guess so."

"Okay, fine, that's enough for now. I just need your driver's license for a minute."

"It's inside."

"I'll come with you."

Greene and Penelope followed Arni into the compact trailer. It was neatly packed with comic books, graphic novels, and a few classics: a compendium of Greek and Roman myths, Joseph Campbell's *The Hero With a Thousand Faces*, everything ever written by Tolkien, and Tolstoy's *War and Peace*. There were a few books from the Point Robert's library, and a hardcover copy of one of Harrington's. While Arni fished out his license from his wallet, Greene leaned down and opened the cover of Lily's book. Penelope peered over his arm and read the inscription: "Arni, Keep your dreams alive, Lily."

Arni handed his license to Greene. He took down the young man's full name and date of birth then handed the plastic card back. "So, you're certain nothing romantic or sexual is going on between you and Ms. Harrington?" Greene inquired again.

"I'm certain," Arni replied, straight-faced. "Sir."

"Okay, but if you hear anything or remember anything more about last night," Greene requested, handing his card to the boy, "you give me or Deputy Thornfield a ring."

"Will do," Arni promised, but was not sure he meant it.

Greene and Penelope alighted from the trailer. Thornfield was leaning against the driver's door, waiting, two of his unseen stowaways already settled again in the back seat. "Did Penelope tell him to ask that, or was it really a coincidence?" Lily asked Marcus.

"I'm not sure, but if I were you I wouldn't trust her. She's got a knack for sticking her nose where it doesn't belong."

Lily frowned. Was Marcus telling the truth, or was it just another snarky comment from a jilted ex-lover?

Arni watched from the doorway as the officers got into the cruiser. He waited until they left, then tried to call Lily. Her phone went to voicemail. Arni didn't leave a message. He went back outside, picked up his sketchpad off the table, and added in Greene's handkerchief and runny nose.

Thornfield left the trailer park and headed back toward Harrington's: Greene wanted to talk to this Owen fellow next.

"Heimirsson and Jonsdottir have different gate codes," Greene pondered aloud as he opened the window for air. "That's helpful: we can do a diagnostic on her system and it should tell us what codes were used and when." He paused, tapping his finger on the window frame. "Heimirsson has a signed copy of a Harrington hardcover book. And he calls her Lily."

"So?" Thornfield asked, failing to grasp the significance.

"So Jonsdottir calls her Ms. Harrington and wasn't allowed to touch the hardcovers. Clearly a hierarchy of servants."

"Or maybe he bought the book himself and she kindly signed it. Isn't that what writers do?"

"Perhaps. But ask around, will you please? People know you; they're more likely to talk to a trusted acquaintance than a stranger."

"Okay, but I really doubt there's anything going on. She's—what?—thirty years older?"

"You never heard of Mrs. Robinson?"

Marcus cast a sideways glance at Lily. She turned her face to the window and smiled. Penelope's expression said nothing, but her mind was turning cartwheels.

A few minutes later they arrived at Richard Owen's property next door to Harrington's. Thornfield knocked but no one answered. He knocked again but still no answer. The third time he pounded his fist on the door. "Richard, open the door. It's David Thornfield," he yelled, but his voice, though loud, was not menacing.

There was a scuffling sound on the other side, followed by the clunk-clunk-clunk of three locks being unbolted. The door opened a few inches, the security latch still in place. A pair of buggy eyes, enlarged even more by high-prescription lenses housed in thick square-shaped black plastic frames, peered out at the deputies. "What do you want?" Owen squeaked.

"There was some trouble at Lily Harrington's house last night," Thornfield answered, maintaining his friendly stance. "We just need to talk to you about what you might have seen."

"I never saw anything. Please go away," Owen pleaded.

"Open the door, Mr. Owen," Green demanded. "We know you've been watching her. So unless you wish to be a suspect, I advise you to cooperate and answer my questions."

Owen looked fearfully at Greene, who stared the recluse down. He looked to Thornfield for support, but the deputy merely gave Owen a look that said *Gotta talk to us*. An impatient Penelope let out an audible grunt and walked through the door. Marcus raced after her, fearful of appearing indecisive in comparison. Lily remained on Owen's doorstep, not knowing whether she should follow her companions or wait to be invited in along with the living.

Owen inadvertently answered her question when he acquiesced to the officers, closed the door, removed the security latch and opened the door again to the men. He eyed Greene with suspicion but the detective kept his expression neutral as he sized up the hermit in return. Owen was in his midforties, Greene estimated, about six feet tall but appeared shorter on account of the way his shoulders were hunched over. Despite his relative young age his attire was decidedly West Coast geriatric: gray knitted wool vest over a wrinkled white cotton short-sleeved shirt, khaki knee-length shorts, white calf-high socks, and moccasin slippers. His face was clean shaven but prematurely deeply lined, and dominated by those buggy eyes behind the thick black frames. He reminded Greene of a cross between Martin Scorsese and a pug.

Owen let the men in then shut the door behind them just before Lily crossed the threshold, unknowingly slamming the door in her face. She passed through anyway, irritated by Owen's rudeness before she reminded herself he could not see her. The thought gave her a sweet sense of revenge, and she smiled as she followed the men down the porcelain-tiled hallway.

The slap-slap of Owen's moccasins echoed along the empty corridor as he led the officers to a living room overlooking the strait. The room was large but sparsely furnished, and like his clothes seemed to have been handed down from an earlier generation: worn area carpet, vintage teak couch with orange tweed upholstery, matching reading chair, gold metal lamp, teak coffee and end table set. The only two signs of modernity—a large flatscreen television and a game console—were positioned away from the glare of the windows. On the opposite wall a large teak bookcase was haphazardly packed with texts and magazines, which Penelope and Marcus were perusing while they waited for everyone else.

Other than this, the expansive room was eerily empty: no art adorned the walls, no knickknacks graced the space. The only item of significance was a large painting, set atop the heavy oak mantelpiece, of Richard Owen standing proudly behind a plump, gray-haired woman whose kindness emanated from the canvas. Heavy vertical blinds, 1980s light pink and frayed along the bottom, closed off the view north to Lily's property, but the windows to the sea were bare.

Owen turned around three times then sat down in the middle of the sofa, forcing Greene and Thornfield to choose who got the reading chair. Neither did; they both stood and looked down at the recluse. He scowled back, his hands tucked beneath his thighs like a naughty schoolboy.

"Mr. Owen, where were you yesterday, all day?" Greene asked brusquely.

"Here," Owen replied, perplexed by the question. He looked over at Thornfield. "Where else would I be?"

The detective's gruff approach bothered Thornfield. Owen was a fragile soul; could Greene not see that? "Richard, can anyone vouch for you?" the deputy asked in a kinder voice.

"The boy from Marketplace delivered my groceries just after six o'clock." Richard wriggled his nose, trying to push his glasses up, before relenting and releasing one hand to do the job.

"Anyone else?" Greene asked, trying to surreptitiously dab his nose.

"No," Owen responded, fearfully eyeing the detective's soiled handkerchief.

"Why were you watching Lily Harrington?"

"I wasn't," Owen squeaked, sitting on both hands again.

"Richard," Thornfield gently chided the recluse, "Runa saw you. Told us how Harrington came here to give you a piece of her mind but you wouldn't answer the door. Said she threw manure on your window."

"And rightly so," Lily huffed, but suddenly she was not so sure anymore. It was obvious to her that Richard Owen was a strange fellow, but there seemed something almost childlike about him, an innocence that belied the rumored millions and large house, empty as it was. Or maybe it was just the effect of the kindly Mrs. Owen looking down on Lily that made her feel badly about judging the woman's son. Lily looked up at Mother Owen. Yup, that was it.

Owen's hands jumped to his face, his bent fingers pressing into his chin. "It was all a misunderstanding," he pleaded. "I wasn't watching Lily. I was watching the birds. A marbled murrelet pair is nesting in her Douglas fir. They produced an egg ten days ago. I've been watching over them. The ravens have been circling. I was worried."

"Why didn't you just tell her that?" Thornfield asked.

Owen wriggled his nose again. "She frightens me."

"She *frightens* you?" Greene said, skeptical. "She's half your size."

"She writes about death." Owen glanced over at his mother. "I don't like to think about death."

"Still, why didn't you just tell me, you silly man?" Lily scolded him. "I wish I'd known I had murrelets in my tree."

"Then you're as weird as he is," Marcus snickered.

"Spoken from experience," Penelope scoffed. She was standing at the north wall and sticking her face through the closed blinds to check out Owen's view of Lily's property. Marcus waited for Penelope's head to disappear through the blinds again then made a childish face. "I saw that," she said when she pulled her head back in, though the accusation was really just an educated guess.

Greene pushed his handkerchief back into his pocket and frowned. Richard Owen seemed genuine, if genuinely bizarre, and the detective wondered if anyone capable of doing Lily Harrington harm would care about a bird, let alone know its name. Owen misinterpreted Greene's expression as disbelief. "I can show you," the recluse anxiously said. "You can see the nest from my bedroom."

Lily eyed Owen's moccasins—worn-down soft suede, blackened along the heels—as he led his interrogators to the upper floor. He paused before his bedroom door and removed his slippers, left foot first, then bent down and set them neatly aside, aligning the heels just so. "Please remove your shoes," he requested after he straightened up. "I don't like dirt on the carpet."

Greene rolled his eyes. "Mr. Owen, I am on duty. I cannot remove my shoes. And neither can Deputy Thornfield."

Owen's face went blank with disbelief. "But ... but then you can't come in," he declared, his voice an octave higher. "It's just not possible."

There was a momentary standoff, then Owen's face lit up. "I have an idea! Wait here, please." He put his moccasins back on, left foot first, then slap-slapped his way along the hallway and down the stairs.

Marcus pushed his hands into the pockets of his trench coat and watched Owen scurrying down the hall. "Just what on earth do you think he's gone after?"

"I have no idea," Lily replied truthfully, her head cocked to one side. Penelope just rolled her eyes as she had earlier at the front door and walked into the bedroom.

Exasperated, Greene turned on Thornfield. "You said he was a recluse; you never said he was nuts. You'd better hope he doesn't return with a weapon."

He did not. Richard Owen returned carrying a box of plastic food wrap. He offered it to Greene. "I can let you in if you wrap your shoes in this."

"Seriously?" Greene said, irritated by the request.

Lily looked at Marcus. "Do we track in dirt? I mean, like, is there ghost dirt on the bottom of my shoes?"

"Would it matter?" Marcus replied, maddened by what he considered a stupid question. "If it's ghost dirt Owen can't see it, and what he can't see can't hurt him."

"Are you sure about that?" Lily asked, and Marcus wondered if she was still talking about germs.

There was another momentary standoff between police and recluse before Thornfield took the lead, taking the box from Richard's hands. Thornfield wrapped his shoes and offered the box to Greene. He refused it. "That's okay. I'll just watch from the door."

Owen removed his moccasin slippers again, left foot first, and set them neatly aside, aligning the heels just so, then entered the bedroom. He led Thornfield to the window while Greene watched from the doorway as agreed. Marcus walked through him into the bedroom. Lily stayed behind with Greene, not wanting to risk offence. She was feeling guilty now for having thrown manure on Richard's bedroom window and did not wish to add injury to insult, visible or not.

She leaned into the room and peered around. The bedroom, like the living room below, was sparsely furnished. The walls were bare except for a lone picture, this time a photograph, of Richard and his mother. It took pride of place above the brown vinyl-upholstered headboard.

Owen picked up a pair of binoculars off the window ledge and offered them to Thornfield. "They're about a third of the way from the top, on the right side near the trunk. You can just make them out through the gap in the branches."

What is? Lily thought before remembering they had come upstairs to view a pair of murrelets allegedly roosting in her Douglas fir. Between the moccasins ritual and the plastic wrap, Lily had become so engrossed in Richard Owen's peculiarities that she had completely forgotten the purpose for visiting his bedroom in the first place. It was the writer in her, the observer of other people's habits and mannerisms, their idiosyncrasies filed away for later use in a novel. She was a shameless thief of others' personalities. No one, whether loved or loathed, was spared.

Thornfield held the binoculars to his eyes and scanned the tree. Penelope shielded her eyes from the light and squinted into the distance.

"Well, I'll be damned. There is a pair," Thornfield confirmed. He held the field glasses out to Greene.

"It's okay, I'll take your word for it," the detective responded: there was still no way in hell Greene was going to swaddle his feet in food wrap. He addressed Owen. "But when you were watching the birds, did you notice anything unusual going on at Harrington's yesterday?"

"No."

Greene chose a new line of questioning. "I noticed you have security cameras on the house. Are they live?"

"Yes."

"Where do you keep the footage?"

"In my office."

"May we see it?"

"My office or the footage?" Owen asked, confused.

Greene's face hardened with exasperation. Between Jonsdottir, Heimirsson, and Owen it seemed most everybody in The Point was either thick or nuts. "Both."

Owen nodded meekly. "Follow me." He returned to the doorway, put his moccasins back on, left foot first, then led the officers back down to the first level. In a white-walled office a bank of monitors kept eye on the world outside: one displayed NASA's live Internet feed from the Space Station, another displayed Google's live camera feeds, currently set to Australia, while yet another displayed the live feed of an osprey nest. But it was only the monitor that watched the Owen property that interested the detective. The screen was split into four frames representing the views of four cameras that together provided a 360-degree watch over the property, but most significant was the small slice of Lily's property at the top edge of the northeast-facing camera's field of vision. Greene and Penelope leaned in for a closer look. Lily did too, breathing over Greene's shoulder. "Is that a bit of my driveway?" she asked no one in particular.

Marcus's forehead wrinkled. He leaned over Lily's shoulder for his own look at the monitor. "I think so." He blew out a sigh. "Let's hope we get lucky."

Greene looked over at Owen. "How long do you keep the footage?"

"Each cycle is twenty-four hours, starting at nine a.m. When I get up in the morning, if nothing looks amiss, I set it to overwrite. I've never had to keep any video."

Greene's face fell and he bolted up from his stooped position, swinging his arm through Lily's body, startling her. "Stop the recording!"

The volume and urgency in Greene's voice also startled Owen, and he jumped back a foot. "Stop the recording!" Greene barked again. "We need the footage before it's completely erased."

Owen scrambled into his desk chair. He grabbed a mouse and stopped the recording. "I'm not giving you my drive, though," he pronounced, his face sullen. "But if you bring me something to upload the contents to, I will oblige."

Greene muttered his displeasure and pulled out his cellphone. He called Sheraton next door. "Hey, we're next door to the south. We need to clone some security footage. You got a spare drive we can use? Uh-huh." He looked over at Owen. "What size?"

"It's about seven hundred gigabytes."

"He says about seven hundred gigabytes. Uh-huh." Greene nodded and put his phone away. "Mick's on his way over."

Moments later came the knock at the door. Thornfield momentarily left the office to lead Sheraton in. When the CSI stepped into the room, Owen looked nervously up and said, "Please give me the drive. I don't like people touching my stuff." Sheraton glanced over at Greene, who just gestured *Let him have it his way.*

"What system you using?" Sheraton asked as he handed Owen a terabyte drive and USB 3.0 cable.

"I've got four one-megapixel cameras recording high-quality MPEG-4 files at thirty frames per second, totaling six hundred seventy-four gigabytes per twenty-four-hour cycle."

"Impressive," cooed Sheraton. The flattery worked: Owen seemed to relax a bit. Sheraton looked over at Greene. "It's going to take a while to copy the drive."

"How long?"

"I'd guess about forty-five minutes, maybe an hour. Depends on his system."

Greene looked put out. "Hell, I might as well get on with things elsewhere. Can you stay?"

Sheraton nodded. "We're pretty much done at the house. Kerry's just finishing the last of the dusting."

"All right, we're done here. Just one last thing, Mr. Owen, I need your full name and date of birth."

The request made the hermit nervous and he visibly squirmed before replying, "Richard Henry Owen, January 27th, 1968."

"Thanks," Greene said, snapping his notebook shut. Penelope did the same.

The officers left Sheraton behind with Owen and walked back out into the bright sun. "Who's next?" Greene asked as both men reached into their pockets for sunglasses. Lily squinted and wished she also had a pair. Marcus lowered his fedora over his eyes. Penelope blinked until her eyes readjusted.

"We can canvass Rex Street and the rest of Marine Drive, maybe even ask over at the golf course," Thornfield stated, pointing east. "But honestly, Detective, I think we'd be wasting our time. We'd likely be better off announcing her death on the radio and posting notices asking anyone with information to come forward. Too many of these homes are weekend getaways for Canadians; they would've been empty on a Wednesday. Besides, I worked the nightshift last night; I gotta get some sleep."

Greene took a deep breath of sea air. Thornfield was right. A complete canvass would take hours. And for what? Lily Harrington had likely committed suicide; despite Greene's misgivings—which were few and unsubstantiated, he admitted to himself—he ought to wait for the medical examiner's report before too much time was wasted on the file. The scene was in lockdown, and Greene had interviewed the three key witnesses; any potential embarrassment for the department had been avoided. And he had real cases to solve, real victims whose only fault was not being important enough to warrant press attention.

"Okay, I'm heading back to Bellingham," Greene announced. "I'll get the report started, then wait to hear from the M.E. and Forensics before I proceed further."

They reached Harrington's house just as Reeds came out with Collins. He helped her place the last of her silver metal cases into her Forensics van, then the two joined their colleagues at the foot of Lily's porch. "What are your first thoughts, Kerry?" Greene asked, gesturing toward the house with his chin.

"Looks like a typical suicide," Reeds speculated with a shrug. "Nothing jumps out as suspicious, but we'll know more once we take a look in the lab. And of course we'll see what Anderson has to say. But right now, I'd say this'll be a quick one."

Greene let out a sigh. "Let's hope so." His thoughts returned to the mishmash of conflicting evidence gathered these past hours, and he sent out a silent prayer to the universe that the M.E. would rule it a suicide and Greene could wash his hands of Lily Harrington.

"You heading back too?" Thornfield asked Greene.

He nodded. "In a minute. I just have to get the sister's number off the cork board." He climbed the porch stairs and disappeared inside.

Reeds got into her van, laden equally with evidence and assumptions—at least that is how it felt to Lily. It seemed no one except Marcus really believed her, but he seemed more preoccupied with maintaining his starring role than he was with figuring out who killed her. Penelope was reticent at best. Greene was clearly biased despite his minor suspicions, blatantly eager to close the case and move on to a victim he felt more worthy of his efforts and attention. A sense of injustice filled Lily's heart, the organ swelling and pressing against her chest. Her head started pounding from the pressure, so much so that when Penelope turned and asked "Are you sure you were murdered?", Lily exploded.

"YES, I'M SURE! And I don't care if you believe me or not! Go back where you came from. Both of you. I don't need you or your ignorant assumptions."

"Good work," Marcus scolded Penelope. "Look how you've upset her. As if she hasn't been through enough." He reached out to Lily and tried to enclose her in his arms. "See, Lily, this is why you need me and not some long-dead detective with an ax to grind."

Lily pushed him away with such force his fedora fell to the ground. "You're a fraud." She turned an angry eye on Penelope. "And you're … you're … I don't know what the hell you are but you're not my friend. So both of you just leave me alone."

Greene returned and made his way to his cruiser. Lily stomped after him. "Just leave me alone!" she repeated as she got into the back seat and let herself be driven away into an uncertain future.

THEY WERE AT THE BORDER IN MINUTES. The Forensics van had been waved through moments earlier, but Jaipal walked out when he saw the cruiser. "Hey, Detective, spot of trouble on Marine Drive, I hear."

Greene nodded wearily. "I was just about to come inside. Lily Harrington's dead. We can all expect a flurry of press soon. I'm on my way back to Bellingham to notify next of kin and then we have to put out a statement. It's going to get weird down here for a few days, I expect."

"Soon? Or already?" Jaipal asked. "Have you seen this?" He pulled out his cellphone and showed the screen to Greene. It was open to Twitter where the hashtag *#Harringtonsuicide?* was already trending.

The news gave Greene an instant headache. "Ah crap, already? Well, I've got two deputies coming in from Bellingham to secure the property and keep Thornfield and Collins free to keep the peace; they should be here within the hour. I suspect Border Protection will send extra hands to watch for anyone trying to sneak across. I'd appreciate it if you guys kept a lookout for anything that looks like it might have been taken off her property, just in case anyone gets past our guys."

"Will do," Jaipal said and patted the top of the cruiser. Greene drove off, his gun still holstered. Jaipal didn't care: it was at his discretion whether or not to demand the gun be locked, and this Greene seemed like a decent fellow. But that new Thornfield guy, not so much.

Greene drove north along 56th Street, the window open, a southwesterly breeze blowing through what remained of his hair.

His stomach growled. He needed another coffee. There were several restaurants along 56th but he didn't have any Canadian money on him, and the exchange rate offered for American cash was never favorable. He made the decision to suffer until he crossed back into Washington, rubbing his stomach to soothe his hunger.

This was only Greene's second call to Point Roberts. He had been part of the team that had hunted down the Canadian wife-killer who used The Point as a stopover on his way from California to his eventual suicide in the ironically named town of Hope, British Columbia; that was six years ago, when Greene had first joined the division as part of the department's mandatory rotation. He was supposed to have been released from the position three months ago and sent back to regular patrol, but then a division colleague was diagnosed with cancer and Greene reluctantly agreed to another year in Homicide.

He had initially wanted the position, had welcomed his kick at the can, but it soon became apparent to him that he was best suited elsewhere. It was not the sight of a dead body, or the smell—not even one in an advanced state of decomposition—that bothered him, it was the banality of the typical murder. Jealous lovers. Vengeful ex-business partners. Psychopaths with a list of grievances from Mommy on down to the sales clerk who didn't show enough respect. Pedophiles. Drug dealers fighting over territory. A robbery gone awry. Lives ended for nothing worth dying over. There was never anything noble about the killers, nothing clever or original. They were all as passé as bellbottoms. Even the notorious ones. Just once he would like to square off with a real opponent, someone smart and worthy of his begrudging respect. A Hannibal Lecter or a Moriarty maybe. The best killers were always fictions.

Greene turned onto the highway, and for the second time in a day Lily looked out over the farmlands of Delta. A strong smell of manure wafted in through the open window of the cruiser. Lily reveled in the pungent odor: it made her feel alive again, and in an odd way it soothed her anger. Greene raised the window and turned on the air-conditioning, but that only made his nose start dripping again, and he reverted to the open-window method of cooling off. He muttered something under his breath and wiped his brow with the back of his sleeve.

He was quiet the rest of the way to the border, giving Lily time to think. Her mind was a tangled mess. Why, for instance, had Runa lied to Greene? Lily had always thought of herself as a kind and generous employer, and she had entrusted her home to Runa; the betrayal struck hard. And what of that odd exchange between her and Thornfield? "Tell me you love me," Runa had whispered to him. And there were contraceptives and a man's shirt in her bedroom. Clearly the two were an item, though they had done a brilliant job of keeping it quiet: Point Roberts was not the place where people minded their own business, and Lily had not heard a thing about Runa and Thornfield becoming lovers. Then again, Lily tended to remain aloof with her neighbors; had the news just passed her by via her own indifference?

And poor Arni. Who would nurture his talents now? Without her he would be on his own in an increasingly difficult industry where personal connections often counted for more than talent. She had been his best hope for a publishing career; he would not have killed her. He could not have killed her, could he? His was a gentle soul, yet there had been that one incident where the ugly specter of jealousy had revealed a darker side. *But don't we all have a dark side,* Lily thought next, shaking off her suspicions.

Then there was Richard Owen. Of all the people in Point Roberts he had the best access to her home. Their respective properties were gated at the front, on Marine Drive, but neither party had ever bothered to build a fence between them: there had never been a reason to. For as long as these two houses had stood, their consecutive wealthy owners had shared the same desire for security, but from outsiders, not each other. Had Lily's trust been misplaced? Had Owen really been watching murrelets in her tree, or were they just an alibi nobody could question? And the man was seriously unbalanced, that was for certain.

Then Lily had the most distressing thought of all: what did it really matter who killed her? Maybe it mattered to her, and maybe to this Greene fellow, but finding out what happened would not change the fact that she was dead. It was over. She was never going to write another word. Her literary novel will never be published. Sellinger will finish *Farewell, My Love* the way they want to and that will be it. They will roll out this fiftieth Mantova mystery to great fanfare, and, while pretending to mourn her death, will welcome the extra publicity to promote the book.

Her lips began to quiver. She was all alone in this world, wherever this world was. And after her outburst and insults, she would likely never see Marcus or Penelope again. Lily wanted desperately to return to The Point and beg their forgiveness, but she lacked the ability to get back there, or any certainty they would be there should she return. She wondered if she prayed would they hear her, or if God—assuming God existed—would relay the message.

Through tears she saw the border ahead. It suddenly felt insurmountable, as if they would see her and deny her entry, would leave her in limbo here in Canada, unable to return home.

She needn't have worried. The southbound lineup at the Douglas border crossing was lengthy as it always is on a Thursday afternoon, but Greene's cruiser was waved forward. After a quick scan of his enhanced driver's license, he and Lily were on their way to Bellingham. She was still unable to relax, yet paradoxically began to feel a deep fatigue. The unremarkable landscape along the highway added its own soporific effect, and Lily succumbed to it and the stress of the day. She laid her head against the window of Greene's cruiser and closed her eyes, grateful for a few moments of oblivion.

David Thornfield tossed about beneath the covers of his worn duvet. Sleep was proving elusive. After parting company with Detective Greene and the others at the Harrington property, the deputy had gone home to rest, but thoughts of the day's events were like a hurricane in his brain. Runa, Arni, Owen, that Martin fellow— all were creating a web of worry that had the deputy's stomach in knots. The Harrington murder had happened on his watch, his turf, and only months after he had successfully petitioned for the post. Now this Detective Greene was snooping around The Point, digging into everyone's secrets and picking away at alibis like they were scabs. What would he find? And would he uncover Thornfield's secrets, too? Would the deputy's own life become collateral damage?

He glanced at the clock. He had been in bed for ninety minutes already yet could not fall asleep. Defeated, he got up and trudged to the bathroom in search of relief. He opened his bottle of sleeping pills but found it empty; he would have to refill his prescription the next time he was in Blaine. Annoyed, he tossed the useless vial into the trash and settled for two acetaminophens, washed them down with tap water, then lumbered back to bed.

Lily awoke with a start. They had arrived at the station on Grand Avenue. Greene had parked his cruiser on Prospect Street, slammed the door, and was now walking into the bowels of the station. Lily quickly collected herself and ran after him. She followed him into the Homicide division where four officers were discussing bullet trajectories, their theories drawn in red pen on a large whiteboard that now featured a mockup of the latest Bellingham shooting. Greene acknowledged his colleagues then moved on to the small cubicle he called his office.

He put his coffee down and took off his coat, revealing wet grey stains beneath his armpits and along his back. His scent was a mix of sweat and sea breeze deodorant, which was clearly not working as advertised. Lily recoiled and covered her nose with her hand. Greene reached across his desk to a box of tissues, wiped his nose with one, then settled into his chair and pulled out his notebook. He found Amanda Clarins' number then checked the area code online. He confirmed it was Santa Clara, then called their local department. "Hello, this is Detective Paul Greene, Whatcom County Sheriff's Office in Bellingham, Washington. I need a notification made to next of kin." He listened a moment, sipping his coffee, then said, "Name's Amanda Clarins. She's the sister of the deceased, Lily Catherine Harrington of Point Roberts, Washington. That's Catherine with a C. D-O-B is 8 July 1962. All I have for the sister is a phone number: four-o-eight, five-five-five, nine-three-six-eight. Can you get an address?" Another sip and then, "Good, good. Cause of death appears to be suicide. We're still waiting on autopsy; won't likely have that until Saturday. If you could give Clarins my number and ask her to contact me, that would be appreciated." Greene gave the Santa Clara police his phone number then ended the call.

Lily's heart sank. *Dear sweet Amanda, I'm so sorry about all this.* Why Lily should be sorry was unclear to her, yet she felt a sense of guilt for the pain her sister was about to feel. They had always been close despite the physical distance, and during every visit Amanda had begged her sister to move to Santa Clara. Lily had always refused: though she never voiced it out loud, she profoundly disliked her brother-in-law, a Silicon Valley entrepreneur who viewed an artist's labor as simply something to exploit with yet another app—every time he used the term *content aggregation* as if it were the Holy Grail, Lily wanted to backslap him into tomorrow. But she loved her sister too much to argue with the leech, instead took the more passive-aggressive approach of refusing to finance any of his startups. There was also a big surprise in her will: while Lily had left a reasonable sum to her sister, Lily's main heir was not Amanda but the Artists' Defense League, notable both for their defense of copyright and their scathing criticism of the likes of Scott Clarins.

But that was for another day. Today Amanda would get the news that Lily is dead, and Lily could only hope the wretched Scott would step up to help his wife when it really counted.

Greene logged on to his computer. Lily put her olfactory discomfort aside and settled into the chair beside him. She was just getting comfortable when Penelope appeared. "We meet again," she said in a friendly tone.

Lily sheepishly looked up. "I'm surprised to see you."

"Don't be. You're not the first victim to lash out at a cop. And I understand what you're going through. I was all over the place too, at the beginning. You're not here of your own free will; it's natural that you're angry."

"Then you believe me when I say I was murdered?"

"I neither believe nor disbelieve you, Lily. I believe the facts, and we don't have all of them yet."

Suddenly Marcus strode into the cubicle, further crowding the tight space. "Ha! I knew I'd find you here," he spit at Penelope. "You just don't know when to quit, do you?"

"You're the one who refuses to take his final bow," Penelope retorted.

She assumed a falsetto voice, mimicking his earlier outburst. "'You were going to *kill* me? You witch!' Bravo. Outstanding performance, Joe. And yet still no statuette. What a tragedy."

"Everyone knows those awards are fixed," Marcus hissed. "And don't call me Joe."

"Forgive me for interrupting, but what's he looking at?" Lily asked, grateful for a reason to divert their attention away from each other. Greene was finished checking his email for urgent messages and, satisfied there were not any, was now logged in to some kind of database.

The diversion worked. Penelope reassumed her professional demeanor, while Marcus tried to affect something similar, determined to perpetuate the charade despite the obvious futility. "It's the Washington Crime Information Center database," Penelope explained, pulling out her notebook and pen from her back pocket. "First stop for checking out witnesses and potential suspects. It'll let him know if anyone has a criminal record or arrests here in the state. Though I'm surprised you don't know this, what with you being a crime writer and all."

"I work in New York," Marcus answered, indignant for both him and Lily. "This isn't our turf."

They watched over Greene's shoulder as he keyed in Runa Jonsdottir's name and date of birth. Nothing. Next he typed in the data on Arni Heimirsson. Nothing again. It was the same with Richard Owen. Greene closed down the WCIC and logged in to another database called NCIC. "This one I recognize," Lily said. "National Crime Information Center. Federal crime database. Also contains the sex offender registry." Everyone wondered if Richard Owen would show up there, but the database returned nothing on him.

The NCIC, however, did get a hit on Runa. She had been arrested but released over an alleged stalking of Stephen Harper, car dealership owner turned state assembly member; and later, after a desire-induced altercation outside the legislature in Sacramento, had been apprehended under section 5150 of the California Welfare and Institutions Code. A psychiatrist had then determined that no one in their right mind would desire a car salesman turned politician with a plastic face and a paunch, and Runa was committed for fourteen days under section 5250. She was released upon a promise to continue seeking help on an outpatient basis, but instead left the state.

"What do you think, Lily?" Penelope asked after they had read the data. "Do you think she was a danger to you?"

Lily knew of Assemblyman Harper, had met him once at a soirée in San Francisco. She shook her head. "No. I think her only crime is a bad taste in men." Marcus glared at Lily. "Oops," she said, feigning regret, "forgot she's a fan of yours."

Penelope let out a chortle then turned serious again. "How well did you know her?"

Lily raised one eyebrow. "Not well enough to know about this."

Greene next tried LexisNexis Accurint, the commercial database of financial and public records nationwide. There was nothing owing on Runa's Corolla, and she owned no real property. She only had the one cellphone, no credit cards, and a single account at the Umpqua Bank in Point Roberts.

The only question, then, was why Thornfield had lied about not knowing the nature of Runa's troubles in California. Surely he must have checked the database? Was Thornfield banging the woman? Greene made a mental note to ask the brass what, if anything, they knew about the deputy.

The records for Richard Owen were even more perplexing. Greene grunted, and Penelope leaned over to take a closer look. "That's odd," she said, drumming her fingers on the desk.

"What is?" Lily and Marcus asked in unison.

"There's no property registered to him, not even his Point Roberts house. He has no car, only one credit card—no outstanding balance—and he has a single bank account in Seattle. You said he was supposed to be a wealthy recluse."

"The house might be registered to a company to keep it safe from seizure," Marcus suggested. "Maybe he's a speculator."

"Maybe. But then he should come up as a director of a company," Penelope responded, standing back up. "And only one credit card? Who with money doesn't have a backup credit card? Weirder still, his financial records only date back to June 2008." She frowned and stared at the screen, her thumb rapidly plunging the thrust tube of her pen.

"That's just before he moved in next door," Lily said.

"It's like he didn't exist before that," Penelope replied, contemplating the possibilities. The pen migrated to her mouth, the thrust tube now wedged between her front teeth.

Lily looked up at Penelope. "Are you thinking what I'm thinking?"

"What?" asked Marcus, annoyed he was not in on their thoughts.

"Witness protection," Penelope postulated with a wave of her pen. "It's long been rumored that The Point is a favorite spot for the federal witness protection program. Most secure neighborhood in the country."

"Witness protection wouldn't give him such a nice house," Marcus scoffed, adjusting his trench coat. "The Feds are way too cheap."

"It might still be his own money," Lily hypothesized. "They might've just helped him hide it."

"From whom?" Marcus asked.

The women shrugged. "That we might need to figure out," Penelope answered, tucking her pen away in the coil spine of her notebook.

Greene sent a copy of the Accurint entry to the printer. As soon as he left the cubicle to retrieve the document, Penelope reached over and scanned his notes. Then, to Lily's surprise and amazement, Penelope picked up Greene's pen and added *WP?* to his notes. "Oh my God," Lily exclaimed, her mouth agape. "You're a poltergeist!"

Penelope smiled. "Stick with me, sister, and I'll teach you a few tricks." She tossed the pen back onto Greene's notebook.

"You're playing with fire, Penelope," Marcus warned. "You know that's frowned upon. There could be consequences."

Penelope shrugged with indifference. "What are they going to do? Send me to the back of the line? I couldn't care less. I'm in no hurry to return. I like things just the way they are. As do you. You just don't have the balls to admit it."

"Really?" Marcus sneered at Penelope. "Seems to me my balls were perfectly adequate when they were servicing *you*."

"Could you two please not start again?" Lily pleaded. "I can't take—"

Their conversation was interrupted by the return of Greene. He filed the paper away then sat back down at his desk. He reached for his pen—and froze. He looked nervously down at his notes and saw Penelope's addition. "What the fuck!" he gasped. He jumped up from his seat and spun around in the cubicle, then slowly backed out, his face white, beads of sweat dotting his forehead.

"Hey, Paul," a man's voice called out from the other side of the squad room. "What's the deal with Point Roberts? The phone's ringing off the hook. Do you need help on the file?"

Greene tried his best to compose himself, but his voice was still a little shaky when he answered, "No. Looks like a suicide. Autopsy's tomorrow. Media Relations will just have to cope until then."

"You okay, Paul?" the man asked as he came into view. He had three chevrons on his sleeve indicating his status as sergeant, and Lily guessed he was the man in charge of the division.

"Yeah, yeah. Just got a bit too much sun today."

"Well, it's the end of the day anyway. Time to get home to Ellie."

"Sure, um …," Greene replied awkwardly.

"How's she doing, by the way?"

"Good days and bad," Greene nodded, still trying to collect himself. "You know how it is."

"How you coping?"

"Good. Good. Um, her sister lives nearby now. She's retired. Helps out."

"Well, off you go," the sergeant said as he patted Greene on the arm. "And you're right. Nothing you can do about the media frenzy; that's Clayton's problem. But let me know how the autopsy goes soon as it's done."

Greene nodded and stepped back into his cubicle, his hands still shaking as he logged out of his computer. He grabbed his coat and walked briskly toward the squad room door, leaving the remains of his coffee behind.

"Now look what you've done!" Marcus scolded Penelope. "We could have just planted the thought in his head, but no. You just had to show off to Lily." He turned to seek her concurrence but Lily had left the cubicle and was hurrying after Greene. Marcus began to walk after her but Penelope held him back.

"Let her go, Joe. There's nothing we can do until tomorrow. Give her some space and we'll meet at the autopsy."

"Where are you going?" Marcus asked. He hated the thought of spending another minute with his ex, but best to keep an eye on her.

"Places," she replied vaguely.

"Where, Penelope?" he asked, suspicious. He adjusted the collar on his coat like some television gangster, as if *that* would intimidate the likes of Penelope Winters.

"Places," she replied again, the rise of one eyebrow indicating she was not about to reveal anything more to *him*. "I've got some ideas I want to explore. You go do whatever you want. Follow Lily, go home, go bed some newbie, I don't care. I'll see you tomorrow."

"Fine. *But stop calling me Joe.*" But Penelope did not hear him; she was already gone.

Marcus pouted for a moment then made his own decision. He had seen the spirit of a hot young redhead rise from a car wreck on Central Avenue just as they had arrived earlier; if he hurried he might still be able to find her and offer some comfort. And if he were really lucky, she might already be a Marcus Mantova fan.

GREENE WAS STILL SHAKING AS HE CLIMBED into his cruiser. His eyes darted nervously about, as if he suspected he were being followed. He needed a drink. Shot of scotch, neat, with a beer chaser. American beer. None of that pretentious European stuff some of his colleagues had taken to, thought it made them look sophisticated. Greene thought it made them look gay. And unpatriotic. Not that he had anything against gays.

He held tightly onto the steering wheel to ground himself. Ford. Crown Victoria Police Interceptor. CVPI for short. Solid. American. Dependable. That it had actually been manufactured in Canada was semantics: they were just the fifty-first state, after all. Besides, the Vic was discontinued, replaced by the Police Interceptor Sedan. Dual exhaust, 305 horsepower, 280 pounds of torque. Chicago built. Greene wanted one of those.

He stopped at a drugstore in a strip mall on Alabama Street. He searched the aisles without assistance until he found the magnesium and the nasal saline rinse, then paid for them at the pharmacy counter, suddenly too self-conscious to go through the general cash registers. He felt like he was a teenager again, buying condoms at Holland Drugs on Metcalf Street in Sedro-Woolley. There had been no pharmacy in Lyman where he grew up on the shore of the Skagit River, and Ellie had made him borrow his father's car and drive the nine miles west on the North Cascades Highway so she wouldn't be "one of those girls." She had promised herself to him on his seventeenth birthday—13 August 1978—after six months of dating and his persistent proclamations of unwavering devotion, the deed performed on a blanket beneath a giant cedar on the shoreline under cover of darkness. He had been too quick and all elbows, her hair caught in his wristwatch, but they were still together when he graduated from high school the following summer and bought his first car with money earned working alongside his father servicing farm machinery. It was in that secondhand 1973 Pontiac GTO—painted green with a black racing stripe—that a year later their luck ran out and Ellie got pregnant the winter after her own graduation when the highway was closed for two weeks due to heavy snow. Their son was three years old when Greene made it through the academy and joined the Whatcom County Sheriff's Office. Another son came two years after that.

Almost forty years now and they were still together, his love as faithful and unwavering as he had professed as a teenager. Sometimes, when Greene was out after work with colleagues, the subject would come up and someone would realize Ellie was the only woman he had ever had sex with, and there would follow a gasp of shock followed by what looked like pity, which Greene never understood. It was he who pitied them, the serial monogamists with their consecutive failures, their adulteries and divorces, always looking for someone better, as if perfection were right around the corner and they just had to be patient and keep their eye open. He had found perfection early in life, and looking around for anyone else struck him as a futile exercise, a waste of time and energy.

He left the drugstore and settled back in the car, a restless Lily tapping her fingers against the window and humming to herself, waiting for him to return. He drove back onto Alabama Street, headed east.

Ten minutes later they finally arrived at his home on Willow Street in the middle-class neighborhood of Roosevelt. He pulled into the driveway of a midcentury rambler with—Lily could not believe it—cedar siding stained leaf green, and left the car outside the attached single-car garage. The lot was small but the landscaping mature and well cared for, with flowering bushes that blossomed in bold pinks and reds. A clichéd but quaint white picket fence bordered the property and matched the wooden ramp that led to the front door where once had stood a few small steps.

They entered the house. It was tiny—no more than twelve hundred square feet, Lily estimated—with wood wall paneling in the living room and a stone fireplace where a cheap gas insert had long ago replaced the original wood burner. The floors were hardwood, damaged by the tacks of wall-to-wall carpet that had been added later then torn out and the floors refinished but not replaced. The walls were adorned with family photos, petit point pictures, and a few pieces of cheap art; books and a few knickknacks sat on built-in shelves. The home, in real estate parlance, was a gut job, yet it was immaculate, cozy and inviting. Lily could not help but make a sad comparison to her own newer, larger and yet less soulful house.

She followed the detective into the eat-in kitchen. A middle-aged woman, attractive face dulled with fatigue, sat outside the patio doors in a wheelchair beneath a covered deck. Its cedar planks were weathered, the corrugated plastic roof littered with tree and bird debris, but the garden was large and also immaculate, its brightly colored bushes fluttering in the breeze.

Greene bent down and kissed the woman. "How are you, my darling?" he gently asked.

"Tired. The ladies came for tea but I'm afraid I didn't last very long."

"You had your interferon today?"

"Yes. They've upped the dose a bit, which explains the aches," she replied, absentmindedly rubbing her arm at the injection site.

Interferon? Wheelchair? Oh my lord, the poor woman has MS, Lily thought. *How dreadful!*

"Where's Carol?"

"At the Legion. Some fundraiser for a man in Dad's regiment. Lost his wife two days ago and needs help with the funeral expenses. She picked up some Chinese earlier. We just need to reheat it."

"Are you hungry now, Ellie, or do you want to wait?"

"Now is fine. But just a little please, Paul. I've not much of an appetite today."

Greene wheeled Ellie into the kitchen and set her at the table. He opened the fridge and removed the takeaway cartons. Ellie watched from her perch at the table as he began to spoon out helpings of sweet-and-sour chicken, fried rice, and mixed vegetables onto plates. He put one in the microwave and set the timer. Lily eyed the food. The sight of it made her mentally hungry as she had been earlier in the day, though she still did not feel the craving physically.

"Tell me about your day," Ellie suggested.

"You're not going to believe this, but Lily Harrington is dead."

Ellie gasped. "Are you serious?"

"Would I kid a fan?" Greene said, smiling.

"But how?"

"Looks like a suicide."

Ellie gasped again. "Oh sweet Jesus. How?"

"Hanged herself." Greene pointed a wary finger at his wife. "But no blabbing that to your book club, Ellie. Cause of death has not been announced yet."

And please, I beg you, do not tell her about the snotsicle.

"Will it be on the news tonight, do you think?"

"Probably. We can't release a statement until we notify next of kin but the Internet is already active. Harrington's got a sister in California. As soon as they call in and let us know they've reached her, Media Relations will put out the official word."

"Are you lead investigator?"

"For now. Once the M.E. confirms it's a suicide, I'll move on to a real case."

"It *is* a real case," Lily blurted out before she remembered he couldn't hear her.

"Her poor family," Ellie lamented. "It's bad enough to lose a loved one, but to do so in such a public way must be very distressing."

"It's the price of fame, my love," Greene said, smiling at his wife. "Be thankful we're ordinary."

"Yes. I suppose no one will be banging down your door when I go. Small miracles, I guess."

Greene's face fell. "Ellie, please don't talk like that. You're not going anywhere." The microwave dinged in agreement. He set her plate on the table but the sight of the food made her eyes well up.

"Ellie, love, what's the matter? Is it Harrington?"

Ellie shook her head.

"Are you in pain? Do you need your medication?"

She shook her head again, and despite her considerable efforts not to, Ellie began to cry. "I-I'm such a burden, Paul. I can barely look after myself, never mind you and our home. I can't even cook you a nice meal anymore. It's not right."

Greene kissed his wife on her forehead, then leaned his own against her hair. "Ellie, you are *not* a burden. You are my joy. I can't imagine life without you."

"But it's not fair to you," she said, struggling to speak. "You should be retired by now. But you can't. We need your benefits. But you wouldn't if I weren't here." She began to sob, convulsions wracking her frail frame, her fingers grasping the edge of the table.

Greene lifted his wife out of her wheelchair and wrapped his arms tightly around her to quell her tremors. "Ellie, my love, please don't say such things," he said, fighting back his own tears. "You're just having a bad day, that's all. It'll pass."

Ellie wailed into her husband's chest, her body swaying on wobbly legs. He held on for dear life, fearful he would drop her into a chasm too deep to rescue her from. She could feel his fear through her anguish, his heart pumping erratically beneath her cheek, and she felt sorry for him, sorry that he was saddled with her, yet deeply grateful that he still held on despite her failings. Eventually her concern for him surpassed her shame, and she nodded her head and slowly recovered her composure. "Yes, I know. I know, Paul. It's just a bad day. It'll pass."

Greene pulled back a bit so he could look into Ellie's eyes. He gently wiped the tears from her face and swept back a stray strand of her speckled brunette hair. "Would you dance with me?" he asked with a wan smile.

Ellie smiled weakly and nodded her head. She steadied herself with the table while her husband walked over to the corner built-ins and turned on a small CD player. From its tinny speakers a soothing orchestral piece began, followed by the silky sound of a woman's voice. Greene returned to Ellie's side and pulled her into his arms. She leaned against him for support, and as they swayed to the music he whispered the lyrics into her ear:

> Finally, my love has come to me
> Finally, my loneliness is over
> And like a bird I am free

Lily watched, embarrassed by her intrusion, and it was moments before she realized she was crying. It was a further few moments before she realized she was angry and jealous that she had been reduced to tears by this portly man—with his bald spot and snotty handkerchief—dancing with his crippled wife. "Damn you, Greene," Lily said as she sniffled and wiped her own nose on her forearm, "just damn you."

Marcus Mantova sat back against the tree and sighed. He wished he had a cigarette. Redhead was curled up in the grass beside him, splendid in her nakedness, and fast asleep after what Marcus was certain was his fastest seduction yet. Bewildered and frightened, she had fallen easily for his soothing words and promise to stick beside her; it had taken less than an hour to get that blue sundress off her.

He had taken her to Maritime Heritage Park, on the bank of the Whatcom Creek Waterway just west of the Sheriff's Office, and bedded her on the inlet's sandy shore. Now the deed was done, and he had nothing more to do but stare out over the water and think.

His mind immediately returned to Penelope. What was she doing here? He hadn't seen her in ages until she showed up in Point Roberts. Interfering witch. He had forgotten how much he despised Penelope until he had walked into the house and saw that unmistakable Amazon frame. What he would not give to put another bullet in her head.

He reached down and fondled his balls. *Seem big enough to me,* Marcus thought, *no matter what insults Penelope hurls my way.*

His next thought was that it might be prudent to check in on Runa: there was something definitely going on between her and Deputy Thornfield, and Marcus wanted to know what. Had Runa been in cahoots with the man? If so, to what end? Was it just a romantic affair, or something more sinister?

But why should I care if Thornfield wished harm to Lily? Marcus thought bitterly. *She was going to kill me, her great detective, her meal ticket. Should have done the deed myself, but I'm way too smart to pull a poltergeist move like Penelope did. That just brings unwanted attention upon oneself.*

He looked down at Redhead. He didn't even know her name. He didn't care. She wasn't even his type. He stood up, got dressed, then willed himself back to Point Roberts with a mind to spying on Runa.

Penelope waited until Marcus left the station, then slipped out from her hiding place in one of the interrogation rooms. She walked down the empty hallway and returned to the Homicide squad room.

The four detectives who had earlier been discussing their case had left the whiteboard and were gone. Penelope ambled over to Greene's cubicle for a look around. He had taken his notebook but left the pen behind. Penelope rolled her eyes: it was not like she had never moved anything before in this place. She had been haunting Homicide ever since she found her feet, dumped Marcus, and got back to work. Death, Penelope had decided, was nothing more than an inconvenience, and she had cases to solve. More importantly, she had sworn an oath to protect the good citizens of Washington State, and she had no intention of quitting just because some gangster put a bullet in her head.

The thought made her rub her forehead. "Yup," she murmured to herself, "still there."

It had become her habit to go through cases overnight when the detectives were gone, and if anything struck her she would leave notes for the investigator or check in on suspects, seeing as she did not need a warrant—or even a key—to enter their premises. Her actions led to the usual "Hey, Frank, did you leave me a note about the Hastings case?" type questions, all of which were denied with a shrug, and soon the detectives stopped asking each other. There were often uneasy looks over one's shoulder, and one officer even set up a hidden camera to catch the intruder, but all he got was a whole lot of static, both literally and figuratively. Literally, because Penelope's presence merely registered on camera as magnetic interference; figuratively, because her insights were often right on the money and nobody was keen to see her depart. Detectives with a particularly troublesome case took to leaving the file on top of their desk in the hope of a lead come morning, and even though nothing Penelope left them was admissible in court, she gave the detectives direction and kept them from wasting their time on dead ends, pun intended. No one was willing to admit out loud that a ghost had helped solve a homicide, each detective got to take sole credit, and the collective clearance rate of the department went up. It was a win-win situation all around, save for the occasional freak-out moments like earlier with Greene. *Okay, okay, that was stupid,* Penelope finally admitted to herself. Joe was right: she had been showing off. She had never pierced the veil in here during the day like that, and she vowed not to do it again except in an emergency.

She busied herself for the next few hours reading the notes on the shooting, then studied the whiteboard. She could not find anything they might have missed, so she took down the name and address of the chief suspect and headed out. She would sit in on him for a few hours and eavesdrop; if anything significant came up she would come back to base and leave another note. Other than that she would rest awhile: tomorrow would be Lily's autopsy, and Penelope wanted to be sharp for that.

David Thornfield awoke with a headache. The painkillers he had taken earlier to induce sleep had worn off, and scary thoughts were rattling around his brain again. He could hear them clanging against his skull, mocking him in the voice of his father: "This here is what we call a fuck up, son, and not in the good sense." Thunderous laughter then turning serious again, moods switching on and off like a light bulb, keeping the boy off balance. Gone for months: Honduras, Chad, Libya, the Persian Gulf. Home again yet still distant until a neighbor happened by and then it was "Look at my son! How big he's grown! Decent grades, too. Expect he'll follow in my footsteps: this country needs more good soldiers. By the way, that pussy boy of yours still on the chess team?" More thunderous laughter, the mocking tone nullifying the "just kidding" slap on the back.

Thornfield turned on the television. Harrington's death was all over it. Bestselling author, worldwide sales, twenty languages, blah blah blah. Her veneered smile filling the screen. But no snotsicle.

He let out a snort: if only everyone knew the world-renowned Lily Harrington had died with a snotsicle hanging off her famous face. He relished that he knew this, that he was only one of a handful who did. That was the thing he loved most about policing: the glimpse into people's real lives, not the ones put out for public display; and he, keeper of secrets, holder of keys, the knight in shining armor who gallantly sealed his lips.

He thought to call his mom. He loved his mom. Her honey blond hair that always smelled of vanilla, her bright red fingernails that lovingly scratched his head. And then just like that she was gone. He saw her only once after she left his father, an apparition on the other side of the courtroom, her legal aid lawyer struggling to be heard over the booming voice of his father's counsel. Accusations of adultery. Unfit parent. Was any of it true? If not, why had she not fought harder for him?

They had reconnected after he joined the police, but there was still a distance blood could not cross even though she was just down the highway in Seattle. She had long since remarried—a grandmother now courtesy of his half-brother—and it seemed her affections were finite and needed to be reserved for the next generation, those she perceived as more in need.

He wondered next if he should go see Runa. That might cure his headache. But he didn't want to risk anyone seeing him there, not tonight anyway, so soon after she had been questioned by Greene. The optics would not wash. He reached to the floor for his laptop. In the absence of a real woman, fantasy would have to suffice.

Marcus leaned against the tree he was hiding behind on Runa's property. He had been watching for a few hours already, but Thornfield had not returned and no one else came to visit or ask further questions. Runa had simply made dinner, watched some television, and washed the dishes.

But then, just when Marcus was thinking he was wasting his time, Arni approached the trailer and knocked. Runa opened the door, a few words were spoken, then Arni fell into Runa's arms, sobbing. He let her hold him close for a moment, then broke away and collapsed onto her couch. Runa sat beside him, her face lined with concern but her eyes weirdly distant, as if her face said one thing but her mind another. Marcus read the words *I'm so sorry* on her lips, then what looked like *I knew you admired her.* But then she turned her face away from Marcus's view and he lost what was said next. He considered sneaking in closer, anxious to hear the conversation, but decided against it, fearful Penelope or Lily might show up with the same idea to spy on Runa, and he would have to explain his presence.

Arni wiped his face and looked at Runa, his eyes searching hers for an explanation, some kind of rational reason why his lover was gone. And then, to the surprise of everyone, including himself, he grasped Runa's arms and kissed her, as if he could kiss the answer out of her mouth, or at least find some comfort there. She pulled back, shocked but not angry, then her eyes deadened again. She stared blankly at Arni, waiting, but whether it was for an apology, an explanation, or another kiss was impossible to tell from her expression. Arni wiped his mouth with the back of his hand, looked anxiously at Runa for a moment, then burst into shameful tears and fled her trailer as swiftly as he had arrived.

Marcus watched Arni stumble down Park Lane, twilight closing in on him. He turned onto Julius Drive and disappeared, and Marcus turned his attention back to Runa. She, too, disappeared from view, then the bathroom light came on. Several minutes passed, and Marcus realized she had likely retired for a soak in the tub. He maintained his distance despite the opportunity to spy on her nakedness, as lovely as he knew her nakedness to be.

An hour later Runa alighted from the bathroom in her terry robe, picked up *Love and Secrets* and settled down on the couch to read. *Oh damn,* Marcus thought as she opened the book to the sex scene between him and Anastasia, his love interest in the novel. He could feel his own lust rising as Runa imagined herself in place of Anastasia, but he chose to fight his desire: it would be a huge mistake to bed Runa now. Besides, millions of women put themselves in this same place every day; he could have his pick of any of them. Sex with live women was never as good as with other spirits—the sensation never managed entirely to cross the divide—but they were a reliable option when no one else was available. He briefly considered looking again for Redhead and thinking of some excuse for his absence, but decided against it: the last thing he needed right now was some distraught newbie clinging to him and getting in his way. He scanned the airwaves for a more suitable conquest, honed in on a lonely brunette reading Lily's *Tragedy on Elk Island*, then headed out to Brunette's apartment a safe distance away.

Lily yawned and sank back in the easy chair in the Greenes' living room. She was exhausted. The rest of her evening had been spent watching game shows and classic television with Paul and Ellie, and try as Lily might she could not successfully execute any kind of mental manipulation to get either of them to change to the documentary channel.

When the ten o'clock news arrived, Lily's death was front and center. The Internet had been lit up like Christmas all day. The nonsense had begun as a trickle of speculation from the moment police had pulled into her home that morning, and over the course of the day Lily had been dead, alive but in a coma, in stable condition in Bellingham, critically injured and airlifted to Seattle, kidnapped by terrorists, held hostage in her home (also by terrorists), and "missing" before the public finally settled definitively on dead. Once that was fixed, the manner of her death became the next guessing game; top picks were shooting, stabbing, strangulation, beheading, drug overdose, erotic asphyxiation, home invasion, and accidental drowning in the Strait of Georgia. Suspects included Muslims of all stripes, the government (all levels), the CIA, ex-lovers, crazed fans, angry neighbors, competing authors and publishers, jealous gigolos, and of course Lily herself by suicide. The official statement, put out by the Whatcom County Sheriff's Office just three hours earlier, would only confirm that Lily Harrington was dead but would not confirm cause, only to say that foul play was not suspected. This, of course, did nothing to quell the rumors, and police refusal to elaborate only encouraged the conspiracy theorists and Internet trolls. "Sources" were abundant but never named.

Greene yawned and slumped down lower into the couch, the cushion sagging beneath his weight. "People are stupid."

"I hear ya," Lily concurred, involuntarily aping his yawn. "I've never hired a gigolo."

Greene's cellphone rang. He picked it up off the coffee table and checked the call display. It was a Santa Clara number. "Ah crap," he mumbled as he turned down the television, "this is likely the sister." Greene hated this part of the job, the discomfort of grieving relatives. It was not that he lacked empathy, but rather that he possessed too much, and each time he had to deliver bad news it left a stain on his soul.

Lily sat at attention, her back stiff, apprehensive. "Detective Greene," he answered then listened for a moment. "Ms. Clarins, I'm very sorry for your loss. Yes, it is indeed a shock. For everyone. Your sister was a valued member of the community." He grimaced and moved the phone a little ways from his ear, and Lily trembled at the garbled sound of her sister sobbing.

"At the moment it looks like a suicide," Greene replied as he pressed the phone back against his cheek and rubbed his forehead. "No, not certain. We won't know definitively until after the autopsy. It's scheduled for tomorrow. I'll have more for you once we get the results … You'll need to liaise with the medical examiner to take possession of your sister's body for burial. I'll have them call you tomorrow with the information … Not just yet. I haven't released the scene. But as soon as I do, myself or someone from the department will contact you … We're doing our best to control the media, but you know how they are. I can assure you that you will be the first to hear of any updates … Yes, yes of course. And again, I am very sorry for your loss."

Greene put the phone down and hung his head. Ellie reached over and rubbed his shoulder. "Well done, my prince. I know how much you hate those calls."

He nodded wearily. "I should get to bed." He turned off the television, alighted from the sofa, then helped Ellie back into her wheelchair.

Lily watched through tears as the two went off together to the bedroom. If only she knew how to relocate she would rush to her sister's side, would hold her and promise her everything will be all right. Amanda wouldn't be able to hear the promise—across the veil or through her own anguish—and it would be a lie, of course, but Lily would utter the words anyway. There were moments when lies were the only compassionate option.

Her hands shook as she wiped her face and tried to compose herself. Greene had reminded her that her autopsy is tomorrow. Would she have the stomach to attend, obvious answer aside?

LILY AWOKE FRIDAY MORNING TO THE SOUND of Paul Greene getting ready for work. Mindful not to intrude any more than she already had, Lily stayed on the couch while the detective showered then dressed himself and his wife. He made breakfast, put the dishes in the dishwasher, made sure Ellie had her emergency call button around her neck, then headed out with Lily at his side.

It was a nerve-wracking drive for her. She fretted the whole way to the Whatcom County Health Department building on North State Street, wondering if she was strong enough for the obvious trauma to come. She hoped Penelope and Marcus would show up, both for their support and to make note of the M.E.'s findings should Lily lose her wits and leave the room.

When they arrived at the morgue, Lily looked in the rearview mirror and nervously fixed her hair. She alighted from the car and straightened her dress in the reflection of the side window. Satisfied she at least looked presentable in death, she took a deep breath and followed Greene inside.

Reeds was there, waiting with her camera gear in the hallway outside the morgue. Penelope and Marcus were also there as hoped; Penelope was leaning against the wall watching Marcus adjust his coat and hat in the mirror-like surface of a darkened office window. "Oh, for God's sake, Joe, stop your preening. How do you even see yourself in a mirror anyway? You're a bloody vampire."

"*I'm* a vampire? You suck the life out of everyone you touch. No surprise they put you in Homicide: probably figured you couldn't do any damage seeing as the vics were already dead."

Marcus looked surprised when Penelope didn't answer but instead straightened up and looked over his shoulder. He turned to see Lily arriving with Greene. "Morning, Lily," Penelope said, beating Marcus to the punch. "You up for this? You don't have to watch, you know."

Lily shook her head. "Yes I do. I don't know why, exactly, but I feel I have to be here."

"We'll get you through it," Marcus assured her with a squeeze of her arm, trying again to upstage Penelope.

At exactly eight a.m. Dr. Anderson and his pathology technologist came down the stairs, and Anderson unlocked the morgue door. Everyone followed him in, a shaky Lily included.

Anderson's assistant fetched Lily's corpse from the "frig" and wheeled her to the center of the room, then opened the body bag its full length. Reeds immediately began taking photographs, shooting Lily from every angle. She felt like she was being murdered all over again.

She swallowed hard as she stared at her face, puffy and pale in death. The end of the noose was still around her neck, the rope having earlier been cut about eight inches above the knot by CSI Sheraton. Her stomach was bloated, and she prayed she would not let out a death fart like the kind she had read about in her years of researching murder. The snotsicle had melted, a sticky yellow residue over her lips the only evidence of the icicle's previous existence. *Small miracles,* Lily thought, unintentionally echoing Ellie Greene.

The detective's cellphone rang. He checked the number but it was not one he recognized. "Greene here," he said, his voice a question mark. He listened a moment then responded angrily, "How did you get this number? Do *not* call this number again. You want information you call Media Relations. *Comprendes?* I repeat, do *not* call this number again. If you do I will find you and beat you with a copy of that rag you work for." He hung up then turned off his cellphone. "Stupid tabloids," he said to his small audience as he put his phone into his breast pocket.

"We've been getting those calls too," Anderson said. "I answer their questions in Latin. *Omnia durantibus afficiuntur,*" he chortled. No one else got the joke. "It means 'all things come to those who wait." Anderson's assistant chuckled. Everyone else remained stone faced. "Tough crowd," the M.E. jested, then pulled down the microphone suspended from the ceiling. He crooned the opening line of "Strangers in the Night" into the mic before turning serious and flipping on the switch.

"Autopsy is begun at 8:05 a.m. on June 5, 2015," Anderson dictated into the microphone. "Case number 2015-483WA. Present are myself, Dr. Clive Anderson, MD; my assistant, pathology technologist Brian Taylor, BS, CLS; Whatcom County CSI Kerry Reeds, forensic photographer; and lead investigator, Whatcom County Detective Paul Greene, Homicide."

"Also present," Penelope added, "are Lily Harrington, victim; Whatcom County Detective Penelope Winters, Homicide; and Detective Joe"—she raised her hands and gestured quotation marks—"'Marcus Mantova' Esposito, Hollywood Division."

"Oh, aren't you the clever one," Marcus responded in a surly tone.

"Don't start!" Lily said angrily. "This is hard enough for me without you two going at each other."

"Sorry," Penelope said, looking genuinely apologetic.

"Sorry," echoed Marcus, if somewhat less convincingly.

Penelope positioned herself beside Dr. Anderson as he began the external examination. "Victim is a Caucasian female, age fifty-two," he intoned. "The body is present in a white body bag. Victim is wearing a white sleeveless lace shift dress; make is"—Anderson lifted Lily's head and checked the label—"Armani. No obvious staining or damage to dress. On feet are white patent-leather slingback sandals with multicolored cork soles."

Lily was impressed: the man knew what a slingback is. She wondered next if he were a closet cross-dresser, if he might be wearing women's underwear at this very moment. To her surprise the thought brought her some comfort: that maybe she, a woman freakishly watching her own autopsy, was not the only oddball in the room.

Anderson removed Lily's shoes and inspected them. "Make is Stuart Weitzman. Leather soles. Minor wear. No damage. Slightly heavier wear on back edge of heels may indicate dragging, but inconclusive." He handed the shoes to Brian, who placed them in an evidence bag.

Lily's face fell into a pout: she had just bought those shoes. The thought made her look down, and for the first time since she died she became acutely aware that she was wearing the same clothes as when she had been so rudely exiled from the living. And then she realized she might now be wearing the same clothes for all eternity. Had she known this she would have changed into something more practical. And not white. Did clothes get dirty in the afterlife? She scrutinized Penelope's black pants and crisp white shirt. They were spotless. *Okay, maybe that won't be an issue.*

But if we are stuck with the clothes we died in, Lily wondered next, would this mean she was going to come across a multitude of people wearing hospital gowns? She imagined a zombie apocalypse of flabby asses and fleshy scrotums peeking out the back of crinkled cotton drapes, and shuddered. Lily suddenly felt a surge of gratitude that she had died in Armani and Stuart Weitzman, not a hospital gown or—maybe just as bad—yoga pants and a mid-priced cotton twinset.

Her thoughts were steered abruptly back to the autopsy when Anderson removed one of her earrings and held it next to a small ruler. "Victim is wearing brilliant-cut diamond earrings of approximately eight millimeters in diameter set in what is presumed to be white gold or platinum, one in each ear. On left wrist is a platinum and diamond watch." Anderson removed the rest of Lily's jewelry and handed them to Brian, who placed the pieces in another evidence bag.

"I guess that rules out robbery," Greene said flippantly, the fingernails of his right hand resting against his teeth.

"At least for now," Lily said. "They had better not disappear between now and probate."

"Face bears lipstick, eye shadow, and mascara," the M.E. continued without replying to either Greene or Lily. "Eyebrows have been augmented with cosmetic tattooing. There is no bruising to face. Skin is pale, consistent with upright position victim was found in." Anderson shone a light in Lily's eyes and measured her pupils. "No petechia in eyes. Irises are brown and corneas are cloudy. Pupils measure 0.3 centimeters." Next he measured her hair. "Hair is straight, dyed dark brown, and measures eleven inches at longest point. Gray roots are approximately one millimeter, indicating recent coloring."

He leaned down and breathed in deeply. "There is a slight odor of floral perfume still on the body despite initial decomposition."

Anderson placed a measuring tape around the rope still tied around Lily's neck. "Around the victim's neck is a noose bearing a hangman's knot. The rope is half-inch twisted-strand nylon." Penelope leaned in for a closer look at the rope, then stood back again and scribbled a few lines down in her notebook.

Anderson's eyes followed Lily's body down. "Fingernails are French manicured and appear to be of medium length. Fingernail beds are blue. There is no damage to the nails or manicure. Toenails are painted red. Lividity in hands, lower legs and feet consistent with death by hanging. Petechial hemorrhages are also present in extremities, consistent with prolonged suspension after death."

With Brian's help Anderson removed Lily's dress. "Removal of dress reveals victim is wearing beige bra and panties. Both are intact and there is no obvious damage."

The sight of her lying there in her lingerie sent Lily's thoughts zooming off to the adage that you should always wear clean underwear in case you got into a car accident. If people only knew it went *way* beyond the hospital. And then she thought of the headline she had read in a recent edition of *Vogue*: "Summer dresses to die for!" If she ever became a poltergeist she would break into *Vogue* and change the headline to "Summer dresses to die in!" And suggest a spread on funeral fashions.

But then Anderson began to remove Lily's bra, and she felt a blinding panic. She jumped in between the table and Marcus. "I need you to leave," she said, her voice trembling: Lily had never felt more vulnerable in her life.

"Lily, I can assure you I am capable of keeping my professional distance," Marcus said as he stretched his neck for a peek.

"GET OUT!"

"Wow, fine," Marcus huffed and strode toward the door. "But it's not like I've never seen you naked before," he added as he left the room.

Lily's eyes widened in surprise. "What?" She looked to Penelope for an explanation.

Penelope shrugged. "Told you he's an asshole."

Still shaking, Lily turned back around to witness her continued humiliation. When her panties were removed she saw no indication of postmortem urination or defecation—something she had read about and which she had feared—and breathed a sigh of relief. She looked nervously at Greene as he looked down at her naked body. His expression was neutral, and she found in his detachment further comfort.

"No obvious bruising to body," Anderson droned on with similar detachment. "No birthmarks, tattoos, or other identifying markings." Anderson handed one end of a long measuring tape to Brian and together they determined Lily's height, then wheeled the cart onto a floor scale.

"Body is that of a normally developed female measuring sixty inches and weighing one hundred one pounds, and appears consistent with the stated age of fifty-two years."

"Really?" Penelope said, skeptical, the butt of her pen resting against her chin. "I think you look at least ten years younger."

"Ah, thanks," Lily replied, truly appreciative. The compliment lightened her mood, and seconds later it occurred to her that this might have been Penelope's intention.

Anderson carefully cut off the noose that encircled Lily's neck. A dark purple version of the rope's pattern was imprinted deeply into her flesh. "Removal of rope reveals a ligature mark (known throughout this report as Ligature A) on the neck below the mandible. Ligature A is approximately one-half inch wide and encircles the neck in the form of a V on the anterior of the neck and an inverted V on the posterior of the neck, consistent with hanging. Petechial hemorrhaging at Ligature A is consistent with perimortem injury."

Brian began scraping beneath Lily's fingernails and tapping the contents into a little bag. A lock of her hair was cut off, and her pubic hair shaved; both were collected and documented. Lily frowned: had she known she was in for a Brazilian she would not have bothered to pay for a French wax just last week.

She was fingerprinted next for a comparison set, then her body washed, the water filtered to catch any bits of evidence that might fall off during the rinse. When Brian was finished washing the body, Anderson picked up a scalpel. He paused, his arm suspended over

Lily's left shoulder. "Okay," he said to Reeds and Greene, "we're going to open her up now. Are you keeping us company or shall we continue on our own?"

"It doesn't seem like you have anything for us so far," Greene replied. "We've got cases to work on. Call me if anything contrary comes up."

Lily felt another rise of panic. *Nothing?* Whoever had done this to her had been exceedingly clever, or exceedingly lucky. She looked to Penelope for help. "Do something, Penelope. Please. They mustn't get away with this. You have to tell them I didn't kill myself."

Penelope scowled and crossed her arms across her chest. "Don't panic, Lily. We'll figure it out. But there's no sense leaving a message until we know what really happened."

"What do you mean 'what really happened'? You don't believe me, do you? Just like before. You think I killed myself."

"I didn't say that."

"But you're thinking it!"

"I am not!" Penelope replied tersely. "Now get a hold of yourself. I have no patience for hysterics."

Lily fought back tears as she watched Greene and Reeds leave the morgue with nothing but incorrect assumptions and a camera full of unflattering photos. And now Lily was again annoying the one person who might really be able to help. It was all going so pear shaped. She could feel her breath quicken, her chest tighten, panic strangling her heart, fearful Penelope would leave and never come back. Lily turned around to face Penelope, to beg her to stay, when Lily saw Anderson's scalpel cut down the length of her torso, and then everything went black.

LILY AWOKE TO FIND HERSELF ON HER BED in Point Roberts. She heard voices and followed them to the media room. Marcus was sitting on the couch watching the news. "I thought you didn't believe in pulling any poltergeist moves?" Lily asked.

Marcus spun around, surprised. "I don't when the living are around," he replied when he got his breath back. "Anyway, I'm bored and it's not like there's anyone around to hear it."

"You mean other than the deputy outside?" Lily said, referring to the uniformed figure walking along the west perimeter of her property.

Marcus waved off her concerns. "He's not allowed inside. The house is still sealed off until Greene releases the scene. Cops are just here to make sure no one steals your stuff. And I've kept the volume down."

"What happened at the morgue? And how did I get back here?"

"You fainted apparently. No worries; it happens to all of us at our first autopsy. Just part of the job, you know?"

"No, I don't know," Lily said, resenting Marcus's nonchalance. "And you're an actor; autopsies are never part of your job. And I never wrote an autopsy scene in any of my books. Too gruesome. Who'd be stupid enough to do that?"

Marcus did not answer. He picked up the remote and began channel surfing, pretending to look for something more interesting to watch, but in truth he was sulking from her actor comment. He wondered if she had been influenced by Penelope: she, too, had always been dismissive of his craft. He recalled the time he had taken her to a play in Seattle, to a modern interpretation of Shakespeare's *Hamlet*, how she had insulted him by falling asleep during the final act. Afterwards, as he was waxing nostalgic about his own time in the theater—often interrupting the conversation to recite lines from his favorite plays—Penelope had simply leaned her head on one hand and did nothing to hide her indifference, even yawning on occasion. The conversation had thus amounted to a soliloquy, as their conversations often did, and when Penelope finally did speak it was only to remark how sad it must be to be him if all he wanted every day was to be someone else. She left him the next morning.

The two women's developing closeness bugged him. It felt like they were conspiring to keep him out of the investigation, and yet it was he who had come to the rescue first! Ungrateful witch. So what if he had been an actor before they met? If anything, Lily of all people should understand him, should understand what it means to live outside your own existence. She spent her days inside her characters' heads; how different, really, was that from what he did?

"Earth to Marcus," Lily said before realizing that might not be entirely accurate anymore.

"What?" he replied, glancing up from the television only briefly to acknowledge her.

"How did I get here?" she repeated her earlier question.

"Oh," he said with another dismissive wave of his hand, "when you fainted, Penelope insisted I bring you home. So I picked you up off the morgue floor, willed myself back here and put you to bed."

"Where is she?"

"Still at the morgue. She's sitting in on the whole autopsy. Said she'll come here later and report."

"What do we do until then?"

"Nothing. Just wait."

"I can't just sit here twiddling my thumbs. I'm going for a walk."

"Suit yourself," he said and continued clicking the remote.

She left him on the couch and went outside. A deputy Lily did not recognize was standing guard at the front of the house. She walked past him and down her driveway toward Marine Drive. As soon as she cleared the trees that fronted her property she came face to face with a throng of reporters camped out at the side of the road.

They were sitting in collapsible chairs in the shade, playing on their smartphones or chatting with each other, and the overall atmosphere was one of boredom.

There was a sudden flurry of activity as a lone car approached the entrance to the golf course just yards away from the gate to her property. The horde of reporters swarmed the car and began shouting questions at the unwitting occupants. Unfortunately they were not locals but two Chinese tourists—a businessman of some renown back in Shanghai and his mistress—who misinterpreted the attention and sped off at high speed, nearly running over a reporter from Foxx News. *Damn, you missed,* Lily thought uncharitably.

The horde settled down again. Lily walked among them, eavesdropping and thinking it quite ironic that she was spying on them after so many years of being on the receiving end of their intrusions. She thought it would be fun to start a gossip blog that reported on the paparazzi; all she needed to do was find a live writer with an open mind and leave her notes like Penelope had for Greene. Just as soon as Lily learned how to do that, she decided, she would pursue the idea.

Her observations yielded nothing, unfortunately: the reporters seemed to know very little in the way of facts, and there was nothing original about their speculations. With nothing much else to do except walk off her anxiety, Lily headed south down Marine Drive with a mind to checking on Runa and Arni.

Penelope leaned over Dr. Anderson's shoulder as he punctured Lily's bladder with a syringe and withdrew the urine. He opened a sterile package containing a drug screen quick test and wrote the file number on the plastic kit. Three drops of urine were placed in each test well, then Anderson tilted the kit up to disperse the liquid. He set a timer to five minutes and the test aside. The remainder of urine in the syringe was labeled and added to the autopsy kit.

Penelope looked down at the drug screen and waited. The act of waiting made her apprehensive, and her concern puzzled her. What was she afraid of? That the test would prove Lily's protestations that she had been murdered, or that it would not? Penelope wanted to believe Lily, had so from the very beginning, but doubts were creeping in: so far no one had found anything to suggest a homicide.

Penelope sat down on a stool, held the edge of the counter with her hands and stared. The slow ticking of the clock brought back memories of sitting on her living room couch and staring down at the white-and-purple stick on the coffee table, her worry increasing with each passing minute. She had just made Homicide after three years of pining for the gig, and a momentary lapse in judgment was threatening her career plans. It also did not help that the culprit was a senior officer, and Penelope was not sure how she would cope with the inevitable accusations that she was sleeping her way to the top. She was also not sure what she would do if the test were positive; about the only thing she *was* certain of was her ambivalence when the negative sign finally appeared in the little screen.

Now she was feeling the same anxiety, and she concluded that it was due to nothing more than an unhappy memory, the resurface of which she also attributed to a momentary lapse in self-control.

Thoughts of motherhood led Penelope to wonder how her own mother had taken the news of Lily's death. Agnes Winters was a huge Harrington fan and after Penelope's death had found solace in Lily's books. It became their time together, with Penelope snuggling down beside her mother in bed and reading over her shoulder, believing that on some level her mother knew her daughter was there. Personally, Penelope found Lily's books trite and thin on reality, but Penelope had not been there for the literature.

She knew she should be checking in on her mom, and Penelope felt guilty that she was too bogged down with this case and others to make the trip to Kansas City, "the one in Missouri," as she would say when anyone asked.

The timer went off. Anderson sauntered over to the table to check the results. Positive for BZO, benzodiazepine. "Well, I'll be damned," Penelope murmured to herself. Had Lily been drugged?

Anderson picked up the morgue phone and called Greene. "Detective, I have two developments to share. Quick screen came up positive for benzodiazepine. Won't know which one and how much until the lab quantitates and confirms with blood, but it is of interest."

"Could she have just taken a sedative to calm her nerves before hanging herself?" Greene asked at the other end, hopeful the drug could be rationally explained away.

"Yes of course. It's a common enough scenario. But I can't answer that until I see how much she had in her system. It's not a fine line between relaxation and unconsciousness."

"How long before we know? We need to shut this down as fast as possible, Doc." *Really, really fast,* Greene added in his head. Media Relations was overwhelmed with inquiries, and though everyone knew the detective could only dance as fast as the facts presented themselves, there was an undercurrent of expectation that he pull a rabbit out of a hat and solve this in record time.

"Believe me, my office is as keen to expedite this as you are," Anderson replied. "We'll put a rush on the results; should have them in forty-eight hours, max, I would expect."

"You said you have two developments."

"Right. Your victim had sex the day of her death. Consensual, or at least it appears to be. There was lubricant used, which might have been used to cover up a rape or may simply have been necessary due to her age."

"You thinking the vic was roofied?" Greene asked, once again hoping this was not headed in the direction it appeared to be.

"Possibly. Again, it's a common scenario, though the culprit is usually smart enough to wear a condom."

"No condoms at the scene. You got DNA?" Greene asked, hopeful for at least a bit of good news.

"We do. And a hair follicle. Your paramour is blond."

"That little shit."

"I take it you have a suspect?"

"I do indeed."

Greene hung up the phone and grabbed his car keys. As he stormed toward his cruiser, he put a call out to Thornfield. "I'm on my way to The Point," Greene said when the deputy answered his cell. "I need you to round up Arni Heimirsson and keep him there until I arrive. I've got a few things I need to ask him."

Lily took a shortcut through the forest north of Park Lane and came up on the rear of Runa's trailer. She walked around to the front; Runa's Corolla was not in the driveway. Lily peered through a window and saw a child of about ten years in Runa's living room. The girl was wearing pink shorts, a pink T-shirt, white and pink sneakers, her blond hair French braided in a plait down her back and secured with a pink ribbon. She was playing with Barbie dolls and chatting to herself, as children do. Lily wondered who the girl was: Runa had never mentioned there was a child in her life.

Lily left the property and was nearing Arni's when she heard the sound of tires on the gravel behind her. She spun around and jumped out of the way just before Deputy Thornfield nearly ran her down with his cruiser. That he would have just driven right through her did not register until seconds later, after she had shaken off her fright.

He parked his cruiser in front of Arni's trailer, strode to the door and loudly banged on it. "Open up, Arni," Thornfield barked.

Arni opened the door and came out swinging. "You lying bastard," he said as he took a drunken swipe at the officer. "You never told me she was dead."

Oh dear, Lily thought as she watched the altercation, *this is going to get ugly.*

It took Thornfield all of two moves to spin Arni around, slam him against the side of the trailer and pin one arm behind his back. "Calm down, son, before you get yourself in a world of trouble. Detective Greene's on his way to question you and he sounds mad. You need to get yourself together. Now get inside."

Thornfield pushed Arni up the stairs and into his trailer before the deputy released the boy's arm. Arni fell into a heap on the sofa. "You said there was a break-in," he moaned as he rubbed his throbbing arm. "You lied. Lily's dead and you lied to me."

Thornfield placed his hands on his hips and stared down at Arni. "First of all, no one told you there was a break-in; you assumed that. Second, next of kin had not been notified, so it wasn't yet your business."

"What am I going to do without her?" Arni cried as he unsuccessfully tried to stand back up.

"I'm sure you'll find other work."

"It's not about that," Arni said as he fell back against the sofa. "She believed in me," he sobbed into his arm.

Lily sat down beside Arni and placed a comforting hand on his back. She wished there were some way she could pierce the veil and draw him to her bosom, to hold him tightly and tell him everything was going to be okay, that she knew he had not hurt her. At least she thought he hadn't. Had he? Lily had not seen her killer, and whoever it was had been strong enough to string her up. Lily looked at Arni's muscular arms, the ones she had been so fond of caressing each Wednesday, the ones that often held her up while he thrust madly inside her. He was such a paradox, her Arni: he possessed the strong, toned body of a gym rat and the lust of a man in his sexual prime, yet also the soft, introspective soul of a writer. His graphic novel was good, its themes far deeper than the superficial smut usually gobbled up by his demographic, and she saw in him some hope for the future of the genre. She had been sincere in her promise to show the novel to Donald Martin. Now she would have to find some other way to get him to read Arni's work. Lily made a mental note to talk to Marcus again about that mind meld trick he was good at.

Thornfield looked over his shoulder to the kitchen counter. There were five empty beer bottles from a six pack, and an open fifth of whiskey. "How much have you had to drink, son?" he asked.

"I-I don't know," Arni stuttered between sobs. "I d-don't care."

"Well I do. You need to sober up. Where do you keep the coffee?"

When Arni did not answer, Thornfield went through the small trailer's few kitchen cupboards until he found a can of instant coffee. There was no kettle, so he found a small pot, filled it with water and set it on the electric stovetop to boil.

"Look, Arni, I know you didn't hurt Ms. Harrington, but if you don't have an alibi for all of Wednesday night you're in for a bumpy ride. You got an alibi, Arni?"

Arni tried to answer but the words would not come forth. He lost his breath and began coughing, which turned into dry heaving as he struggled to breathe—and then Arni's face turned purple and he threw up onto his shoes. He would have thrown up onto Lily's shoes, too, were it not for the gulf between their worlds. Odd, Lily thought, how one minute she wished she could breach the chasm and the next minute be grateful for its existence.

"Ah Jesus, Arni," Thornfield said as he surveyed the mess. He looked around the kitchen for paper towels, found some under the sink and tossed the roll across the room. "Clean yourself up before Greene gets here. You look pathetic."

Arni flopped about on the floor until he slowly regained some control of his limbs. The act of vomiting had sobered him up a bit, or at least enough to haphazardly wipe up the mess. Lily's nose wrinkled, both from the smell of vomit and the sight of her former lover in such a sorry state. She watched with dismay as Arni removed his shoes and pants and put on clean ones, tossing the soiled items into the shower stall in his tiny bathroom.

The water on the stove began to boil. Thornfield made Arni a cup of coffee while he rinsed his face and mouth in the bathroom sink. Reasonably presentable again, he stumbled to the small Formica dinette and sat down. Thornfield put the steaming cup of joe in front of the boy and sat down across from him.

"So, what do you think Greene wants to talk to you about?" Thornfield asked, grasping the edges of the table as if he were about to lift it off the floor.

"I don't know," Arni pouted and took a sip of coffee.

There was a moment of awkward, angry silence between the men before Arni quietly asked, "How did she die?"

The sight of Arni's mournful face made the deputy feel a bit guilty about his earlier gruffness. "I'm sorry, son, I can't answer that."

"Did she suffer?" Arni asked, his blue eyes dark with worry.

"I don't know. But I think she was suffering before, you know, emotionally."

"Why do you say that?"

Thornfield stopped cold. He realized he had already said too much. If anything got out ahead of schedule, his head was going to be served up on somebody's platter. He was struggling for something plausible but purposely vague to say, when the deputy heard the gravel drive crunching under the wheels of Greene's cruiser. *Thank God*, Thornfield thought and got up to let the detective in.

Greene stomped up the two metal stairs and into the trailer.

He took one look at the rumpled mess of a man, at the beer bottles and half-empty fifth of whiskey on the kitchen counter, and said, "Rough day, Arni?"

Arni bent low over the table and scratched his head, pushing his blond hair as far down over his eyes as it would reach.

"Yeah, me too," Greene said, his voice soaked with sarcasm. "See, I started off my day thinking I was going to close this unfortunate matter. I started off my day thinking the department was going to be done with all this celebrity nonsense and nonstop phone calls to Media Relations, and tomorrow the world would get back to talking about real issues like global warming and government corruption. But guess what, Arni? My day went to shit when I got a call from the M.E. telling me that a blond motherfucker had been banging my victim just hours before she died. And when I say 'motherfucker' I mean 'motherfucker,' Arni, because Lily Harrington *was old enough to be your mother.*"

Lily bolted from the sofa and slapped Greene hard across the face, but her hand merely went through his head. Her ineffectiveness made her angrier. "You sexist troglodyte," she spit at him. "If I were a man you'd be patting my corpse on the back. And how dare you berate this beautiful soul just because you now have to actually get off your fat ass and do your job!" She was shaking now, her fists banging noiselessly on the table. She wanted to slug the detective so badly she could taste her fury. She clenched her eyes shut, trying to contain her rage—and what happened next no one saw coming, not even Lily: the last, unopened, beer bottle from Arni's six pack exploded, spraying glass and warm beer all over Greene.

"What the fuck!" he yelled as beer soaked into his dress shirt.

Everybody froze. And then slowly, as the surprise wore off, Lily smiled.

12

"WHERE'S LILY?" PENELOPE ASKED MARCUS when she returned to the house on Marine Drive.

"Went for a walk," he shrugged and continued watching *Cops*.

Penelope grabbed the remote out of his hand and turned off the television. "You were supposed to keep an eye on her."

"No, you said bring her home and put her to bed. Which I did."

"Well, we need to find her."

"Why? Something show up at the autopsy? Did they find a clump of granite where her heart was supposed to be? Or am I confusing her autopsy with yours?"

Penelope shook her head and rolled her eyes. "You're an idiot," she said and disappeared. A second later the television turned back on. Marcus jumped. *Damn! That was good, even for a poltergeist.*

Penelope appeared in Arni's trailer just as Greene was wiping the last of the beer off his face. His shirt stank, and he was grateful he was not wearing his suit jacket. His pants bore some brunt of the attack, but it was nothing he couldn't spot out later. Luckily the glass had missed his face and hands, the shards still scattered around the trailer.

Greene threw the wet towel aside. "Hold on a second," Thornfield said and reached over to pick a shard of glass out of the detective's hair. Greene slapped the deputy's hand away.

"What happened here?" Penelope asked, surveying the mess.

"Oh, Penelope, it was *amazing*!" Lily exclaimed, her face glowing. "He got me really, really angry, and I was thinking how much I wanted to smash a bottle over his thick skull, and next thing I knew the beer just exploded. Just"—she mimicked the explosion with her hands—"boom! And then glass and beer all over the jerk." She paused and let out a wistful sigh. "If only you'd been here to see it."

"Lily, you need to be careful," Penelope admonished her. "You can't do stuff like that."

"I didn't mean to. And besides, you do stuff like that all the time."

"It's different for me."

"Why?"

"It just is. Now promise me you'll not do this again."

"Fine. I promise." *For now.*

"Anyhow," Penelope said, resting one hand on the kitchen counter and the other on her hip, "they know about you and Arni."

"I know."

"How long had you been bedding the boy?"

"He's not a boy."

"Lily, this is me you're talking to, not Greene."

As if on cue, the detective sat down at the table across from Arni. "How long had you been having sex with Ms. Harrington?" Greene asked brusquely, still fuming about the beer.

"About a year now, I guess. Started last summer," Arni answered, his head bowed.

"Was that wise?" Penelope asked.

"Look at him. Then you tell me," Lily replied, laughing. There was joy in her laugh: she was still floating from the exploding beer despite Penelope's disapproval.

Penelope ran her eyes over Arni. "I see your point."

"Who initiated the relationship?" Greene asked.

"Um, no one, really. It just happened one day. She offered me a drink at the end of my shift and next thing I knew we were naked."

"And how often did you and she hookup?"

"Every Wednesday. Always at the end of my shift but sometimes before, too. And during lunch. And we didn't 'hookup.'"

Ah, Wednesdays, Lily sighed inwardly. Wednesday, day of Woden. Germanic Mercury. Patron god of commerce, poetry, messages and communication. What could be a more perfect day for literary sex? Also patron god of travelers, luck, trickery and thieves, keeper of the boundaries between the two worlds, and guide of souls to the underworld. Okay, those latter attributes were unintentionally ironic.

Greene ignored the criticism. "This past Wednesday, did you use lubricant during sex?"

Arni's eyes went wide, shocked by the question. He looked to Thornfield for assistance but found none. "Chivalry isn't dead, son," the deputy responded with a shrug, "your lover is."

"And if you don't answer my questions," Greene threatened, "I'm going to arrest you for obstruction."

"Yes," a reluctant Arni admitted. And then, finding his nerve, he added, "Would you like to know what flavor?" Lily let out another laugh but it was aborted by a snort. She had never adored Arni more than she did right now.

Greene ignored the question and persisted with his own. "Did you ever use drugs with Ms. Harrington, either to relax or enhance the sex?"

Arni glared at the detective. "No."

"Did she ever offer you money in exchange for your sexual services?"

Arni's face went dark. "It wasn't like that. I *loved* her."

Oops, Lily thought and grimaced.

Her expression did not pass by Penelope. "I take it the feeling wasn't mutual?"

Lily looked guilty. "Maybe not love, but I was fond of him. Genuinely fond. He—" She stopped short.

"He what?"

"He made me feel … hopeful again. I even read my novel to him. My literary one. He said he loved it. And I chose to believe him." She reached over and brushed the back of her hand down the side of Arni's face, and mourned the fact that neither of them could feel it.

"Why did you lie to me yesterday when I asked you if you were in an intimate relationship with Lily Harrington?" Greene demanded. He had been angry when he arrived, made angrier still by the exploding beer, and now he was going to reach across the table and knock Arni's head into the Formica if the boy lied one more time.

"Because I knew you wouldn't understand. Nobody would. They would just gossip and judge and shake their heads in ignorance."

"So you were just protecting her honor, is that it?" Greene asked sarcastically.

"Yes. Maybe honor is something *you* don't understand anymore, but *I* still believe in it." Arni sat back and crossed his arms in defiance. The exploding beer had sobered him up real quick like, and there was a small part of him that had imagined Lily had done it. It was weird, but he could almost feel her presence, could have sworn he heard her laugh at the sight of Greene's dripping face. The thought had sent Arni hurtling back two days previous, to his last time with Lily, to the throaty laugh that escaped from her mouth when he did that thing with his tongue. And then he remembered she was gone, and he sank his front teeth into his lip until it bled, the physical pain a welcome diversion.

"What time did you leave the Harrington property on Wednesday?" Greene continued probing, scribbling down the answers in his notebook, the pressure of his pen creating lines so deep on the paper they could be seen three pages down.

"A little before seven, I guess. The ball game was just starting when I got home."

Greene checked his notes. Penelope leaned over his shoulder to read them, then scribbled the missing (for her) information down: Harrington's last opened email had been read at 8:38 p.m. Looked like Arni was telling the truth. "Still, he might have drugged her, set her up for an accomplice or went back later himself," Penelope said as if Greene could hear, and Lily wondered once again if Penelope was infiltrating his thoughts.

"When did you join your neighbor Jimmy?" Greene asked.

"As soon as I got home. He was waiting for me."

"And when did you leave his trailer?"

"Game ended around ten o'clock."

"Where were you the rest of the night?"

"Home."

"Alone?"

"Yes."

"You got any way to prove that?" Greene challenged Arni, the accusation hanging heavy in the air.

"You got any way to prove I wasn't?" he tossed back.

"I'm not the one suspected of murder."

Arni's face went white. "Murder? How?" He looked to Thornfield for answers but the deputy just maintained his silence.

"Why don't you tell *me* how, Arni?" Greene soldiered on.

"I did *not* murder Lily! I *loved* her." Arni looked angrily at Thornfield. "You're a right dick, you know that? And to think people around here trust you." Arni summoned up his courage and stared Greene down. "Get out of my house. If you think I killed Lily, then arrest me. Otherwise leave."

Greene stood up, angry. *Ah crap,* he thought. He had nothing to make an arrest with. Nothing. *Nada.* He resorted to bravado. "I'll be back. I'll find something to link you to this and then I *will* be back." Greene stormed out of the trailer. Seconds later the sound of flying gravel was heard.

Thornfield stood up. "Don't be stupid, son. Secrets have a way of coming back to bite."

"You should know, shouldn't you?" Arni retorted.

Thornfield opened his mouth to respond then thought better of it. He turned and left the trailer, slamming the door behind him.

"Do you think he was capable of killing you?" Penelope asked, gesturing with her chin toward Arni.

"No. At least I'd like to think he wasn't," Lily answered sadly as she sat down across the table from her former lover and stared into his face. "But …"

"But what?"

"You asked me the same question about Runa. I thought I knew these people. Apparently not as well as I imagined."

"I think everyone has a secret part of themselves they never share with anyone, not even their lover or best friend," Penelope mused. "Everybody has a secret life, Lily. Absolutely everybody."

13

"THERE'S SOMETHING ELSE YOU NEED TO KNOW," Penelope revealed once she and Lily had left Arni's trailer: Penelope suspected Lily's fondness for the boy ran deeper than she admitted, and this next bit of news needed to be delivered away from the influence his mere presence seemed to have on her. "You were drugged."

The news brought Lily to a halt. Her eyes went wide and swept back across the trailer park to Arni's door. "He didn't ..."

"What do you remember about Wednesday night?" Penelope asked. She turned Lily back around and forced her to start walking again.

Lily could feel a hot flash of anxiety creeping along her spine. "We had sex, like he said. He left. I opened a bottle of red to breathe, then had a long bath and dressed for a party at the marina. I poured myself a glass of wine and went into my office. Checked my email, then tinkered with my novel for about an hour. By then it was time to leave for the marina but I was feeling a bit nauseous. As soon as I stood up I felt really dizzy, so I ..." Her voice trailed off and her expression turned dark.

"You what?"

"I remember thinking that something was really wrong and I should call for help but I couldn't move. My body felt like lead. I fell down, onto the couch I think. I don't remember a thing after that except that I heard a scream—or maybe just a yell, but definitely a raised voice—and woke up hanging from the damn rafter."

"Then let me ask you again: Do you think Arni could have done this?"

Lily's lips began to quiver. She tried to quell them with the fingers of her left hand but it was shaking just as badly. "What aren't you telling me?" Penelope gently probed.

"He ... he wanted to go public with our relationship," Lily admitted. "He was imagining himself escorting me to the fiftieth Mantova book parties and such."

"What did you tell him?"

"I said no." Lily looked at the detective, imploring her to understand. "Can you imagine the press, Penelope? He's my gardener, for heaven's sake. And he's twenty-five years old."

"Was he angry?"

"Yes. But not angry with indignation. More ... disappointment."

"Then what happened?"

"He yelled at me, said some things I'm certain he regretted. And then he just gave up and left. He was ... crying." Lily's eyes welled up as she recalled the hurt in his azure eyes, the way the color had drained from his flawless face, the shock of blond hair that fell down when he bowed his head to hide his tears. "Oh, Penelope, what did I do?"

"You didn't *do* anything. You're the one who's dead."

"But ..."

"But what?"

"But I hurt him, didn't I? I was selfish and I hurt him."

Sudden anger like a bolt of lightning flashed across Penelope's face. She grabbed Lily by the arms and shook her. "Dear God, Lily, women like you drive me crazy. No one deserves to be murdered just because she broke someone's heart. These men need to get over themselves. Women do not deserve to be raped or beaten or murdered just because some guy gets rejected." Penelope let Lily go with a mild shove, as if disgusted by her presence.

"I'm sorry."

"Stop it!" Penelope shouted, jabbing her hands in the air. "Don't be sorry, Lily, be angry. Somebody *killed* you. And if it wasn't Arni, who was it?"

"I don't know." Lily dropped her head and cried, the weight of Penelope's anger and disgust too much to bear.

Her tears had no effect. Penelope grabbed Lily by the shoulders again and stooped down to look her hard in the eyes. "Stop crying,

Lily, and think. Who had motive? People usually kill for one of two reasons, money or love. Arni might have been love. Who gains financially?"

"My sister and the Artists' Defense League are my heirs," Lily answered, struggling to recover her composure. "But they wouldn't know that. Only my lawyer knows the contents of my will." Lily shuddered: the thought that her beloved sister might have been behind this was too ghastly to think about. If so, that husband of hers was the culprit.

"Anyone else?" Penelope asked, letting go of Lily.

She scanned her brain for possible culprits. "My agent. My publisher. If I die they get to finish the last Mantova book the way they want and bury my novel. Penelope, do you think that's it? Do you think they killed me to get their way?" Lily's face brightened: she was much more comfortable suspecting them than her sister, or even her sister's husband.

"It's possible. You met with your agent on Wednesday, yes? And he was there at the house on Thursday after they found you. Killers often return to the scene and insinuate themselves into the investigation, makes them feel important."

Um, isn't that what you did? Lily thought, then quickly cast the idea aside: Penelope may be a poltergeist but it was doubtful she could hang a live human body. Could Donald? "If Donald did this," Lily speculated, "he must have had help. He's a scrawny thing. I can't imagine he was able to string me up like that."

"Your publisher is a multinational corporation. Killers can be hired. Maybe all Martin had to do was confirm the deed. Does he have the code to your security system?"

"No." And then Lily remembered the time Donald had visited two summers ago when he was rushing her to finish *Love and Secrets*. "Wait, Penelope, he did! He stayed with me two years ago. I gave him his own entry code and never deleted it."

"It's possible he gave it to the killers. And if they used his dedicated code, that should be in your system. Let's investigate this further and if necessary I'll leave Greene a note."

Greene pulled up to Lily's gate and was immediately swarmed by the media camped out front. He pressed on his car horn to clear a path but no one cooperated. Greene was in no mood to put up with their nonsense. He put on his emergency lights, rolled down the window and bellowed, "Get the hell out of my way or I'll fine you for impeding an emergency vehicle."

A reporter responded by pushing a microphone into Greene's face. "Deputy, do you have any information on the death of Lily Harrington."

"No!" Greene barked at the reporter. "And it's *Detective.*" He turned his attention to the two standing in front of his car. "Get out of my way or I'll run you down," he hollered at them. He rolled his window back up and moved his cruiser forward like he meant business. And he did.

Seconds later one of the two deputies guarding Lily's property appeared through the trees. The officer ran over to the gate and triggered the release. Greene drove through while the deputy stood as a warning to the press not to follow. Greene gestured his thanks and drove up to the house. He parked his car and strode across the lawn to Richard Owen's house.

Greene banged on the door. A few moments later the recluse peered through the peephole then opened the door. "You've returned," he said, scowling. "Why?"

"On Wednesday, did you see Harrington's gardener, Arni Heimirsson, on the property?" Greene asked impatiently, misdirecting his anger with the media onto Owen. There was a small part of Greene that wished Owen would say something stupid so the detective would have an excuse to slam the door on the hermit's head.

"Yes. He comes every Wednesday."

No kidding. "Have you ever observed them together?"

"Yes."

"Have you ever noticed anything sexual between them?"

"Yes."

"I thought you said nothing went on there on Wednesday?" Greene's anger with the press was being replaced by equal exasperation with Richard Owen.

"No, you asked me if anything unusual happened," Owen corrected the detective. "It wasn't unusual. Quite the opposite. They've been at it for about a year now. Disgusting really. And on the kitchen counter yet. Most unsanitary."

Greene glanced over at the Harrington property. The windows in her kitchen did not face south. "How do you know they had sex on her kitchen counter, Owen?"

The color drained from Richard's face. "I ... um ..."

"Spit it out or I'll arrest you for voyeurism."

"I watched them sometimes. So what?" Richard whined defensively. "She's the criminal. He's just a boy. And she didn't close her drapes."

"The only view into her kitchen is from the patio on the east or through the great room on the west. So you went onto the property, Richard. How did you do that without anyone noticing?"

Owen squirmed in his moccasins. "I watched from her back stairs. At low tide you can walk from my stairs to hers."

The wheels in Greene's head were turning. Richard Owen was supposedly a recluse who never left his house; everyone assumed he was agoraphobic. But he was clearly capable of leaving his refuge if the incentive were big enough. Had he secretly been in love with his neighbor? Had he imagined himself a more proper suitor than her young gardener? Had Owen propositioned Harrington and her rejection sent him over the edge?

Greene's day was going from bad to worse. "You'd better hope I don't see you leaving your house on Wednesday night on your security video." He pressed a finger into Owen's chest. "Am I going to see you leaving the house, Richard? Huh?"

Owen was shaking. "I want you to leave now," he said in a tremulous voice. "If you don't leave I'm going to call them."

"Call who, Richard?"

Owen didn't answer. He slammed the door in Greene's face and locked all three deadbolts before scurrying off to his office. His heart was thumping as he watched the security feed of Greene storming back off north to Harrington's.

Lily and Penelope were passing Runa's house when Lily remembered the little girl. "Penelope, I forgot to tell you, I saw a little girl in Runa's trailer earlier. She never said anything about a child. Do you think we ought to investigate?"

Penelope nodded and the two women approached the trailer. There was no one inside. They went around back and there she was, sitting on the tree swing and letting the breeze push her about. "Oh, it's you," Penelope said to the girl. "Whatcha doing here, Ripley?"

"Ripley?" Lily asked.

"Mother was an *Alien* fan," Penelope explained.

"Just swinging," Ripley mumbled sadly, staring at the ground.

"Wait a minute," Lily said, perplexed. "She can hear you?"

"She's dead, Lily. Has been for over a decade. Drowned during a birthday party at a friend's house in Blaine. No one was minding the pool." Penelope turned her attention back to Ripley. "How long you been hanging out here at Runa's?"

Ripley shrugged. "Dunno. A while."

"Why?"

"She's nice. She reads to me."

"Penelope, is she saying that Runa can see her?" Lily asked, intrigued.

Penelope nodded. "Appears so."

"But if Runa can see Ripley," Lily asked, "could Runa see us when Greene was questioning her yesterday?"

"Not necessarily. It's a mutual thing: the spirit must want to be seen, and the seer must feel a connection."

Lily glanced back east toward the RV park. "So if I wanted someone to see me, how would I go about that exactly?"

Penelope gave Lily a look that said *I know what you're thinking.* "Don't be stupid," Penelope warned. "And you're missing the point of this."

"Which is?"

"Which is ... Ripley, honey, does anyone else visit Runa?"

"She has a boyfriend."

"Who's that?"

"A policeman."

"What's his name?"

"Dunno."

"It's Thornfield," Lily whispered.

Penelope elbowed Lily to be quiet and continued questioning Ripley. "What's he look like?"

"Dunno."

"Then how do you know she has a boyfriend?"

"She tells me about him. But she makes me leave whenever he comes over." She looked at the ground and pouted. Clearly the arrangement was not to her liking.

"Ever spy on her and her boyfriend?" Penelope gently asked.

Ripley looked up, alarmed. "No! Then she won't be my friend anymore. I don't have many friends here."

Lily frowned. Back at Sunny Side she had seen six children kicking a ball around the small field in the center of the park, laughing and screaming as kids do. The sight of Ripley alone on the swing broke Lily's heart.

"You've got me," Penelope assured her.

Ripley's eyes fell to the ground again. "You're never around. You're too busy with cases and stuff."

Penelope grimaced. It was just like a child to point out the obvious. Penelope felt doubly guilty that her next words were, "We have to go now, Ripley. But if you need me, you just call out, okay?"

Ripley nodded but her face said it all. And now even Lily was starting to feel guilty.

"HOW DID YOU GET THIS NUMBER?" Greene yelled into his cellphone. "Do *not* call this number again. You want information you call Media Relations. *Comprendes?* I repeat, do *not* call this number again. If you do, I will find you and force-feed your cellphone to you." He hung up on the caller, then turned off his phone. Greene swore he was going to kill someone today if things kept going in this direction.

He had just opened the front door when he heard the voices from above. He pulled out his gun and crept slowly through the foyer toward the stairs. He slowly ascended the steps and was just about to turn into the media nook when he recognized the unmistakable sound of a sitcom laugh track. He peered around the corner and saw the television on. "Who's there?" he called out.

Marcus jumped in his skin. "Damn," he muttered to himself and instinctively dived below the couch as if Greene might see. Marcus reached over and, without lifting the remote off the coffee table, hit the off button. Then he slowly reached onto the couch for his hat and put it back on, as if Greene might see it, too.

The detective entered the room and crept around to the front of the couch. No one. Which was a really good thing because his hands were shaking and he did not want any suspect to see that. Marcus's hands were also shaking, and he was equally glad he could not be seen. At least by Greene. But then Marcus heard Penelope yell out "What the hell is going on?" and he knew he was even deader than he already was.

Marcus poked his head above the couch. "He caught me with the TV on."

"Oh for heaven's sake, Joseph, how stupid can you be?"

"Stove calling the kettle black, don't you think, Ms. Let's Leave Him a Note in Broad Daylight?" Marcus shot back. "And don't call me Joseph!"

"What do we do now?" Lily asked, staring at Greene. He was continuing to sweep the house, gun still drawn. He headed in the direction of her bedroom.

"Nothing," Penelope replied. "There's nothing we can do." She glared at Marcus. "You're an idiot."

The three stood there staring down the hallway as Greene entered then left each guest room. Satisfied everything was clear, he headed downstairs. They followed him down and waited in the living room while he checked the main floor. Nobody spoke, as if afraid Greene might hear them.

He returned a few moments later, his gun holstered. He pulled out his cellphone and turned it on. No sooner did he do so than it rang, and Greene almost had a heart attack. He jumped back, dropping the phone onto the hardwood floors. "Crap!" Greene cursed as he picked up the still-ringing phone. He checked the number. It was Kevin Monk, a colleague from Homicide.

"Hello?" Greene said into the phone, hoping his voice didn't sound as shaky as he feared it did.

"It's Kevin," Monk replied. "Are you okay?"

"Yeah, sure, just a little out of breath, that's all. Gotta work out more often, I guess."

"More often?" Monk joked.

"Shut up, Kevin."

"Where are you?"

"At the Harrington property."

"Can you come back to the office? That video surveillance I offered to look at, there's something weird on it that's hard to explain over the phone."

"Is it going to ruin my day?"

"It probably would have," Monk said with a laugh, "but I hear Anderson beat me to it."

Greene shook his head wearily. "Oh sweet Jesus, somebody just shoot me now." He sighed. "I'll be there in an hour. Do me a favor? Call ahead to the border and tell them I'm coming through and I'm in a hurry."

"Will do," Monk promised and hung up.

Greene put his phone away and looked around the room. His eyes flickered for a moment when they passed over the three ghosts, but no one could tell if it was a flicker of recognition or something far less significant, like his rhinitis. To their relief Greene pulled out his handkerchief and wiped his nose. His hands were still shaking as he tried to cast off the creepy crawlies that were climbing along his back, then decided he had been imagining it all. It was either that or Lily Harrington was haunting her house—and his investigation—and he decided he preferred the idea of suffering hallucinations more than he fancied suffering Harrington's ghost. It was bad enough the Homicide unit was haunted by a former cop; to have his victim on him too was too much to bear.

Greene hurriedly left the house without looking over his shoulder. "Hey," he called out to the deputy on guard, "get in. If those fuckers are still at the gate when I leave, I'm going to need you to keep me from shooting them." The two men got into Greene's cruiser and he headed down the drive.

"What do we do now, Penelope?" Lily asked as she walked over to the kitchen window and watched Greene speed away.

"He asked if it was going to ruin his day. That means someone found something."

"We clearly need to find out what it is," Marcus asserted, adjusting his hat for emphasis. "Do we know where he's headed?"

Penelope shook her head. "No. But also, why did he return to the house? What was he looking for?"

"Well," Lily said, "he had just found out about Arni and me. Maybe he came back to see if he could find anything to place Arni here when I was killed."

"What are you two talking about, Arni and you? What did I miss?" Marcus demanded, but his voice came across more whiny than authoritative.

"Oh, you mean while you were lazing about, watching television and scaring the hell out of our investigator?" Penelope sniped. She was not finished with Joe yet. Actually, she was. "Take my hand," Penelope said to Lily without explanation, and next thing she knew she and Penelope were in the back seat of Greene's cruiser as he raced toward Canada.

Thornfield parked his cruiser in the shade in front of the gates to the tiny Point Roberts cemetery, then walked through the pedestrian entrance and into the sun. Runa was in the far corner, tending to the twin graves of ancestors long gone and whom she had never met outside of the family picture album: Oddný and Hjálmar Jónsdóttir, dead five years apart, Hjálmar first in 1939. Thornfield always wondered if Oddný got picked on for her name, even then.

Their graves were overgrown with crab grass and thistles that Runa was patiently digging out from the roots. Beautifying the graves had become something of an obsession, a righting of past wrongs: Oddný Solvason and Hjálmar Jónsdóttir had eloped in Victoria in 1893 and run away to Point Roberts to work in the cannery, and neither family spoke to them ever again. The source of the friction was never fully disclosed; from the pieces Runa cobbled together over the years, Hjálmar's father had allegedly stolen a cow—vehemently denied, never proven—from the farm of Oddný's paternal uncle, Ingólfur Solvason, and the families became sworn enemies. The affair was an Icelandic immigrant version of *Romeo and Juliet*, minus the nobility and fatal ending.

"Hey, Runa. Thought I'd find you here."

"Why?" she asked blankly.

"You're not answering your cell. You never do when you're here."

"Oh," she replied, uninterested in her own habits.

"How you holding up?"

"I'm fine," she said, as if the day before had not happened, or the memory and associated emotions had already been relegated to the Recycle Bin in her brain.

Thornfield was not sure how to handle her obvious lack of trauma. He had come to rescue Runa from her distress but his damsel didn't seem to be in any. "Um … I want to apologize for yesterday. I do love you, you know that, right?"

Runa looked indifferent. "Okay."

"I'm on a break. Do you want to get something to eat?"

Runa looked at the torn landscape around the graves then up at Thornfield, her forehead wrinkled. "Can't."

"Do you want to meet up later?"

Runa shrugged. "Okay."

"Um, right, then, I'll call you later."

Runa nodded and turned her attention back to the graves. Thornfield watched for a moment, silent and awkward, as if expecting her to remember he was there and change her mind about his offer of nourishment. She didn't, and he left without further intrusion, wandering off in a fog back to his car.

Greene had just arrived at the station in Bellingham when Marcus suddenly appeared in the back seat. "Very funny, Penelope. Did you think I wouldn't find you two?"

"I had no illusions to that effect," she retorted. "Just needed the break. Again. And it's not like you've been particularly helpful so far. Anyhow, what took you so long? Had to finish watching *The Young and the Restless*?"

"Don't be ridiculous, Penelope. It was *Seinfeld*. That show never gets old," Marcus laughed to himself as the four alighted from Greene's cruiser.

The trio followed Greene into the station. He went straight to Kevin Monk's cubicle. The detective was sitting in front of his computer monitor, his eyes flicking between the four camera frames as he fast-forwarded through hours of footage. "Hey, this is for you," Greene said, handing Monk a double latte. "What you got for me?"

"Thanks. It's weird, which is why I wanted you to see it in person."

Monk rewound the digital video taken from Richard Owen's computer and pointed to the frame from the northeast-facing camera, the one that caught a sliver of Harrington's driveway. At exactly 7:27 p.m. a pair of legs could be seen crossing the driveway;

when they passed through the shade of Lily's Douglas fir, faint sparks that resembled static in the air appeared in front of the legs, a flash of light that was gone in the second it took the intruder to walk back into the sun.

"What the hell was that?" Greene asked.

"That's the weird thing," Monk replied, swiveling his chair to face Greene. "It's like an electrical charge in the air that the camera picked up. I have no idea from where. The weather was perfectly clear."

He rewound the video and played it again, frame by frame this time. Greene bent down for a closer look. Lily, Marcus and Penelope all leaned forward behind him.

"What do you think it is, Penelope?" Lily asked, curious.

Penelope shook her head, uncertain. "I don't know. What do you think, Joe? Have you seen anything like this before in any of your cases?"

Marcus shook his head. "Nope."

Penelope and Lily cast a sideways glance at each other. There had been an obvious hint of sarcasm in Penelope's voice—and she had called him Joe again—but this time Marcus chose not to take the bait. Why? Could it be he was finally taking the case as seriously as they were? Or was he just finally showing some maturity? Neither scenario seemed likely.

Greene frowned and took a sip of his own double latte. "Could the person have been holding some sort of electrical device that was emitting a charge?"

"Possibly. Maybe some sort of jammer. Maybe the killer tried to jam the cellphone signal to prevent the vic from using her phone. Or at least her mobile phone. Land line would still work."

"Killer? How do you know it's a homicide?"

"Oh sorry, jumped the gun. You need to call Sheraton at the lab."

"Thank God," Lily sighed audibly. That the authorities were finally arriving at the truth gave her some hope.

Greene also sighed audibly and hung his head. "Okay, my day has officially gone to hell." He lifted his head back up and zoomed in on the legs on the screen. "Were you able to get a close-up of those legs?"

"A bit. Not too much. It's a really small part of the image." Monk opened a folder where he had stored still images captured from the video, then opened them in imaging software. The image details were greatly improved, but unfortunately there was still no way to tell if the legs were male or female, or what kind of pants were on them, only that the fabric was dark and the side seam appeared to look like that on a pair of blue jeans. The shoes were white, but what kind was not obvious.

"Please tell me you have more than this," Greene said, his expression glum.

"Sorry, nothing. The killer doesn't appear again onscreen, so we don't know when he left or in which direction."

"Did the homeowner, Richard Owen, leave at any time during the day or night?"

"Yes. He leaves through the back patio doors at 11:00 a.m. carrying binoculars and disappears down the stairs to the beach. He returns about forty-five minutes later."

"Low tide," Greene said. "He must've been watching her and the gardener."

Lily's jaw dropped. Just after eleven that morning she had been naked on her back on the sofa. "What are you talking about?" she demanded as the image of Richard Owen with his binoculars flashed through her mind. Greene of course did not answer, and Lily looked to Penelope for an explanation.

"I don't know, Lily," Penelope said, shaking her head and pulling out her notebook and pen. "Greene obviously found out something today that we didn't."

Marcus gave Lily a lascivious look. "Were murrelets the only thing up your tree?" he inquired. "Is this what you and the ice queen were talking about earlier?"

"It's none of your business!" Lily snapped at him.

"Calm down, Lily, please," Penelope quietly requested, though it still sounded like a command. "We don't need any more exploding bottles. Let's just wait and see what more they tell us. If necessary I'll read Greene's notes this evening."

Lily complied as instructed, but if Richard Owen had been spying on her and Arni there was going to be hell to pay. Mark her words.

"Then there's a delivery person at 6:06 p.m. at the front door," Monk continued. "That's the only activity on his property until you showed up this morning."

Ah crap, Greene thought, *that all but eliminates Richard Owen.*

"Did we get anything from the security company?"

"Yes." Monk picked up a paper off his desk. It was a log of Harrington's security system, emailed over from the monitoring company. Penelope stepped behind Monk and began quickly copying the information down. Marcus stepped beside Penelope and pretended to be equally interested in the log sheet.

"They ran a remote diagnostic of her system and the house alarm was off at the time of the murder," Monk said, interpreting the log entries. "It was last set Tuesday night at 9:15 then turned off at 8:44 Wednesday morning. It wasn't put on again after that. Gate code three-seven-two-zero was used to open the gate on Wednesday at 8:59 a.m."

Greene downed the last of his coffee, tossed the empty cup into the trash and pulled out his notebook. He flipped through the pages. "That was the gardener. It's consistent with his story."

"The gate was then triggered from the property side at 12:04 p.m.," Monk continued through the log.

"That was me leaving for Richmond," Lily offered.

"That would've been the vic leaving for her meeting with her agent," Greene said.

"Gate code eight-three-zero-two was used to open the gate at 5:12 p.m."

"That must've been Harrington returning from Richmond."

Lily looked at Penelope and nodded in agreement. "He's right; it was."

"Gate was then triggered from the inside at 6:47 p.m.," Monk said.

"That would've been the gardener leaving. Exactly as he said." Greene slapped his notebook against the palm of his hand. "Crap."

"Next time the gate was opened was Thursday morning at 8:55. Code used was seven-nine-four-eight."

Greene looked at his notes again. "That's the housekeeper's code. Again, consistent with her story. Nothing else?"

Monk shook his head. "No. But Mick tells me the property really isn't that secure. There's little to stop someone from jumping the fence at the road. Killer left the body, so he didn't need a vehicle on site. Our perp could've just walked in then walked away."

Greene closed his eyes and shook his head. This was going downhill faster than his pension plan. God only knows what Sheraton would have for him next.

GREENE TRUDGED OVER TO HIS CUBICLE. This was not good. Everyone's stories were checking out, though neither Arni Heimirsson nor Runa Jonsdottir had alibis for the evening. Greene had instructed Thornfield to check in with Arni's neighbor about the ballgame; Jimmy Griggs and Arni had indeed watched the Mariners play the Blue Jays until ten o'clock, but that alibi ended when Arni left Jimmy's trailer. And Arni had lied about his relationship with Harrington. If only that damn air-conditioning had not been on, Anderson might have been able to get a better idea of when Harrington was killed. It was going to take more work to poke holes in Arni's story. Then there was Runa; she didn't have an alibi at all for last night. But what could her motive possibly be? Arni was the lover, and lovers often become killers. But housekeepers? Not so much.

Greene called Sheraton at the lab in Marysville. "Can you switch to video phone?" the CSI asked when he answered. "It would be easier to explain."

Greene hung up and called Sheraton back over the Internet. "I hear you've got something for me," Greene said into the webcam.

"Bad news. It looks like a homicide."

"So Kevin tells me. What did you find?"

Sheraton took a handheld webcam and pointed it at the rope that Lily had been hanging from, snaked out over a long worktable; sections of the rope were marked with red plastic ribbons. "First up, the rope. Half-inch white nylon construction, used mostly to anchor boats to the dock because nylon has a bit of stretch and good energy absorption. It can be bought by the foot or precut in fixed lengths. This one is thirty feet long and precut: you can see how the end is spliced with a twelve-inch eye and heat sealed. It's widely available commercially both in store and online. They even sell it at the marina in Point Roberts, so it could have been sourced locally."

"Great," Greene deadpanned. "Nothing like a popular item to narrow down suspects. But what points to murder?"

"We found anomalies. The rope was strung over a cedar truss, and we found microscopic wood fibers embedded in the rope, as one would expect in a hanging. But the pattern is all wrong."

"How so?"

Sheraton pointed the webcam at a portion of the rope about fifteen feet above the end where the noose had been. Penelope bent down behind Greene to get a closer look. Marcus jockeyed for position beside her but it was pointless, and he stepped back to listen, his expression sullen.

"First there's a line of fibers deeply embedded in the rope for about three feet. Then there's a cluster of fibers found here, even more deeply embedded in the rope. Finally, we see another line of fibers that spans for about another five feet below the cluster."

"Interesting," Penelope murmured.

"What do you think it means?" Lily asked.

"Explain the significance," Greene requested.

"In a normal hanging," Sheraton replied, "you would see a line of fibers for a foot or so on the rope from when the victim first drops, scraping the rope against the wood. Then a cluster of fibers as their body spasms and dies, digging the rope deeper into the wooden truss. And then that's it." Sheraton paused to pick up a sheet of paper with a printout of a chemical test. "Anderson found benzo in her system. We tested the empty bottle found in the recycling bin but it had been rinsed out well—a little too well, in my experience. Same with the glass. So on a hunch I tested the small wine stain we found on the carpet at the foot of the vic's writing desk. Positive for traces of benzodiazepine."

"So what's the scenario?"

"My theory is this: The wine was laced; victim drank it while working at her desk. She got up, was dizzy, and knocked over the glass, spilling the last little bit. Passed out in her office. Perp carried or dragged her to the dining chair we found placed beneath the truss. The rope was tossed over the truss and attached to the victim. The body was raised a few feet, just high enough to strangle her; the weight of the victim's body accounts for the first line of cedar fibers in the rope. She was held in place while she died; her spasms account for the cluster of deeply embedded fibers. Then the body was raised high enough to look like a hanging; that's the second line of fibers where the rope scraped hard against the wood. Perp then cleaned out the bottle and glass, not realizing there was some wine in the rug. It was easy enough to miss: dark wine on a dark carpet."

Hearing Sheraton recount her final moments sent a chill through Lily. Memories and sensations began flooding her mind: The way her vision had started to blur as she tried to read the computer screen. Her wobbly legs as she tried to stand. The glass falling as a dysfunctional limb knocked it over. The fear as she stumbled forward and the dull thud as she collapsed onto the sofa. The way her head fell forward, pulling her body down with it. The prick of the stem of her earring as her head rolled against the cushion. A pair of running shoes—

"Running shoes!" Lily blurted out.

"What about them?" Penelope asked.

"My killer was wearing running shoes!"

"Did you see what kind?" Marcus eagerly asked.

Lily closed her eyes, tried to conjure up the details from her subconscious. Frustrated, she shook her head. "No. Just white. White running shoes."

"How strong would someone have to be to pull that off?" Greene asked, his mind awhirl. "To move an unconscious body and then hang it?"

"The vic was only a hundred and one pounds," Sheraton replied. "So you'd have to be strong but not Arnold Schwarzenegger."

"But the rope was anchored around a post," Greene said, creases snaking across his brow. "How does one person hold the body in place so it doesn't drop, then tighten the rope around the post?"

"That I can't answer. Either this was a two-person job or someone very dexterous managed it."

Greene grimaced. "This can't leave the lab. The media is already in a frenzy; this will just set things off like a rocket. I need to talk to the brass about what they want to release and when."

"Our lips are always sealed; you know that."

"Yeah, of course. Sorry. Just thinking aloud." Greene paused to regroup. He reached over his desk for a tissue and wiped his nose. "Okay. Let's assume the vic was hanged to make it look like a suicide. Why such an elaborate scheme? Clearly there are easier ways to kill someone and make it look like a suicide."

"Reeds said something about the vic hanging a character in her novel," Sheraton speculated. "It's consistent with the research folder we found. Why the killer used the same method is a mystery though."

"And how did he know? According to her agent, only him, the vic, her editor, and maybe her publisher knew about the plot line. So either this is some really weird coincidence or somebody was making a point."

"The agent was in town."

Greene dismissed the idea with a scrunch of his nose. "Weak little man. But he could have had help, or he *was* the help. I'm going to have to talk to the Canadians, see if he left his hotel that night." Greene paused, scowling. "What's the motive, Mick? Would somebody really kill over a book?"

"Sorry, motive is your job. But Iverson in Olympia may be able to shed some light on that. Did you get his report? He said he sent it already."

Greene sighed in resignation. "All right. I'm off to check his findings."

"Before you go, there's something else. I found bits of dirt embedded in the rope, but no touch DNA anywhere except in the noose where it came into contact with the vic's neck."

"Huh?" Greene and Penelope said in unison.

"Precisely. The rope was bought precut and is sold shrink-wrapped, so we would expect no skin cells from the sales staff. But if Harrington hanged herself, skin cells from her hands should be all over this rope, and they're not. And nothing from the killer, either. So he used gloves, gloves with dirt on them."

Lily's eyes widened with alarm. Greene's eyes widened with

anticipation. "The gardener is my prime suspect. There were gloves in the gardening shed. Get someone up there to grab and test them. Can you match the dirt?"

"Well, yes, but if we find epithelials from multiple people inside the gloves, we won't be able to prove it was the gardener who used them to hang Harrington."

"You let me worry about that. Just get the gloves."

"I'm on it."

Greene closed down the video link and checked his email for the technology report from the Investigative Assistance Division in Olympia. A division of the Washington State Patrol, the IAD and their High Tech Unit provide forensics assistance to forces across the state; Sheraton had sent them Harrington's laptop and other electronics. They had pushed the investigation to the top of the pile as per the chief's request, hoping, as everyone was, to shut this file down as fast as possible.

Greene scanned the report but, as usual, found it indecipherable: technology was not his strong point. He always found it easier to discuss these things in person, but Olympia was a long drive away and Greene needed to be expeditious with his time. "Hey, Kevin," Greene called out over the cubicle wall, "can you come here a moment?"

Monk appeared in the doorway. "You understand this stuff better than I do," Greene said. "Would you mind listening in while I call Tech?"

"Sure."

Greene checked the report for Keith Iverson's direct line, then called the investigator and put the man on speakerphone. "Detective Iverson, it's Paul Greene, Whatcom County Homicide. I got your report. Do you mind talking to me in laymen's terms?"

Iverson chuckled. "No problem. We ran some tests on your vic's laptop, backup drive, and modem. Found a few items of interest. First up, someone plugged in a USB flash drive at 9:42 Wednesday night. And they copied the manuscript that was open on her computer."

"What?!" Lily shouted. "Someone stole my novel!" She began pacing back and forth behind the detectives. "How dare they? Kill me, fine, but steal my book? That's just beyond low."

"How do you know that?" Greene asked Iverson.

"When I checked the recent documents list in the vic's open Word window, there were two copies of the open manuscript: one in her documents folder, as one would expect, and another in an external drive no longer attached to the computer. Whoever copied the manuscript used the Save As function instead of sourcing the file on her drive and copying it. Had they done that, I would not have been able to tell what file or files were copied. But by using the Save As function, they left me a trail in Word. So then I went hunting for the device. Whenever you plug in a new device, Windows goes looking for a driver to run it. The new driver that Windows installs shows up in the system. The driver was for a FastBack brand USB 3.0 device. Such a device wasn't found by your people in the vic's office or anywhere in her personal effects."

"Can you tell if anything else was copied?"

"Not if, as I said, they simply copied it through the file system. But I can tell you that something was deleted."

Penelope and Lily looked at each other, shocked. They turned to Marcus, but he simply stared back, equally surprised.

"What was deleted?" Greene asked.

"There was a document she was working on called Farewell_My_Love; it's in the documents list but it was deleted and the Recycle Bin emptied. It was also deleted from her external backup drive that was plugged into one of the USB ports. But you're in luck; the file wasn't overwritten yet and I managed to retrieve it."

"First things: Which manuscript was open and copied?"

"Something called *Waves*."

"What's it about?"

"I don't know; I didn't read it."

"It's an exploration of one woman's inner world as she struggles with the loss of her father and the disintegration of her marriage," Lily recited from memory.

"How long did it take you to write *that* logline?" Marcus snickered.

"It was just a draft," Lily replied indignantly.

"Can you check it for me?" Greene requested. "Is there a character called Mantova in it?"

Iverson did a quick search for *Mantova* in the Word document. "No."

"Then this isn't Harrington's last Mantova book," Greene concluded. "This is probably her literary novel, the one that was causing all the fuss." He tapped his fingernails on the counter, thinking. "Which document was deleted?"

A few keystrokes later and *Farewell, My Love* opened up on Iverson's screen. "Ah," he said, "this opens with someone called Mantova."

"Can you hold on a second while we check something?"

Greene opened a browser on his computer and checked online for a list of Harrington's forty-nine novels. "What are you looking for?" Monk asked.

"I want to see if this *Farewell* is an old book or the latest one."

"No need," Lily responded. "I can tell you. It's my latest book. Why did someone erase my damn book! Do you have any idea how long that took to write?" She turned to Penelope. "How do I tell them?"

"You don't, Lily. It's easy enough for them to figure out. Be patient."

Greene checked Sellinger's website. An ad for Harrington's upcoming fiftieth book was already prominent on the site. *Farewell, My Love*: large white lettering, red background, a stricken Marcus cradling what appeared to be a dying woman, her shiny blond hair flowing back from her porcelain face, lithe arms lying limply at her side. The pathos dripped off the cover and down the screen.

"Nice cover," Marcus said, genuinely impressed. Penelope rolled her eyes but refrained from commenting: she needed to hear this conversation, not have one of her own.

"So, somebody stole Harrington's literary novel and erased her new mystery novel," Greene said to Monk. "That doesn't make any sense."

"Why?"

"Harrington was writing the final book in a very successful series. Imagine if it leaked online ahead of publication. Publisher might lose millions. You could hold that one for a tidy ransom."

"That sounds like motive to kill the thief, not the writer."

"True. But the point is, *that* book had value. But her literary novel? No one wanted it."

"That is *not* true," Lily argued. "I had interest from several publishers."

"*Somebody* definitely wanted it," Monk said with a rise of his eyebrows.

Greene turned his attention back to the phone call. "Detective Iverson, when was the file deleted?"

Iverson checked his recovery log. "At exactly 10:48 Wednesday night."

"So someone copied her literary novel at 9:42, and then over an hour later they deleted her mystery novel. Why? And then sometime before or after, she was killed. Again, why?"

"Maybe the one book was copied at 9:42. Vic caught the thief, so he had to kill her. An hour later the deed is done and he copies the second, more valuable book, and then deletes it, ensuring he has the only copy, or so he thinks."

"Except there were no signs of a struggle. Nothing to indicate surprise. She was drugged and then killed." Greene grimaced. "This is not making any sense."

"Well, aren't we assuming, perhaps wrongly, that the killer and the thief are one and the same?" Iverson suggested, muddying the waters further.

"Good point." Greene turned pensive again. "Well, thank you, Detective. And thanks for expediting this. Much appreciated."

"Let me know if you need anything further," Iverson said and hung up.

"Okay, I'm going to print this out then head home," Greene announced, hitting the print sequence on his keyboard. "I'll give the brass the heads up then get out of here. I'm done with this day. I need to think this through. Try to make some sense of it."

Lily's face went white and she sank onto the carpeted floor of the cubicle. "What's wrong?" Penelope asked, her expression a cross between concern and mild confusion.

"I understand someone stealing my Mantova book, maybe holding it for ransom. Someone who needed money. But my literary novel ..." She looked up with wide eyes at Penelope. "He wouldn't, would he?"

"Who and what?" Penelope replied.

"Arni. He wouldn't steal my novel and pass it off as his own, would he?"

"Does he know you already shared it with Martin and Sellinger?" Marcus asked.

Lily shook her head. "No. I read it to Arni, but I never told him about the negotiations."

"You mean the blackmail," Marcus corrected her, the judgment evident in his voice.

"Call it what you will," Penelope chided Marcus, "it's not the point."

"Then what is? Arni had access, Arni knew about the novel, and maybe he wasn't waiting around for Lily here to get his graphic novel published. Maybe he got impatient."

Lily's eyes welled up and she covered her mouth with shaky fingers. "Oh my God, Penelope, Arni wears white running shoes."

"DEEP BREATHS, LILY, DEEP BREATHS," Penelope said, trying to calm Lily down. She was hyperventilating now. The news that her novels had been stolen, and that her lover was her killer, was overwhelming.

"Why, Penelope?" Lily asked through tears. "I understand he was upset, but if he really loved me like he claimed, why would he kill me?"

"Like Greene said earlier, most homicides are committed by an intimate partner or family member," Marcus said.

Penelope glared at him. "You are *not* helping." She squatted down to look Lily in the eyes. "Lily, honey, you don't know for certain that Arni killed you. Lots of people wear running shoes."

Lily looked around the cubicle. She was wearing sandals, Penelope was in short black boots, Marcus had his loafers on, Greene was in brown dress shoes. Only Monk was wearing sneakers. That was only one out of five. So there was an eighty percent chance that Arni was the killer. Lily did not like those odds.

Penelope glanced at the detectives' shoes as Greene and Monk left the cubicle, and knew what Lily was thinking. "Lily, we five are hardly a representative sample. There are suspects with a lot more to gain by your death than Arni."

"I don't know, Penelope," Marcus chimed in again, "I agree with Greene. Arni appears to be our prime suspect. And what about the dirt-covered gloves? That points to Arni."

Their conversation was interrupted by Greene, who called out to Monk just as he returned to his own cubicle. "Hey, Kevin, one more thing. What's a RAT?"

"I believe it's a rodent."

"No, I mean this." Greene walked from the printer to Monk's desk, the Tech Unit report in hand. "I forgot to ask Iverson about this. It says somebody was spying on her using a RAT," Greene said as he handed the printout to Monk.

"It stands for remote administrative tool. It's a piece of malicious software installed by hackers, usually to gain access to personal information like banking passwords, but this one specifically targeted the webcam: it turned the camera on but disabled the LED light. The software is popular with peeping Toms and low-level blackmailers who use the camera to record compromising images then blackmail the victim over them."

Everyone's thoughts turned to Richard Owen, to his buggy eyes, bank of computer screens, and secret income. Lily's mouth fell open and her face turned to ash. "I think I'm going to throw up," she said and let her head fall forward over her knees.

"Is there any way to know who did it?" Greene thought it prudent to ask before he rushed back to The Point to ring Richard Owen's neck.

"Not likely," Monk shrugged. "The software is usually installed either through an email attachment or from visiting a malicious website. I'll call Iverson and ask him to go through her emails, see if anything came with an infected attachment. If so, they can try to trace the email. But if the Trojan came from an infected site, you're out of luck. There's no way to know which one she visited."

"Do they know how long ago the program was installed?"

Monk scanned the report. "Yeah, two months ago. But more importantly, whoever was spying on her was doing so the night she died."

Greene's eyebrows shot up: this was an interesting development. "How can they tell?"

"The RAT was executed through her Wi-Fi." Monk saw the blank look that quickly replaced Greene's budding enthusiasm. "Every time someone accesses a modem," Monk explained, "they leave behind their MAC address in the device. IAD found six MAC addresses in Harrington's modem, which could be anything from a smartphone to a laptop: every wireless device has a MAC."

"MAC address?" Greene asked with a roll of his eyes. "RATs? Why do you techie types always have to speak in acronyms?"

"Sorry. Media access card. Every one of them has a serial number called a MAC address, and every time you access a modem with a wireless device, the modem logs the address."

"Harrington's got a weird neighbor who admitted to spying on her through her windows. Could he have done this? He seems computer savvy."

Lily's head shot back up. "Owen's been peering through my windows?" she said in disbelief. So it was true! Her cheeks puffed out as she fought back the threat of vomit, then her body fell forward again.

"Of course. The software is readily available on file sharing sites. But a MAC address is useless without the device itself to confirm it. IAD have Harrington's laptop and mobile phone so they have those MAC addresses for elimination, but that's it. You can match an address but you can't look one up. It's not like there's a phone book out there. But someone with a MAC address that did not belong to Harrington's devices was online the night she died."

"Okay," Greene said, his voice weighed down with fatigue, "just to recap: someone copied one manuscript and deleted another, someone installed spyware to watch her through her webcam, and that someone may be our killer or star witness."

"That about sums it up, yes," Monk concurred. "And we don't know if everything was done by the same person, or even if the actions are related. And your star witness could be anywhere in the world."

Greene felt an overwhelming exhaustion. It was just like technology to complicate an investigation, and he longed for the good old analog days when witnesses could not spy through webcams from anywhere in the world.

"And not to make things worse for you," Monk added, "but there's a segment of the dark web that's devoted to weird shit like watching crimes committed in real time online. It's usually sex crimes like rape, but there have been a few homicides. And the vic's famous, so that would have been a drawing card. People get off on the creepiest stuff these days."

"You think someone killed her for an audience?" Greene asked, trying to wrap his head around that one.

Lily, too, was speechless. Back in New York she'd had some stalkers, and over the years a few angry fans had sent her hate mail when she refused their amorous advances, but the idea that someone might have killed her for the pleasure of others to watch was just too demeaning to think about.

"It's possible," Monk replied. "I know a guy with the Feds who monitors the dark web. I'll ask him to check for chatter about a murder show. I'll let you know if anything comes up."

"Great," Greene sighed. "Now I'm really going home. I need a drink. This is a lot to digest." He turned and headed for the door.

"It's a lot for *him* to digest?" Lily said, incredulous. "My pervert neighbor has been spying on me through my windows and webcam, my lover stole my book and killed me and might have put it on the web, but *he* needs a drink?!"

"I disagree with your conclusion," Penelope said, shaking her head. "Except the drink part. I could use one myself. Kind of miss those after-work beers." She shook the thought away and looked down at Lily, clinging for dear life to the edge of Greene's desk. "Lily, you know how hard it is to get published these days. Arni had more to gain by keeping you *alive*. If he stole your novel, what would he do with it? Spend the next two years just trying to find an agent, that's what."

"He could self-publish," Marcus suggested.

"Joe," Penelope said between clenched teeth, "unless you have something useful to add, please keep quiet."

"Stop calling me—"

"He's right, though," Lily interjected, defiant. "Arni could publish it himself. It's all the rage now."

"And then what?" Penelope argued back. "Arni writes graphic novels. That's where his heart lies. And you were his entry ticket to the big boys. No, I think it more likely Sentient was behind this. They have the money and the power and they can afford to hire hackers and assassins. Maybe the webcam was just for proof before payment."

"What do you propose?" Lily asked. Her anger had quelled the queasiness in her stomach, restoring her equilibrium.

"I think we should go to New York. Eavesdrop on Sellinger and Martin. If we find out anything of use we can leave a message for Greene."

"That's a great idea!" Marcus exclaimed. "We could go see *Wicked*."

"Really, Joseph?" Penelope said, throwing one hand up in frustration. "You want to go to the theater? We're investigating Lily's murder, which if I recall correctly is allegedly why you came here in the first place."

Marcus wrinkled his nose in reply. "That *is* why I'm here. I just don't see why we can't do both. Not everyone is a workaholic, Penelope. And for the last time, stop calling me Jo—"

"Oh for God's sake, please you two," Lily moaned. "If I weren't already dead I'd beg you to kill me."

"Sorry," Penelope said. "I don't know why I let him get under my skin like that." She paused, then asked, "What would you like to do? This is, after all, your case."

"I agree we should go to New York, spy on that weasel Donald. But it's Friday night there already; the offices won't be open again until Monday."

"On the contrary, Lily, one of their star writers is dead," Penelope pointed out. "You can bet they're in the office brainstorming how to make this work for them."

"That's probably true," Lily admitted. "I keep forgetting I'm dead to them. But it's already evening there; I suggest we head out in the morning. I want to observe Greene tonight. He tells his wife stuff about his cases; it would be good to know what he's thinking and, if necessary, direct it as you both have suggested."

"Fair enough," Marcus whined. "You do that and report back. I'll meet you in New York tomorrow."

"You're off to see *Wicked*, aren't you?" Penelope said with an accusing eye.

Marcus didn't answer; he just sneered at Penelope and was gone.

"Well, I guess it's just us two," Penelope said with feigned resignation.

"No, Penelope, it's just me. I want to do this on my own. I feel … badly that we're spying on Greene in his home. I know it's necessary but … I feel if it's just me then somehow that mitigates the intrusion."

"I understand. I've got other cases I can catch up on. Let's meet at Greene's house tomorrow morning and I'll take us to New York."

"Um, there's just one problem."

"What's that?"

"Greene's gone. How do I get to his house?"

"That's not a problem. I'll take you there now and pick you up in the morning."

Lily shook her head. "No, Penelope, teach me instead. Please? It's time I learned. I was self-sufficient in life; I want to be the same in death."

"Well then, my protégé, put on your seatbelt. We're going for a test drive."

Lily grinned, and for a moment she forgot the troubles of the day.

An hour or so later Lily had got the hang of relocation. It was easier than it had seemed at first: you conjure up the image of either a person or landmark, then you clear your mind of all other thoughts until your spirit connects with the energy of the person or place and—voila!—you are there. The tough part, Lily discovered, was clearing her mind of her present environment. It was easy enough to close her eyes to the sights but shutting out sound, and focusing her thoughts, was trickier. She wished she had practiced meditation or at least a bit of yoga.

After several false starts, one of which landed her on a ferry in the middle of the San Juan Islands—Penelope had had to find Lily and bring her back—she got her thoughts under control and successfully transported herself to the back of Greene's cruiser. Penelope came along only long enough to confirm the time and place for their next meet, then she was gone, likely back to the Homicide squad room. Lily wondered if Penelope ever slept.

Greene was driving the last leg home. He was quiet. Judging by the range of expressions that crossed his face, Lily concluded he was deeply perplexed by the turn of events. As was she. She wished she could strike up a conversation with him, bounce some ideas around and see what he thought. Her initial dismissal of the detective had been replaced with a grudging respect and growing appreciation of his efforts.

When they arrived home, Ellie was dozing beneath the shade of the porch, the wheels of her chair locked so she would not roll away. Greene tapped lightly on the patio door glass to wake her, then walked over and gave her a gentle kiss on the lips. Ellie looked up dreamily and said, "My prince, how was your day?"

"It went from hopeful to bad to worse. But now"—he smiled at her—"it's good again. How about you?"

"I had a good day today. I even managed some baking. I made your favorite cookies."

"You're a saint."

"And I made chili."

"Wow! You really had a good day."

Ellie beamed. It felt wonderful to be useful. "It's keeping warm on the stove. If you make a salad we can eat out here in the cool breeze."

Greene did as suggested. Half an hour later he and Ellie were seated at the plastic table on the patio, eating chili and a fresh salad of greens, cucumbers, and tomatoes picked from the small vegetable garden in the corner of the property. Lily sat on the nearby settee and tried not to look at the food: the sight of homegrown produce was making her nostalgic.

"What went wrong today, Paul, or is it confidential?"

"It's confidential, but you're my confidante so I see no harm." He laughed and squeezed Ellie's hand.

"Is it the Harrington case? It's been the talk of the day on the news. You'd think the president just died."

Lily smiled. She knew she had been a popular author but no one had ever compared her to the president before. And she liked the president, so that was a plus.

"I wish he had," Greene replied. "Then it would be someone else's problem."

"How did the autopsy go?"

"Badly. It's a homicide."

Ellie gasped. "Oh, Paul, that's terrible. That poor woman. What happened to her?"

"So far it looks like someone drugged her then hanged her to make it look like a suicide."

"Oh sweet Jesus. Do you have a suspect?"

"I'm liking the boyfriend. Forensics have a few other ideas but they sound too complicated. It's been my experience that most homicides are actually simple acts committed by angry or desperate people: robbers, lovers, family members."

"Lily Harrington had a boyfriend?" Ellie asked with a smile. "That was never mentioned in my *Crime Fiction* newsletter."

"She was banging the help. Her gardener. And he's all of twenty-five years old."

Ellie let out a spontaneous howl of delight. "Good for her! Is he hot?"

Lily smiled mischievously. *Honey, you have no idea.*

Greene gave his wife a sideways glance and smiled despite himself. "If I told you he was hot, would I do as a substitute this evening?"

Ellie leaned forward, slipped one hand beneath the table and began caressing her husband's groin. "You're never a substitute, my love. You're always the real deal."

Greene leaned over and kissed Ellie, tenderly at first and then more passionately. Lily could see where this was headed, and her voyeurism made her uncomfortable. It also reminded her of her other agenda for the evening, the one she had not wanted to tell Penelope or Marcus about. Lily went into the house, sat in a living room chair, closed her eyes and concentrated. Moments later she was back in Point Roberts, sitting on Richard Owen's couch, waiting for her prey.

RICHARD OWEN CAME INTO THE LIVING ROOM with his dinner on a tray. His meal consisted of a microwavable chicken-and-mashed-potatoes platter, some fresh fruit, and a glass of milk in a World's Best Mom coffee mug. He set the tray down on a collapsible TV tray, rotated three times then sat down and turned on the television to *Wheel of Fortune.*

Lily moved off the couch and into the chair opposite Richard and tried to think of what, exactly, she wanted to do to him, and how. The exploding beer at Arni's had been unintentional, and Lily could not ask Penelope how she moved stuff, especially after she had warned Lily not to. But there was no way in hell—or whatever this place is—that Richard Owen's spying would remain unaddressed.

She eyed the coffee mug. *Now that would be karmic,* she thought. Lily focused her thoughts on the mug, imagined it exploding, imagined the shards flying in all directions and the milk covering the recluse in a sticky residue. She imagined his screams of terror—but the only sound Richard Owen emitted was "Bedknobs and Broomsticks" in answer to the television. Lily turned her head. He was right. As was the contestant when another spin later she asked for a *B.*

Lily sat back in the chair and folded her arms, cross with her ineptitude. Richard Owen munched on his chicken and slurped his milk, oblivious to her, pausing his noisy chewing only to blurt out more answers to the game show puzzles. Lily could not take any more of the sound of his chewing or his falsetto voice, and *Jeopardy* was on next. Richard would likely become even more intolerable then.

She got up and stomped out of the living room and down to his office. She sat at the bank of monitors and let her eyes flitter between the osprey nest and the Space Station. The birds were sleeping, faces tucked beneath wings, the fluffy down of the chicks just visible behind their parents. Not much more was taking place on the Space Station: it was currently over the Atlantic, headed for South America, nothing but a cloud-speckled blue sky appearing beneath the station's wing. There were 580 people watching for reasons Lily could not fathom, and on the Social Stream somebody named straycat94 was discussing the merits of juicing with jane68, whose icon was a medieval princess, while sswatcher666 quoted Isaiah 40:22: "It is He who sits above the circle of the earth, and its inhabitants are like grasshoppers." The effect almost put Lily into a stupor.

Fifteen minutes later the station had reached darkness and Lily heard banging in the kitchen, then the telltale slap-slap-slap of Richard's footsteps on the porcelain tiles. He came into the office and sat down on Lily, forcing her to get up and move to the spare chair in the corner, muttering obscenities at him under her breath.

She watched as he opened an encrypted file folder on one of his three desktop computers. He clicked on a file, and a media player opened a video. It was of Lily and Arni having sex on the couch in her office. Lily freaked. She lunged for the monitor, but in her haste lost control of her body and it merely passed through the desk, and she fell face first onto the floor beneath. She crawled out and scrambled to her feet again, then threw herself with more accuracy onto the desk between Richard and the monitor. It was all to no avail. She was invisible. Invisible and powerless.

"Oh no," Lily groaned when Owen undid his trousers and pulled out his pathetic little member. "Really, Richard? Must you?"

He did. Richard began energetically spanking the monkey as he watched Lily and Arni on the monitor. She pulled herself off the desk and turned her back to the insult, unable to watch him violate her yet equally unable to leave. She closed her eyes but could not block out the sound of Richard's heavy breathing and occasional grunts. The heavier he breathed and the more he grunted the angrier Lily became, and just before Richard achieved orgasm the video image on the LED screen burst into bands of color before shorting out to black, then the glass on the monitor cracked. Richard jumped back in fright, knocking his chair to the ground. His member went limp. He scrambled to put it back in his pants, as if he had been caught by his mother.

Lily opened her eyes to the commotion. She turned and saw Richard's fear and the spider web of glass, and burst into derisive laughter. "Ha! Take that, you effing pervert. And if you watch that video again I'm going to break everything in this room. Do you hear me?"

Richard's face was deathly pale. With the back of one trembling hand he wiped away the sweat that had formed on his upper lip. He looked anxiously around the room then over at the security monitor. All was quiet outside. In the office, though, Lily was still yelling at him, her fury peaking and threatening to explode again. Inside Richard Owen's head he heard the shrill voice of an angry woman, and was certain it was his mother. He burst into tears and fled the office with Lily in hot pursuit. He stumbled down the porcelain hallway and up the stairs. "You can hear me, can't you, you disgusting piece of flotsam?" she shouted at him, her angry energy nipping at his worn-out moccasins.

Richard ran, terrified and whimpering, down the hallway to his bedroom. He fled into the room without removing his slippers, then panicked further when he realized what he had done. He shrieked and fell to the carpet, frantically pulling off his moccasins, screeching as if they were on fire. He crawled to the threshold, fumbling with the moccasins as he struggled to set them down on the hallway floor with the heels aligned just so. Finally he got it right, then pulled himself back to his feet and raced to his bed. He threw himself under the blankets, grabbed his teddy bear and curled into a fetal position. "Please, Mother, I won't do it again. I promise. It's dirty. I'm sorry."

The sight of an hysterical Richard Owen battling his disorder, and now curled up and whimpering like a wounded dog, stopped Lily dead in her tracks. Her anger evaporated and was replaced with guilt, guilt she knew she should not feel. And yet she did.

"What did you do to him, Lily?" said a voice from behind her.

Lily's stomach leapt into her chest. She spun around to find Penelope standing in the doorway. "Damn it, Penelope, you nearly scared me to death," Lily gasped in anger.

"You're avoiding the question," Penelope said evenly.

"He *had* been spying on me through my webcam, just like Greene thought," Lily said in her defense. "Little creep even recorded it."

"That still doesn't tell me what *you* did."

Lily's eyes went round as saucers, like a naughty child scolded by her parents. Penelope said nothing more, just stared Lily down until regret crept in and she was duly subdued. "Well … I'm not entirely sure," she slowly answered, looking away. "I tried to break his coffee mug but I couldn't." But then the image of Richard masturbating in front of the screen came flooding back, and Lily rediscovered her indignation. She looked up, defiant. "But then he was watching a sex video of me and Arni and I couldn't handle it. I was so *angry*. Then the monitor exploded. It was like the beer at Arni's; it just happened. I wish I could control it like you, but I can't seem to get the hang of it."

"Stop trying to, Lily; it's forbidden. I told you that already."

"But why? You do it. Marcus does it, at least when he thinks no one is watching. Why can't I?"

"Because there are penalties, Lily, especially if you bring harm to the living. Your rebirth can be postponed."

"Then why do you do it?"

"Because I don't want to be reborn, that's why." Penelope blurted the words out before she had time to think of something more considered, and the misstep embarrassed her. She looked away and raised the fingers of her left hand to her mouth, as if trying to decide if she should elaborate or not.

Lily's brow knotted. She had not given rebirth a single thought, had been so focused on her death and finding her killer that the idea of a new and different life had not entered her consciousness. Did she want to be reborn? Or did she want to stay here, like Penelope? And Marcus. He didn't seem in a hurry to go anywhere, had been living in her novels for the past twenty years. And if torturing Richard Owen was cause for delay, would it be worth it?

"Why don't you want to be reborn?" Lily asked, curious.

Penelope's lip quivered. It was the first sign of weakness Lily had seen in the detective since she had arrived to save the day, and Lily was intrigued by the involuntary gesture. She repeated the question but more gently this time: "Why, Penelope?"

"Because I *know* this life," she answered, her voice unsteady. "I *like* this life. I'm *good* at it. What if I'm not in the next? What if I'm a loser like Richard here, or a selfish bastard like Joe?"

"But what if you're even better in the next life? More successful? Happier?"

"There's no guarantees, Lily. None. You play the hand you're dealt. I know this hand. I play it well. That's all I need right now."

"But aren't you relegated to the sidelines? You solve all these cases but you never get credit. No one thanks you."

Penelope shrugged and smiled. "You will."

"But don't you miss the recognition?" Lily could not imagine anyone wanting to work without credit.

"I *am* recognized. Maybe not by the living, but I am by the dead I help. And when you think about it, I get *more* recognition now by those I help than I did working Homicide when I was alive. Here I actually get to meet the victims. I get to know them. Not just vicariously through family and facts and snooping through their former life, but face to face. Like with you."

Lily nodded her understanding. She sat down on the end of Richard Owen's bed and looked over her shoulder at him, still whimpering into the head of his teddy bear. Lily frowned with remorse. "All right, I promise to be good."

Penelope walked over and sat down beside Lily. "It's different for you," Penelope said, her eyes imploring Lily to understand. "Your talent needs a live audience."

"But will I take my talent with me?" Lily asked, suddenly fearful that her gift had ended with her death.

The question caught Penelope off guard. She had never thought about that. "I haven't a clue," she admitted. "I don't recall my past lives so I have no idea if I share any similar characteristics with my former selves."

"What about Marcus? Why does he stay?"

Penelope let out a dismissive laugh. "Joe is a bottomless well of need. Your books gave him the fame he craved and couldn't find in life. He can't risk losing that in the next one. Though now that you're dead he may have to."

"How did he die?"

"Suicide."

Lily gasped. "Really?" The revelation was unexpected. Marcus was so arrogant and sure of himself, and his looks alone would have carried him in life; did he even need talent?

"Uh-huh. Though if you ask him he'll tell you it was a tragic car accident," Penelope replied with a snicker. "Claims he was killed by a drunk driver. Turns out, he *was* the drunk driver. I know; I read the file. He'd lost a part to another actor, and the show was a huge hit, and then Joe's girlfriend left him because she couldn't stand the pity party. He started drinking heavily, and then one night he decided the worst thing he could do to the world was leave it, so he drove his car into a pole. The funeral was smaller than expected. He never got over that."

"Can I trust him?"

Penelope snorted. "I don't."

"Why do you think he's here?"

"Like I said, he's a bottomless well of need."

"But do you think we should trust him with this investigation?"

"I think Joe's a pain in the ass but he's harmless. And useless. He's off watching a play while you and I are actually trying to solve this case. What does that tell you?"

Lily thought about that a moment, then smiled. "It tells me my stories were mine."

"There you go."

Lily's smile quickly faded. "Except ..."

"Except what?"

"If Joe became Marcus, even if just in his own mind, and if he is able to use that mind meld trick of his to manipulate people's thoughts, how do I know he didn't manipulate mine? That he didn't influence my stories in some way?"

"You don't. I suppose you just have to have faith in your own talent."

"But if he didn't influence me, then how did he become Mantova so effectively? I mean, maybe I did connect with him on some level. Maybe somebody's imagination is connecting with us now. That would be cool, don't you think?"

"No!" Penelope exclaimed, aghast that Lily should think otherwise. "My life is *not* some silly fiction. And I'm a *real* cop, not a bogus wannabe like Joe. I work on real cases, help real victims."

"Speaking of which …" Lily began another question but the words fell silent off her lips.

"What?"

"Can I beg a favor of you?"

"Sure."

"Will you erase my sex video off Richard's computer?"

Penelope blew out a heavy sigh. "Oh, I don't know, Lily; it's potential evidence. If Owen murdered you in some weird fit of misguided jealousy, you could potentially be destroying a key piece to nail him with."

"I-I know. But I don't think he killed me. He's not well, that I concede, but my gut tells me he didn't do this. And the video … it's so invasive. And embarrassing." Lily stared, her brow furrowed, eyes hopeful, in what she hoped was her best doleful expression.

Penelope tried to fight off the blatant manipulation. "Lily, you have to admit your gut has been all over the place on this one."

"Pleeeeeease," she begged, laying it on as thick as she could muster.

Penelope looked over and realized Lily was not going to give in. Though it went against every bone in her investigator's body, Penelope relented. "Oh for heaven's sake, all right."

She arose and strode out of the bedroom, headed for Richard's office. Lily ran excitedly after her, grateful for the act of faith and friendship. They went downstairs to the office. Penelope crawled behind the desk and disconnected the broken monitor from the computer Richard had been using when he was watching the video. Then she disconnected the computer running the osprey nest video from the monitor displaying it, then hooked that monitor up to the first computer. "I hope you appreciate just how much work this is," she said from her spot on the floor.

She crawled out from behind Richard's desk. Windows had recognized the monitor and the sex show was back onscreen. Penelope picked up the mouse, closed down the media player, then went into the still-open folder Richard had stored the illicit video in. She selected the file then hovered the mouse over the delete button. "Are you absolutely certain about this? You could be letting your killer off."

Lily nodded. "Yes. Having others watch this would be worse. Besides, I have you to haunt him afterwards if he turns out to be the culprit."

"Don't count on it." Penelope hit the delete button, then she checked the other files in the encrypted folder.

"What the hell?" the women said in unison as the next video opened on screen. It was of Thornfield and Runa in Lily's office. Runa was on her knees, and despite Thornfield's ecstatic mutterings of "Oh God, oh God," neither of them was praying.

"WELL THAT EXPLAINS A FEW THINGS," Penelope said as Runa's head continued to bob up and down in front of David Thornfield's groin.

"Do you think it has any significance?" That Runa had been vacuuming Thornfield when she was supposed to be vacuuming the house did not bother Lily so much as the possibility that sex on the job was not Runa's only transgression.

"Hard to say at this point. But it's good information."

"I think we should stop watching this."

"I *want* to stop watching this," Penelope said and closed down the file. "I hate the sight of a woman on her knees."

"What? You mean you've never done this?" Lily asked, skeptical.

"No, I've never done it *on my knees.*"

Penelope checked the other files in Richard's encrypted folder. There were two other videos but they were regular porn, downloaded off the net. She left those and the Runa–Thornfield rendezvous untouched, then went into the Recycle Bin and emptied it. She checked Richard's backup drives and deleted the Lily–Arni movie there, too. "Oh, drats," she said after a moment. Her tone sounded ominous.

"What is it?" Lily asked, worried.

"He's got cloud backup. It'll be password protected."

"Damn."

"It doesn't mean he backed up all his files to the cloud. You'll just have to pray he kept his playmates isolated here at home. There's nothing more I can do. We've probably done more than we should have, anyway."

Lily reluctantly agreed. "Thank you for trying."

"No problem. At least we'd better hope so." The sound of footsteps was heard on the floor above. "And I think we'd better leave before you lose it again on Owen."

"Let's go to my place. We can watch a movie if you like."

"Don't you think we ought to investigate this relationship first? Honestly, Lily, I'm beginning to wonder how you managed to write detective novels for over twenty years."

"Now you're just being unkind."

Penelope ignored the criticism. "Do you want to relocate on your own or do you want me to take you?"

Lily reached out her hand. "Let's save us both some time."

Penelope chuckled and took Lily's hand, transporting them to Sunny Side.

They arrived in the trailer park to the smell of meat on the grill and the shrill cries of children running about with water guns. Lily smiled at the sight of the kids' infectious energy, but her smile evaporated when she saw Arni walking down the path toward them. He looked lost despite the familiar surroundings. Lily took a step toward him but Penelope held her back. "Let him go. If you remain attached it's going to be doubly hard if he's involved in this mess."

"I thought you said he didn't do this?" Lily asked, genuinely confused, if a little hopeful.

"I said I thought he didn't *kill* you. But that doesn't mean he's entirely innocent. We don't know all the facts yet."

Lily watched with a heavy heart as Arni walked past her toward his trailer. What would happen to him now? To his graphic novel? He had talent, and he deserved a better life than the one he had here, living in a trailer park and pruning other people's hedges. During their moments together she had tried to boost his confidence, had encouraged him to imagine the fame and recognition his talent warranted, but there was always a seed of doubt in Arni, and it would sprout despite Lily's efforts to kill it off like a weed. She had always wondered what fed it, what had given it life in the first place, but she never asked, had wanted Arni to tell her in his own time. But that time never came, and now it never would.

And then Lily wondered why she still cared. After all, just hours before she had learned he was the chief suspect in her murder. Even Penelope was not entirely convinced of his innocence. How could Lily still care at all about someone who might have killed her? Was it because she knew, deep down, that he was not responsible? Or was it something far more sinister: that she was actually making excuses for the hate? She prayed it were the former because the last thing she wanted was another good shaking from Penelope.

Lily let Arni go as instructed, and the two women turned and headed for the western side of Julius Drive. As they came upon Runa's trailer they saw her inside on the couch, clutching her copy of *Love and Secrets* and talking to a man. But it was not Thornfield. It was Marcus.

"What the hell?" Lily and Penelope said in unison for the second time in less than an hour.

"Can she see him?" Lily asked, surprised by the sight.

Penelope shrugged and shook her head. "I can't tell from here. She could just be imagining him, and he's there lapping it up like a lovesick puppy. He's prone to that."

"What are you talking about?" This was yet another element of the afterlife Lily did not understand.

"When you read a book, you often imagine yourself in it, either as a main character or as yourself but a part of the narrative, yes?"

Well, now that was true. Lily also often imagined herself singing her favorite songs, especially as in reality she didn't possess an ounce of musical talent. She would lie in the bath and listen to Joni Mitchell, imagining herself with the same lyrical voice. "Okay, yes," Lily admitted.

"Well, Marcus has a habit of visiting women who are reading your books, especially if they're reading the sex scenes."

Lily's face fell. Suddenly Marcus seemed no better than Richard Owen, spying on women and getting off on it. "Penelope, do you mean he watches women fantasizing?"

"Actually, it goes further than that. He has sex with them."

"Like an incubus?" Lily asked, stunned. She had always thought them nothing more than ancient superstition.

"You could say that. Though he's not so much a demon as just an asshole."

Lily was floored. This afterlife gig was becoming more complicated by the day.

"So now what?" she asked after they had watched for another minute or two. "Do we confront him or just stand here like two nosy neighbors?"

Marcus inadvertently answered their question when he removed his coat and hat and leaned over Runa, his hand on her breast. She rose from the couch and closed the drapes, putting an end to the spying. "Okay, this is really creepy," Lily declared. "I am never talking to Marcus again."

"On the contrary, Lily, keep your friends close and your enemies closer."

LILY AWOKE THE NEXT MORNING to the sound of birds outside her bedroom window. After discovering Marcus was "sleeping" with Runa, Lily and Penelope had called it a day. Penelope had gone back to Bellingham to read up on current cases, and Lily had come home and gone to bed. She would have preferred to read or perhaps watch a movie, and despite Penelope's warnings not to, Lily had tried to open a book and handle the remote. Unfortunately all efforts proved fruitless. She had then briefly considered visiting Arni in the hope that perhaps he would fantasize about her and she could have her way with him like Marcus did with women, but the temptation proved brief and was quickly replaced with disgust with herself for even contemplating the idea. And so, with nothing else to do, and with boredom an unwanted companion, Lily had simply lain down on her bed and drifted off into nothingness.

But now it was morning and the birds were singing, and for a moment Lily completely forgot she was dead. She was halfway through planning a day of writing and gardening when she suddenly remembered she was due in New York. As if on cue, Penelope appeared in the bedroom. "Get up, bedhead. We have work to do."

"Morning, Penelope. Do you ever sleep?"

"Why bother? It really isn't necessary anymore. Just pure indulgence." Penelope said this with an unnatural energy in her voice, as if she had just downed three espressos. Was there coffee in the afterlife? Or could you ingest it vicariously through the living, like Marcus did with sex? Such thoughts ran through Lily's head but she kept them to herself. She crawled out of bed, put her shoes back on, and straightened her hair and dress. Satisfied she was presentable, she lifted one feeble hand out to Penelope and let her transport them to the offices of Sellinger Press in New York.

The swoosh of relocation woke Lily up like a cold shower. She and Penelope had landed in the boardroom of Sellinger's offices on Fifth Avenue. Marcus was not yet there and Lily felt some relief: she was not sure if she could even look at him now.

Her relief was short lived, however, for moments later Marcus arrived. "How was *Wicked*?" Penelope asked with a straight face.

"Fantastic," he lied. "You two should have come with me."

No pun intended, Lily thought sarcastically. *And no thank you.*

"Not my thing, thanks," Penelope said, and Lily knew Penelope was not talking about the theater.

"Culture never was your thing," Marcus retorted. "That's always been one of your deficiencies."

"Musicals aren't culture, they're entertainment," Penelope replied. "Kind of like porn. Wouldn't you agree?"

"What's porn got to do with anything? Feeling a bit hungry, are we, Penelope?"

"You certainly got your fill last night," Lily said, unable to remain silent any longer. "And not of a musical."

"What *are* you two talking about?" Marcus asked as he checked his reflection in the window and adjusted his fedora. "I'm beginning to think you've been spending too much time together, feeding each other nonsense."

"We saw you at Runa's last night," Lily said, the accusation clear. "You're a pig."

"*I'm* a pig?" Marcus replied, irate. "*You* wrote those scenes, not me. Just because your readers appreciate a visit now and then does not make me a bad person. In fact, it makes me a *generous* man. And why were you watching anyway? What is wrong with you two? Or is it just you, Penelope?" His voice turned sarcastically babyish. "Still need your big daddy, Penelope?"

"I need you like I need *another* hole in the head," she growled, her face hard. She looked like she was going to hit Marcus, and Lily worried he was pushing the detective too far. And then in the next breath he did. "That wasn't the hole I was talking about" was all Marcus managed to say before Penelope hit him square on the nose with the flat of her hand, and Marcus sank to his knees on the broadloom.

"Ow! You broke my nose! You stupid witch."

Penelope stood over him, her arms crossed, one foot tapping the boardroom carpet. "It's not broken, you big baby. But keep it up, Joe, and your nose will be the least of your problems."

"Hey wait!" Lily said. "*I* wrote those scenes? So you admit it now, don't you? Those *are* my stories, not yours. You just came along for the ride."

"Oh for God's sake, are we there *again?*" Marcus asked, rubbing his face. "What I meant was—"

He was interrupted by the sound of the boardroom door opening. In came Donald Martin and five others, four of whom Lily knew. First in was her editor, Jarod Ross, followed by Nancy Weissmann, the head of marketing for Sellinger. Then came Brad Kline, in-house counsel, and Adam Liebowitz, the CEO of Sellinger. The last one in, a stout man with a wizened face, Lily did not recognize.

They came in carrying takeout coffees and deli breakfast sandwiches, notepads tucked under arms. They arranged themselves around the end of the long table, with Liebowitz at the head. Everyone looked tired, as if they had been up most of the night, and judging from the look on everyone's faces this was not a good morning.

"Where are we with all this?" Liebowitz asked. He was dressed in a suit despite the weekend, which did not surprise Lily in the least: Adam Liebowitz was old-fashioned that way, still believed that when a man left his home in the morning he should do so in his Sunday best, and he set the tone for the office. The only time she saw him out of a suit was during a weekend writers' retreat at his home in the Hamptons, and even then his linen trousers and silk shirt were immaculate. Lily suspected that even his pajamas were pressed each morning.

"The police have not released the cause of death," Nancy Weissmann informed the group, shaking a special-edition fountain pen between manicured fingers. "They're just saying that foul play is now suspected. The tabloids are on fire, as expected. We can use it to our advantage. Everyone's mentioning Harrington was at work on the fiftieth Mantova book. You can't buy that kind of publicity."

"Please don't talk like that," Jarod Ross said quietly, rubbing his temples. "She was a human being. And a respected colleague."

Lily melted. Ross had been one of her favorite editors, an accomplished writer himself whose criticisms and suggestions were always intelligent and kindly delivered. Their debates on literature were many but always friendly, and they shared a common passion for the finer points of grammar, his fierce defense of the Oxford comma a source of many jokes between them. Lily would miss his red pen. She wanted to reach out and hug him but then—

"This is no time to be sentimental, Jarod," Nancy replied, the criticism deflecting off her tanned Teflon skin. "Except in your epitaph, of course. How's that coming?"

—and the moment shattered, the shards cutting Lily to the bone. If she did not know just how much of a commodity she was before, she knew it now. She eyed Weissmann's fancy pen. It was ivory colored and platinum plated, with a cushion-cut pink tourmaline on the end that glittered in the light from the large boardroom window. The pen was a point of pride for Weissmann, had been bought on a recent trip to London at the incredible sum of £650.00, over one thousand dollars at the day's exchange rate. Lily vowed to convince Penelope to steal that pen on the way out. It would serve Weissmann right.

Ross did not answer and Weissmann turned her attention back to her boss. "If we put out a statement now that the book is still on track, it will feed the public's appetite well before the title is released."

"But *is* it still on track?" Liebowitz asked Brad Kline. "What's our legal position?"

"The contract clearly states that we have the right to publish anything we paid Harrington an advance on," Kline assured his boss. "Her copyright and earnings will go into probate but we *can* release the work." With fat fingers he grasped his greasy breakfast sandwich and took a bite.

"Great. Where is it?"

Kline hurriedly washed the partially chewed food down with a gulp of his coffee. "I'm afraid the police have Harrington's laptop and backup drive and they're refusing to release them to us. But I'm on it. I've got a guy in Seattle."

"You've got a *guy*?" Liebowitz asked, incredulous. He turned a piercing eye on Donald Martin, who shrunk beneath the CEO's gaze. "Clearly you must have a copy. You're her damn agent."

Martin shook his head. "Lily never sent it to me. She wasn't finished writing. But we're working on it." Donald tried to sound optimistic but his voice, thin as the napkin he used to wipe his lips with, revealed his anxiety.

Lily's eyes narrowed. She wished she had a can of insect spray so she could douse the little cockroach.

"Working on it? How?" Liebowitz asked.

Martin squirmed and looked for help from the stout man Lily did not recognize. "Ralph?"

"Sir," Ralph addressed Liebowitz, "it's important that we keep you at arm's length on this. Plausible deniability and all."

"Never mind that. I want a report. *Now.*"

Ralph shrugged and said, "Fine. But don't say I didn't warn you."

Liebowitz stood up and pressed his knuckles into the table. "Just tell me where the damn manuscript I paid a million dollars for is!"

"He wants half a million for it," Ralph replied nonchalantly and took a bite of his ham and egg on a toasted bagel.

"Who does?" Liebowitz asked, his eyes bulging.

"The cop I paid to copy it," Donald Martin squeaked.

The three ghosts looked at each other, eyes wide. "Thornfield?" Lily asked. "Do you think he's talking about David Thornfield?"

"What?" Liebowitz asked, thoroughly baffled.

Martin wiped his hands on his napkin, and Lily couldn't help but think of Lady Macbeth. "When this sordid business with Lily first started, I called Ralph. He found a Whatcom deputy who was willing to keep an eye on her for us for a reasonable sum. On Wednesday when Lily still refused to cooperate, I paid him ten grand to copy the manuscript. But now Lily's dead and *he's* blackmailing us. He may even be the one who killed her."

"YOU SON OF A BITCH!" Lily screamed and lunged for Donald Martin.

Penelope grabbed Lily and held her back. "No, Lily, no!" She kicked and screamed but Penelope held her firmly. "Lily, please calm down. You know what happens when you get upset. We need information. You freaking out everybody in the room will be counterproductive."

Marcus stood back, avoiding Lily's flailing extremities: he was not going to risk another shot to the face. But his expression suggested he was enjoying the show, which infuriated Lily more and exasperated Penelope. "Joe," she warned him, "stop goading her or this time I *will* break your face."

Liebowitz's legs gave out and he sank into his chair, the subtle sigh of the leather heard in the silence that followed Martin's confession. Jarod Ross's face took on the color and consistency of wet paper. "You did *what*?" he quietly hissed.

Donald Martin looked like a cornered animal: ears perked at attention, dark circles around glassy gold eyes opened wide, like a lemur startled by a nature photographer's flash. "He was just supposed to copy the manuscript. I swear!" he whined in his defense.

Ross looked over at his boss. "This is crazy. We need to call the authorities."

"And tell them what?" Ralph asked, casually slurping back another sip of coffee. "That you hired someone to steal her manuscript? If he killed her in the commission of a robbery, that's first degree murder. And anyone who was involved gets charged too. Washington has the death penalty. Still want to call the cops?"

"*We* didn't do this," Ross argued back. He looked like he was about to reach over the table and throttle Ralph.

Ralph and Martin exchanged a glance, then Ralph said, "That's not how we remember it."

Jarod Ross's complexion went from gray to green. "You're one sick bastard, you know that, Donald? And you're finished in this town. I hope you've got your money squirreled away because you'll never see another dime from us. Brad will see to it."

"I'm entitled to a portion of Lily's royalties for the next seventy years," Martin said, summoning up what courage he had left. "*I'll* be long dead before the well runs dry." He stood up and motioned for Ralph to join him. "I just did what nobody else in this room had the balls to do: get Lily Harrington under control. You're mad now but you'll be thanking me later when the sales start rolling in. I'm sure Brad will find a way to get the manuscript for you legally, but your Christmas launch will be long overdue. I suggest you pay the ransom, you cheap bastards; it's not like you can't afford it."

Martin and Ralph headed for the boardroom door. "Let us know what you decide, gentlemen," Ralph said. And with that the two men left the room.

"I'M GOING TO KILL HIM!" Lily screamed. "LET ME GO!" Penelope released her grasp, and Lily stormed through the boardroom door and down the hallway after Martin and Ralph.

Adam Liebowitz, Jarod Ross, Brad Kline, and Nancy Weissmann sat in silence, stunned by the turn of events. Liebowitz buried his face in his hands, thinking. A moment later he looked up and quietly said, "Nancy, call accounting. I need a cost–risk analysis done of delaying the release of Harrington's book. Once we have the figures in I'll make a decision about this crooked cop. Brad, get onto your guy in Seattle; I want a timeline for a legal way out of this mess. Jarod, put together some names of ghostwriters for me. And Brad, find me a way to cut that little prick out of the royalties."

The three executives solemnly nodded their agreement. Liebowitz stood up. "Okay, everyone, that's it for now. And nothing leaves this room. This goes no further than we four." *We seven, actually,* Penelope thought as the four executives began packing up their things.

"Let's get Lily and go back to Bellingham," Penelope said to Marcus. "I want to leave a note for Greene."

An alarming yell was heard from outside the boardroom, and the six occupants raced out to see what was going on. In the foyer they found Ralph kneeling over the unconscious body of Donald Martin, slapping his face and trying to revive him. "Call an ambulance," Ralph pleaded.

"What did you do to him?" Jarod Ross demanded, eyeing the heavy bookend lying beside Martin's leg.

Ralph shook his head, his face ashen. "I didn't do anything. That damn thing just flew through the air and hit him in the head."

"That's not how I remember it," Lily said smugly, then stepped over Donald Martin's body and walked out the doors of Sellinger Press.

20

PENELOPE AND MARCUS FOUND LILY on Fifth Avenue, gazing into a window at Tiffany & Co. "Are you all right?" Penelope gently asked.

Lily's face lit up as if she just had a great idea. "I think we should go see *Wicked*. It's playing at two o'clock at the Gershwin. What do you think, Marcus? Or would you prefer another rendezvous with Runa?" Lily added the latter bit without so much as a hint of sarcasm, which seriously unnerved Marcus.

"I think you need some time alone," he replied then disappeared.

"I'm going to pass on the show," Penelope said. "I need to return to Bellingham and leave a note for Greene. Do you want to come with me or stay here awhile?"

"Give my regards to Greene," Lily said, and Penelope sensed she was being dismissed. The gesture was insulting but Penelope chose the high road: she had seen such behavior in victims before, the disassociation that follows the tornado of hurt and anger. Best just to give Lily some space. A day in New York would be good for her. There were a lot of distractions, and designer stores she could go window shopping in. And the theater. She could live vicariously through the actors for a few hours.

Penelope left New York and landed in Paul and Ellie Greene's garden. It was still early on the West Coast, and the house was quiet. Penelope walked through the patio windows and looked about for a piece of paper and a pen. She found both near the phone in the kitchen. She listened for a moment to make sure no one was about, then picked up the pen and wrote:

Wednesday: Donald Martin 10K to W.C. deputy to
copy 50th Mantova manuscript. Thornfield?

She tore the paper off the pad and put the note on the kitchen
table. And then Penelope lay down on the living room couch and
waited for Paul Greene to wake up.

Marcus sat in Runa's bedroom, watching her sleep and
contemplating his next move. Should he tell her that her lover was
under suspicion? Should he tell her to run? But if so, where to? Where
do the likes of Runa run to where they will find peace and security
instead of constant mistrust? Point Roberts was the closest she had
found to such a place; could he take that away from her?

And Thornfield is a cop. He would find her; Marcus was certain
of it. What would Thornfield do to Runa if he caught up with her?
Would he kill her?

Runa rolled over and moaned in her sleep. She was dreaming. Of
what? Marcus wondered. Me? Thornfield? Lily Harrington and the
sight of her body hanging from the rafter? Runa moaned again, her
face creased in pain, and a trickle of remorse seeped into Marcus's
heart. Funny that. He had thought he didn't have one anymore.

Penelope opened one eye and looked around, reorienting herself.
She had dozed off out of boredom but now someone was in the
bathroom. She heard a loud fart and realized that was what woke her
up. *Poor Ellie,* Penelope thought, *he's a farter.* But then Greene came
into the living room from the bedroom, and Penelope realized it was
Ellie in the bathroom. *What a pair. I'm so glad I never married.*

Greene opened the living room drapes to let in the light then
went into the kitchen. Penelope followed and waited for him to find
the note. He was still half asleep, puttering about in his bare feet and
cheap plaid flannel robe. It wasn't tightly closed, and Penelope got an
unwelcome peek at his hairy pot belly and flaccid junk. "Oh, thanks

for that," she said and averted her eyes. Greene hit the start button on the coffeemaker and wandered over to open the patio doors. He took a deep breath of fresh morning air, leaned against the door frame and closed his eyes.

It was not his favorite time of day. He was a night owl through and through. As a child he fell asleep in class so often he was suspected of having narcolepsy. A school nurse suggested he was staying up too late, so his mother, embarrassed to have her parenting skills called into question, sent him to his room by eight each night with a warning to keep the lights out. When that failed she loaded his morning oatmeal with sugar (brown, telling herself it was not as bad), and snuck candy ("Shhh, don't tell your sisters") into his lunch bag to get him through the afternoon. Each day was something different: a Mars bar perhaps, maybe a jawbreaker, a Blow Pop, Chiclets, Tootsie Rolls, or Gobstoppers, his favorite as much for the name as the taste.

Unfortunately the sugar rotted his molars, and after his fourth filling his more pragmatic father settled the matter one morning with a stern "Damn it, Carolyn, just give the boy a cuppa joe." The legal drug stained his teeth, but that did not require a trip to the dentist, and could be remedied somewhat by dipping his toothbrush in baking soda. He had been an addict ever since—of coffee, that is. Baking soda he now only used to treat occasional bouts of indigestion.

"Oh for heaven's sake, wake up," Penelope said. "We've got work to do."

Her impatience turned the next few minutes into an eternity. She folded her arms and tapped her foot against the floor, she paced and sang a Grateful Dead song to herself—anything to keep her from tapping her colleague on the shoulder and handing the note to him. Finally the coffeemaker dinged that it was finished. Greene opened his eyes and turned around.

He caught sight of the note, fluttering in the breeze from the open patio door but weighed down by the pen. He frowned and walked over to pick up the paper. "What the fuck?" he exclaimed as he threw the note down as if it were burning his fingers. He looked down and realized his robe was open. "Ah crap!" he muttered and quickly covered himself up.

He looked anxiously around the room. "Did you have to come here?" he asked in a plaintive voice. "Couldn't you have left this at the office?"

Penelope weighed the pros and cons of revealing her presence. Greene had read the note, so clearly he knew he needed to get a move on, yet he was glued to the floor. And then Donald Martin's weasel face came back into focus, and impatience won the day. Penelope closed the patio door: No.

Greene's eyes bulged and he clutched his chest. "Ah crap. I-I'm sorry."

Penelope walked over to the coffee pot, poured Greene a cup, and pushed it toward him. She hoped the message was clear: *I'm not here to harm you but we have work to do*. "Now get dressed," she said even though he couldn't hear her. "You need to go to Richmond."

Greene stared at the coffee mug. "It-it's okay," he stammered. "I'm awake."

Thirty minutes later they were on their way to the chief's South Hill home. Greene had called ahead and requested an emergency meeting with his boss, who, despite his initial reluctance to let business intrude upon his Saturday, eventually gave in to the urgency in his officer's voice and agreed to a visit.

Greene pulled out his handkerchief and wiped his nose, then wiped the sweat off his forehead. He was not sure which was more disconcerting, that The Homicide Haunter—as someone had once called Penelope, and the moniker stuck—had left him a note at home, or that a fellow deputy was now a possible suspect. Either way, things had clearly escalated: The Homicide Haunter had never invaded anyone's personal space before like that, had always confined its notes to the security and relative sanctuary of the division offices. And then that thing with his coffee—sweet Jesus, it damn near gave him a stroke.

He looked in the rearview mirror, expecting somehow to see Penelope there. He did not, partly because he simply could not see past the veil, and partly because she was actually in the front seat beside him. "So, um, are you here with me?" he asked, looking again in the rearview mirror.

Penelope chose not to answer. She had gone too far already and she knew it; perpetuating her mistake would not further her aims.

"So, um," Greene persisted despite the silence, "who are you, anyway? We've always wondered. It would be nice to know your name."

Penelope bit her lip and clenched her fists. She fought the need—never admitted to but always present—to reveal her identity. She had not been entirely honest with Lily when she had asked about recognition; the truth was that Penelope still hungered for the acknowledgement of her peers. She knew that some suspected it was her because the haunting had begun not long after her unfortunate demise, but no one knew for sure, and Penelope chose to keep it that way. There was a certain freedom in remaining anonymous, as if in their blindness she remained perfectly impartial, like Justice with her blindfold and scales.

When nothing moved, and the only sound was his own staccato breathing, Greene decided The Homicide Haunter had not come along for the ride, and he finally relaxed. He called Ellie to make sure she was all right after his hasty departure, and, satisfied that she was, put his phone away and sat back for the drive to the chief's house.

"What's this about, Detective?" Chief Clarence Babbitt asked when Greene and the unseen Penelope walked into the small but immensely private backyard of the two-story heritage home. The chief was standing in front of a gas barbecue, the scent of beef wafting out from the exhaust vent. The smell made Greene hungry: he had raced out of the house without any breakfast, a fact he was now regretting.

Chief Babbitt was a tall, fit man with a heavy southern accent that remained despite over a decade up north, and whose speech was still often peppered with Southern slang. He came from a family of lawmen, had never really known anything but law and order, and could not imagine any other career. He had moved to Bellingham when his wife was hired to teach at the university there, joined the Whatcom force, and after five years ran for election. He was an outsider but one with solid credentials, and the good people of

Whatcom County had gambled on the relative newcomer. He had his detractors but they were a minority, and his supporters had recently reelected him for another four years.

"What can you tell me about Deputy David Thornfield?" Greene asked cautiously.

"Why?"

"It's concerning the Harrington file. I received an anonymous tip this morning that Harrington's agent paid a Whatcom deputy ten grand to copy an unfinished manuscript by the vic. IAD confirmed yesterday that the manuscript was deleted from the vic's computer at 10:48 the night of the murder."

"How do you know it was Thornfield?"

"I don't. But something's off. That's why I'm asking."

"Hmmm." Chief Babbitt rocked back on the heels of his cowboy boots, thinking. He opened the barbecue and tinkered with the meat. "The trick, Detective, is a real slow roast all morning," Babbitt said, and Greene was not sure if the chief was just talking out loud or if it was a metaphor for something else. Babbitt then scrutinized Greene, trying to determine if this was a legitimate tip or a personal vendetta. The chief evidently decided the former, for he closed the barbecue lid and said in a low voice, "Thornfield's got a gambling problem. Spent time in rehab for it. That's why he asked for The Point; needs to keep away from the casinos."

"That's motive."

"But not proof, Detective," Babbitt said, shaking a barbecue tong at Greene. "And I'm not letting you take down a fellow officer without a shit load of proof. You find it, you bring it to me. And now I'm going back to my beef. Fine Washington prime rib, aged twenty-one days." He smacked his lips. "Nothing like it."

Greene nodded nervously and left the chief's yard. "So our David likes the tables, does he?" Penelope said as they got back into Greene's cruiser. "And it's not just Lily who's banging the help. Haven't told you that part yet, but it looks like I might have to. We'll see how this plays out."

Penelope knew he could not hear her, but she appreciated the sounding board anyway.

21

AN HOUR LATER THEY WERE at the Peace Arch State Park. Greene locked up his gun in the trunk of his cruiser then crossed into Canada. After passing through the NEXUS lane, on a hunch he pulled into the parking lot and went in for a chat with the Canadian border guards.

Greene held up his badge. "Hi, folks, who's in charge today?" he asked the agent at the desk.

"Nickelson. I'll get him for you."

Brent Nickelson, Chief of Operations for the Douglas border crossing, came out and shook Greene's hand, damn near crushing it. "Morning, Detective. How can I help?"

"Is there somewhere we can speak in private?" Greene asked, rubbing his throbbing hand.

Nickelson nodded and gestured for Greene to follow, then led him to an office in the back of the border station. "What's up?"

"I've got a delicate situation in The Point—"

"Is this the Harrington case? Heard about that."

"Actually, yes. And I need to know if one of our deputies, David Thornfield, went through your border there on Wednesday."

"Good thinking, Greene," Penelope said, perched on the window sill of Nickelson's office.

"You got a plate number?"

Greene nodded and recited the vehicle license number of Thornfield's cruiser. Nickelson punched it into the system. He shook his head. "Nope. Sorry."

"He may have come through in another vehicle. Can you check by name, please. It's David Edward Thornfield. D-O-B is September 8, 1981."

A few taps later and Nickelson said, "There he is. Crossed the Point Roberts border on a motorbike at 4:16 p.m."

"So he crossed into Canada at Point Roberts but not back into Canada through here?" Greene asked. This was not looking good.

"Correct. Doesn't look like he went to the mainland, which is what you'd expect."

Greene stood up and held out his hand. "Thank you, sir. Your cooperation is much appreciated."

Nickelson stood and crushed Greene's hand again. "No problem. I'll see you out."

Forty minutes later Greene and Penelope arrived at the Vancouver airport. Greene parked in the short-term lot, and the two joined the throngs heading into the terminal. Penelope followed Greene's lead as he made his way to the airport office desk of the Royal Canadian Mounted Police. He identified himself and asked for the senior officer. The desk clerk made a call; about ten minutes later the staff sergeant was seen walking from the direction of the international terminal.

"Morning, Detective. You asked for me?"

Greene offered up his badge. "Morning, Sergeant. I'm investigating the Harrington homicide in Point Roberts and I'm here to check out the alibi of an American who was staying at the Fairmont. Wanted to give you a heads up that I'm on your turf."

The sergeant scanned Greene's identification and handed it back. "Appreciate it." He pulled out a card from his breast pocket and wrote a telephone number on the back. "This is my cellphone number. I'm too busy to escort you, but if you have any problems just call me. I'm here until three."

Greene glanced at the card—it read "Staff Sergeant Dale Morgan"—and pulled out one of his own. "And this is mine." The men shook hands and Greene headed for the Fairmont. Penelope left the news agent where she had been perusing the magazine covers, and followed him.

He bought himself a latte and a slice of banana bread at a coffee shop—the adrenaline rush from earlier had subsided, leaving him sluggish—then walked past the international check-ins toward the hotel. He paused momentarily in front of the U.S. check-ins to appreciate the monumental Haida carving there, its boatload of travelers paddling away yet getting nowhere, anchored by their own weight to the floor of the terminal. Greene felt like the man in the middle of The Jade Canoe, the shaman who is supposed to pull the truth out of his hat and lead the way even as those around him squabble over competing agendas and chew on each other's limbs. Greene wondered which one Thornfield would turn out to be, and imagined he would be Wolf, chewing on Eagle's wing while Eagle, in turn, took out his frustration on Bear.

Greene shook himself free of these melancholic thoughts and moved on, his unseen companion beside him. They left the U.S. check-ins behind and took the elevator up to the hotel. He went to the concierge desk, identified himself and asked for the head of security. Moments later a burly man appeared at the desk. "How may I help you?" he asked in a thick French accent. His nametag read "Jean-Luc Lavoie."

Greene explained the situation and was discreetly taken to the security room where two men watched a bank of monitors. "Pierre," Lavoie said to one of the men, "this is Detective Greene from Bellingham. I need you to pull up Wednesday's feed, *s'il vous plaît*."

Pierre did as requested. "Do you have a specific time and place?" he asked.

Greene pulled out his notebook. "Our victim had lunch here with her agent between one and four p.m."

"Most likely at Globe," said Lavoie. He pronounced *Globe* like the *e* was a separate syllable.

Pierre clicked on the feed from "Globe 1" and up came a view of the restaurant. "There they are," Greene said, pointing to Martin and Lily. Pierre fast-forwarded through the feed: seafood salad for Lily, pan-seared salmon for Martin, washed down with a seventy-dollar bottle of Pinot gris. Lily passing on dessert while Martin nibbled at a berry cheesecake. What appeared to be an intense conversation: Martin shooing away the waiter when he attempted to refill the water glasses.

Lily left the table once during lunch, and Pierre followed her via the cameras to the outside of the ladies room. She later left just before four o'clock as Martin had claimed, her walk brisk, just shy of storming off.

Pierre then followed Martin to the bar where he pulled out his cellphone and made a call, waving off the bartender. Greene checked the time code: 4:03:56. Just thirteen minutes before Thornfield crossed the border on his motorbike.

At 4:15:38, a young brunette woman, dressed in a pencil skirt and twinset like a 1950s secretary, joined Martin at the bar. "Can I get a still of that?" Greene asked. "She must be the first of the two writers he claimed to meet."

Pierre hit capture and print, and seconds later the image was in Greene's hands.

Martin and the woman moved to a table where he ordered two glasses of wine, a chardonnay this time, the cheapest on the menu. "You can forward through the chitchat," Greene suggested. "I'm looking to see if he met anyone else."

Pierre nodded. He fast-forwarded until, at 4:45:27, Martin got a call on his cell. He answered, offered what appeared to be an explanation to the young woman, gestured *two minutes* then left the bar carrying his soft leather briefcase. Pierre switched effortlessly from camera to camera, following Martin to the men's room door.

"Pierre, can you bring up that camera for the five minutes prior to Martin going into the washroom?" Greene requested on a hunch. Pierre nodded and rewound the video. And there, just one minute before Martin got his call, was David Thornfield, carrying a backpack and his motorcycle helmet. "That son of a bitch," Greene whistled between his teeth.

"You want a photo?" Pierre asked.

Greene nodded. "And would you be willing to give me a copy of the video?"

Pierre looked over at his boss. Lavoie nodded. "Come back tomorrow and we will have it for you," he said.

They watched the security feed for a moment more, watched Martin alight from the restroom first and head back in the direction of the bar. Thornfield came out two minutes later and walked in the opposite direction. "Okay," Greene said with a sigh, "I've seen what I need. My thanks, gentleman. I will see you again tomorrow."

"*C'est bon,*" Lavoie said. "*Au revoir.*"

Greene left the airport with a heavy heart. It was never a good day when you discovered a corrupt colleague, even worse when he was now the chief suspect in a homicide. Thornfield had accepted money to spy on Harrington, had been paid ten grand to copy her manuscript, had likely been the one who did so at 10:48 the night she died. But did he kill her? Even if Greene could get Thornfield for theft of the manuscript, that did not prove murder. And Thornfield knew all their tricks; would he crack under the pressure of questioning? Not likely.

And then there was the matter of the "anonymous tip." Greene could not use it: it had not been sent by email, or snail mail, or phoned into the tip line. Everyone would know where it really came from, and that it was inadmissible.

How best, then, to proceed? Bring Thornfield in for questioning, or let the chief do it? Greene decided that was not his call. He would have to see the chief again.

Greene was just about to call when his cellphone rang. It was the medical examiner's office. "Morning, Detective," Anderson said in a sing-song voice. "I have some news for you. When I found the benzodiazepine in your vic's system I decided to keep the body for a couple of days to see if any bruising developed postmortem. I came in this morning to check. There are now pronounced bruises on her upper chest consistent with handprints. I suspect that after she was drugged the killer picked her up under her arms and dragged her to the spot beneath the rafter where she was hanged. Oh, and the lab came back with the benzo test. It's lorazepam. Commonly prescribed to treat anxiety and insomnia but easily obtained on the black market. And it was enough to drop a horse, figuratively speaking."

Suddenly from behind came the sound of a siren. "Ah crap, Doc, I gotta go. I'll call you later," Greene said and hastily put his phone away. He pulled over onto the shoulder. An RCMP vehicle pulled in behind him, and a lone officer walked up to the driver's door. "License and registration please, sir," the officer politely demanded.

He was young, likely a new recruit, and Greene figured he could easily talk his way out of this one. "Can you tell me why I've been pulled over?" Greene inquired, trying to match the officer's courteous tone.

"Distracted driving. Holding a cellphone while behind the wheel is illegal in the province of British Columbia."

"As you can see, I'm from Washington," Greene said, feigning ignorance.

The constable's face remained expressionless. "It's illegal there, too." Greene smiled and held up his badge. "I'm on police business. You understand, *officer*." Greene emphasized that last word, hoping to invoke a sense of professional camaraderie.

"Not here you weren't. License and registration, please."

"Officer, I'm in my official vehicle, so obviously I'm on official business," Greene said, struggling to keep his tone agreeable.

The constable was having none of it. "I know for a fact you get this car as a perk of the job," he said, his tone turning surly. "It's likely your *only* vehicle. Now, I must insist you produce your license and registration. And where is your gun, sir?"

"It's locked in the trunk, as per protocol."

"You are not permitted to transport your weapon in British Columbia except when traveling between mainland Washington and Point Roberts. You are in Richmond. I need you to step out of the vehicle, please."

Greene muttered "Are you effing serious" under his breath but knew better than not to comply. He stepped out of the car.

"Turn around and put your hands behind your back, please."

"Ah, really?" Greene said but did as directed. He inwardly groaned as he was handcuffed and walked over to the side of the road. The last thing Greene needed was to embarrass the department, and right now he was one locked gun away from a diplomatic incident. He blamed his stupidity on The Homicide Haunter, on the near stroke it gave him that had obviously restricted the blood flow to his brain. It was either that or the events of the day before when he had thought this case closed only to have it explode wide open with multiple suspects and phantom witnesses. This case was going to be the death of him, of that he was certain.

The officer went back around to the driver's side, took the keys out of the ignition and opened the trunk. There was the gun box. He lifted it up, felt the weight of the piece, then put the box back down and closed the trunk.

"Do not move, sir. I need to call my sergeant about this."

Greene closed his eyes and prayed. *Please, God, let this blow over. Ellie needs my benefits.*

Penelope got out of the car. At first this was funny but now Greene was in deep trouble, and that meant delays. But what to do? If she moved something she might just spook the rookie into shooting Greene. She decided to wait for the sergeant.

She walked over to watch the constable through the windshield of his cruiser. He was on the radio to someone, and then a moment later he put the radio down and was on his cellphone. She saw him nodding and his lips read *Yes, sir.* Then he alighted from his cruiser and walked over to Greene. "Turn around, please," he said. Greene complied and the officer removed the cuffs. "Sergeant Morgan sends his regards. But don't do it again." And with that the officer marched back to his cruiser and drove away.

Greene let out a heavy gasp. "Oh sweet Jesus," he said, clutching his chest, "that was close."

"No kidding," Penelope said, annoyed. "Good luck calling your chief from a Canadian jail cell to tell him your *colleague* is a disgrace to the force."

They got back into the car. Greene buckled up and took a few more deep breaths. He found his water bottle and took a long drink. He turned his cellphone off, just to be on the safe side. And then he put on his signal light and merged back into traffic, headed for home.

Lily lay on the couch, staring at the cedar truss from which she had been hanged. Her mood was predictably somber. New York had done nothing to lift her spirits. An hour wandering around Fifth Avenue had soon become torture when Lily realized she could not buy anything she liked, and a trip to the hospital to check on Donald revealed she had concussed him but nothing worse. Lily had then given up, decided against waiting for the play to open at two o'clock, and come home.

She wondered where Penelope was, and whether or not she had managed to communicate with Greene. Lily decided she would accomplish nothing just lying here and staring at the ceiling, so she closed her eyes, focused her thoughts until she picked up Penelope's energy trail, and transported herself to the back seat of Greene's cruiser. "What did I miss?" she asked.

Penelope jumped in the front seat and spun around, surprised. "Damn it, Lily, you startled me."

"Sorry," Lily said sarcastically.

"No you're not. How's Martin?"

Lily shrugged nonchalantly. "He'll live."

"And a good thing, too. Do you have any idea of the price you would have paid if you had killed him?"

"No, but something tells me you're going to lecture me again."

"Lily," Penelope sighed, exasperated, "murder is murder, no matter which dimension you're in. Now, I've done my best to keep you safe and smart, but if you keep this up you're on your own. I understand you're angry and upset, I was too"—she pointed to the hole in her forehead—"but you have to find your way past that or you'll be doomed to wander this place for eternity."

Her words fell on deaf ears: Lily was determined to continue pouting. "I thought you liked it here. Maybe I do too."

"Nobody *likes* it here," Penelope said, raising her hands as if she were going to throttle Lily. "It's just that some of us … oh, never mind. I've already explained myself to you." She turned around to face the windshield, giving her back to Lily.

"Did Greene find anything?" Lily asked, changing the subject.

"Yes, but I'm not sure it's a good idea to tell you anything, what with the mood you're in."

"If I apologize, will you tell me what he found?"

"Thornfield met up with Martin at the hotel after you left. It looks like that's where the payoff took place."

"What's Greene going to do?"

"Talk to the chief, I suspect. Bring Thornfield in for questioning. Problem is, the payoff was for the manuscript, not your assassination. The money doesn't prove he murdered you, if indeed he did."

"We should tell Greene about the sex video."

Penelope shook her head. "To what end? It's just a sex video. It has no connection to your murder. It might embarrass Thornfield but that's about it. And what about Runa? Do you really want to embarrass her too? What did she ever do to you?"

Lily sat back, silent. Penelope was right, of course. She always was. But Thornfield had been spying on Lily for Donald, had stolen her manuscript, was blackmailing her publisher—okay, that last part was funny—but what? She should just let Greene bring Thornfield in and make him sweat a little? Big deal. Thornfield had to pay, and if all Lily managed to do was embarrass him, that would have to do.

Penelope felt Lily's energy leave the car. She briefly considered going after her, but decided Lily's skills were not adequate enough to do much harm. Sure, she might manage to throw another bookend at someone, but Thornfield's thick crew cut head could probably take the blow. Penelope wanted to stick with Greene, to see where the investigation was headed. It would prove a costly mistake.

22

LILY SAT AT RICHARD OWEN'S BANK of computers and concentrated. The broken monitor was still on the desk; it looked like Richard had been too afraid to return to his office. The thought made Lily laugh and momentarily broke her concentration. She shook those thoughts away and focused again on the task at hand.

She wrapped her fingers around the mouse connected to the computer with the forbidden folder on it and stared at the little device, willing it to move under her control. At first nothing happened, and in her frustration Lily's concentration broke again. "Focus!" she ordered herself. *Before Penelope catches you,* Lily added in her head.

It was another hour of stops and starts and then, to her surprise, the mouse moved beneath her hand without careening off to the right or jumping off the mouse pad. Lily beamed with pride, even if no one else witnessed her accomplishment. And then she marveled at how little it took to make her happy these days, and thus how much she resembled a simpleton. *Ignorance is bliss,* she concluded, somewhat ironically, as she clicked on the encrypted folder.

A window opened, prompting for the password. Lily closed her eyes and recalled the image of Richard at his desk, the movement of his hands over the keyboard, then tried to type. Her fingers went through the keys. "Damn it," Lily muttered to herself. She worked on her typing for the next fifteen minutes until she figured out the right pressure to apply, and that she had to imagine each keystroke before she applied it. It was a tedious process. So how did Penelope make it look so easy?

Lily typed *Mother* in the password window. The folder opened. "Ha!" Lily called out, pleased with herself again.

She grabbed the mouse, opened a web browser, and navigated to her webmail account. There were about fifty unopened messages. Lily ignored them and clicked on Compose. In the New Message window she clicked on the attachments icon and navigated to the video file. "Damn it," she muttered to herself again: the video was one hundred megabytes, far too large to email. She would have to send it through a file sharing account.

Lily navigated to her ShareIT! account, created a new folder and uploaded the file. She clicked on the file and selected Send Link. And then it hit her: she did not have Greene's email address. Who did? He had given his card to ... Runa. Arni. Anyone else? *Oh wait!* Lily thought next. *There should be some cards on his desk.*

She willed herself into the Homicide division but missed Greene's cubicle by two, landing in the paper recycling bin beside the photocopier. *Clearly I need further practice,* she thought as she hauled herself out of the green plastic silo.

She was just inches from the doorway to Greene's cubicle when she froze: Marcus was in Greene's chair, sifting through Lily's case file. A rush of adrenaline coursed through her veins and she quickly stepped into the adjoining cubicle to hide. What was Marcus looking for? Lily realized she could not confront him, would have to explain her own presence here, so instead, with her heart still pounding, she crept up onto the desk and peered over the top of the cubicle.

Marcus was reading the notes from Greene's interview with Runa and tapping his fingers on the desk. He seemed anxious, and Lily wondered what it was about the interview that was making him so nervous. She thought back to the day but could not think of anything that stood out as particularly worrisome. Could this simply be the concern of a lover? Was it possible that Marcus *cared* for Runa, actually cared for another human being? Lily could not quite imagine it, so she made a mental note to tell Penelope about this—maybe have her take a look at the file herself—and crawled back down off the desk.

Oh shoot, was her next thought when she realized she still needed Greene's email address and would not be getting it here. *Okay, Plan B,* and willed herself to Runa's trailer.

Lily landed in the kitchen. The sound of grunting was coming from the bedroom. Lily crept to the doorway and peered in. Thornfield and Runa were having sex, though judging from the look on her face she was not enjoying the act. She looked bored, like she was writing out a grocery list in her head or maybe contemplating the laundry. Thornfield seemed oblivious to her distance, thrusting away with his eyes closed in ecstasy.

Runa looked over at the doorway. Her eyes flickered with surprise. Lily jumped back, her heart hammering in her chest. Did Runa just see her? Lily summoned her courage and peered back around the doorframe. Runa smiled wanly as if to say *I've been waiting for you,* then turned her face away and kissed Thornfield's cheek.

Lily backed away from the door again, unsure of what she had seen. Was she imagining this connection with Runa? Was Lily simply misinterpreting the gestures of a woman in the throes of lovemaking, as detached as she might seem? Maybe that was just how Runa rolled. Whatever it was, Lily was not keen to stick around. She crept back to the kitchen in search of Greene's card, found it on the counter, memorized his email address, then willed herself back to Richard Owen's office.

She could hear the television on in the living room. The office still seemed untouched. Lily went back into her ShareIT! account and clicked on the video to send to Greene. There was a box for adding a message. She pondered this a moment, then decided she still *could* control the narrative, even if it were only a few words: "With my regards, Lily." And then she hit Send, and there was no turning back now.

Greene pulled into a vacant parking spot a few doors down from the chief's house. After crossing back into Washington, the detective had called ahead and requested another emergency meeting. Babbitt did not sound happy about it but had relented.

"How's the prime rib coming, sir?" Greene asked when he entered the yard, hoping to keep things light before he hit his boss with the bad news.

It didn't work. "In one hour it will be perfectly medium rare," Babbitt answered, his tone unwelcoming. "In two hours it will be well done and I might as well feed it to the dog. So I hope you don't need me to come into the office."

"Well," Greene answered carefully, "that of course would be your call, sir. I met with security at the hotel Harrington's agent was staying at. David Thornfield was seen on camera entering the men's room in the lobby just one minute before the agent received a phone call and also went to the men's room. They left separately, a few minutes apart. I believe that's when Thornfield picked up the ten grand."

"Did anyone witness money changing hands?"

"Not that I'm aware of. But it doesn't look good."

Babbitt shook his head. "Darn tootin' it doesn't. Do you have any idea of the source of the anonymous tip?"

Greene's face went blank. "I ... I received a note at home, sir."

Babbitt rocked back on his heels and let out a cynical laugh. "Don't tell me, The Homicide Haunter? I thought it only left you boys notes at work. Anyhow, that dog won't hunt, and you know it."

Penelope bristled at that last comment. She knew it was just Southern slang for "that argument won't fly," but being compared to a dog was nonetheless particularly irritating.

"I know, sir," Greene said. "That's why I'm here. I don't have enough for an arrest, but you have the authority to at least bring Thornfield in for questioning. He's under your command."

Babbitt considered the request. "Okay, Detective, I'll bring him in. But not till Monday. This here is eighty dollars worth of beef and I've got important company coming."

"With all due respect, sir, this is the Harrington file. Could we compromise and make it tomorrow?"

Babbitt shook his head. "Going fishing tomorrow with councilmen Harris and White. Been planning it for weeks. No dead celebrity is going to change that. And don't you have a wife, Detective? Wouldn't you rather spend a quiet Sunday with her than chasing after circumstantial evidence?"

The reference to circumstantial evidence did not pass by Greene. "Yes, sir. Monday it is."

He turned to leave, and Babbitt gave Greene a reassuring pat on the shoulder. "It'll all work out, Detective. These things always do."

With Babbitt's attention momentarily diverted, Penelope reached over and turned the heat up on the barbecue. "Hope you enjoy your lunch," she snickered, "or at least the dog will."

Lily left Richard's house, headed for home. There was nothing to do but wait until Greene got the video. She began to feel nervous. Had she done the right thing? Penelope would not think so, had counseled against it. Lily wondered how angry this would make the dead detective, and if this would be the final straw she had warned about. But in the next breath Lily didn't care if Penelope abandoned the case, for ultimately it would be live detectives and a live judge who would enact justice on Lily's killer.

She was about halfway across the lawn that separated her house from Richard's when two cars pulled up in her driveway. Two large men in black suits stepped out of the one car, and from the other came Clarissa Brody, Lily's attorney from Seattle. From the back seat of Clarissa's car Lily's brother-in-law, Scott Clarins, alighted, followed by her sister, Amanda.

"Amanda!" Lily cried and broke into a run. She raced across the expanse, her arms open to embrace her sister. But when Amanda looked across the lawn and her expression did not change, it hit Lily square on: She was dead and gone. There would be no embrace. There would be no more wine-fueled late-night chats, no more pleadings to move to Santa Clara. Lily stopped at the edge of the driveway, looked longingly at her sister, and began to cry.

Everyone greeted the two deputies on patrol, thanked them for their service, and watched them drive away down the dirt-and-gravel road. From the conversation that followed, Lily learned the two large men were private security officers hired to protect the property. One took up his post on the western side of the house while the other stood guard on the porch. Everyone else went inside. Lily followed as they gathered in the great room.

"Lily left you the house and all her personal effects," Clarissa said to Amanda. "You may keep what you like and sell or donate the rest. There are heavy estate taxes here in Washington, but there are sufficient funds to pay those without having to liquidate any physical assets or real property. The remainder of the estate goes to the Artists' Defense League, including Lily's copyright."

"Are you *serious*?" Scott Clarins asked, infuriated. "She left us a house in this backwater hole and a bunch of used crap but not her copyright?"

"Not now, please," Amanda begged her husband.

"Not *you*," Clarissa responded pointedly to Scott, "Amanda. Lily didn't leave *you* anything."

Lily laughed, and her laughter dried her tears. She could kiss Clarissa right now. The woman was a no-nonsense attorney with a fine legal mind and a backbone to match. She had been Lily's lawyer for as long as Lily had lived in Point Roberts, had come recommended by one of the wealthy marina crowd she socialized with over the summer months. Over the years the two women had become friends, had lunched whenever Lily found herself in the Emerald City.

"By law I own half of anything Amanda inherits," Scott declared. "May I remind you we live in California. And Washington is also a strictly communal property state."

"I see you've done your homework," Clarissa said with a forced smile. She turned her attention back to Amanda. "Contrary to Scott's conclusion that this is crap, I've already been approached by two New York auction firms about liquidating the contents of the house. Both believe there would be a market for Harrington memorabilia, especially all her original hardcovers. Many of the artworks you see have increased significantly in value since Lily bought them. There's also her jewelry, currently insured for over four hundred thousand. And of course there is the house itself, last valued at 2.3 million."

"How long do you think this will take to complete?" Amanda asked.

"Lily has no children or other siblings to contest the will, so I'm expecting this will be straightforward. Nine months on the outside, I would think. The estate will pay for the security and the property taxes in the interim. But we may wish to consider emptying the house just to be on the safe side and to reduce security costs. Both auction houses are willing to store until sale."

Amanda slowly sank into the sofa. She looked lost. Lily sat beside her sister and reached out a hand to caress her face. Lily searched her memory for the right sensation, something to make the soft skin real beneath her fingers. "I'm so sorry about this, Nanda." Nanda: it had been Lily's nickname for her elder sister ever since Lily was two and could not pronounce the *m*. Amanda closed her eyes and breathed in deeply, and Lily imagined her touch had been felt, that they were inseparable even in death.

"Two peas in a pod," as their mother would say whenever she was cross at their latest shenanigans. Amanda usually took the brunt of the accusations—"You're older, young lady, you should know better. At least *try* to set a good example for your sister"—which she stoically bore despite the fact that their schemes were most often hatched in Lily's head. She had always been the one with the more vivid imagination: old Mrs. Wellington down the lane was a witch who ate children, *But if we steal her magic raspberries and eat them they will protect us.* Mr. Finnegan next door chopped up stray animals in his workshop and buried them in the garden: *What do you think all those noises are, Nanda? And look*—peering down from their tree house—*fresh dirt on his shovel again. If we investigate think of all the lives that will be saved; we'll be famous!* Their attempts to solve the mystery were thwarted by house detention after they were caught trying to break into his workshop, but were vindicated two years later by the arrest of Mr. Finnegan after a neighbor's cat went missing. It was no surprise to anyone, least of all Amanda, when Lily grew up to write about murder.

"Have you thought about the funeral?" Clarissa asked.

Amanda opened her eyes and nodded. "Next Saturday. The medical examiner is releasing the body to us on Monday. Lily wanted to be buried here in Point Roberts. The church is too small for the service and a procession across two borders will be a nightmare, so I thought we would clear out this room and use it. We can open the patio doors and add more chairs in the garden if necessary. I found a funeral home in Bellingham willing to work with me here, and Brewster's will do the catering. The problem is the media. How do I keep this a private affair?" The group had been accosted on the way in; the deputy on duty had had to race to their rescue as he had previously done for Greene.

"You let me worry about that," Clarissa assured her. "Give me the name of the funeral home and I'll liaise between them and security."

Clarissa sensed this was all Amanda could handle for one day. "I've got an appraiser coming on Monday to itemize and evaluate the contents. I'll have more for you after that. Why don't you return to your hotel and get some rest. I'll head back to Seattle and start the paperwork."

"I'd like to stay here for the night, if that's all right," Amanda replied. She looked over at her husband. "Alone."

"Do you really want to be alone in this house, considering what happened here?" Scott asked. "What if it's infectious? I wouldn't want you doing anything rash." He tried to appear concerned about his wife but the sour look on his face suggested he was more concerned about her inheritance.

"Lily did *not* commit suicide," Amanda replied angrily. "The police told us foul play is now suspected. And murder is not a virus either, though I *am* starting to feel a bit of a fever."

Scott startled at the look in his wife's eyes. "Fine, my darling," he cooed. "Whatever you think is best. Clarissa can drop me off at the hotel and I'll have your bag sent over in a taxi."

The lawyer nodded. "I can certainly do that."

Amanda managed a weak smile. "Thank you, Clarissa, for everything. You've been wonderful."

Clarissa gave Amanda's arm a comforting squeeze. "Lily was my friend, too. You just let me know what you need."

Scott and Clarissa left Amanda to her solitude, or so they thought. She looked around the room, up at the four cedar trusses, and wondered which one her little sister had spent her final moments hanging from. And then Amanda curled into a ball on the couch and wept, wrapped in Lily's arms.

Greene sat beneath a café patio umbrella, coffee in hand, contemplating what to do next. The chief was behaving like an ass. All Greene had heard from the moment he landed this case was "Shut this down!" Ever since Harrington had died it had been media pandemonium and intense scrutiny; the department was inundated and on edge. It was fine for Greene to work overtime, to have his weekend messed up, but God forbid should the chief have his barbecue interrupted or his politics rescheduled. Maybe Greene should run for the position next election. He would do a better job than this, he was certain of it.

He should just go home to Ellie, he knew, but the situation was eating away at him. Every organization has its bad apples, yet there was something particularly distasteful about a crooked cop. And nobody wanted to be the one who had to cut the apple down from the tree. Why oh why did it have to be Greene's turn to catch a case the day Lily Harrington was found hanging from the rafters?

He finished his coffee and made a decision. He would go into the office for a few hours, see if there was anything else he could dig up on Thornfield, anything Greene could give to the chief for Monday.

23

GREENE LOGGED ON TO HIS COMPUTER and opened his email. "Huh?" he grunted. At the bottom of new emails was one from "Lily Harrington via ShareIT!." The body of the message read "Lily used ShareIT! to share some files with you! Click here to view DavidandRuna."

Penelope peered over his shoulder at the email. "Oh damn it, Lily, what did you do?"

Greene's heart skipped a beat. What kind of a sick joke was this? Somebody, probably the same hacker who had been watching Harrington through her webcam, had now hacked into her ShareIT! account and was sending out files on her behalf. Somebody was toying with him, trying to goad him into downloading an infected file, one with a Trojan horse like the kind used to commandeer the vic's computer.

He called the after-hours emergency number for the IT department. "Hey, it's Greene in Homicide. I just got an email with a link to a ShareIT! folder that may contain important information, but I'm concerned about a virus. Is there any way you can check this for me right away?"

Greene listened for a moment then nodded and forwarded the link to IT. He busied himself with other email while he waited for the call back.

Penelope paced the hallway between cubicles. Should she locate Lily and find out from the horse's mouth what she had done? Or stay here, get the same information and Greene's reaction? Penelope decided upon the latter: it was his reaction, and what he would decide to do afterwards, that mattered most.

The call back came five minutes later. Penelope stopped pacing and returned to Greene's cubicle. The link and the video file in the folder were clean; he could open it. "And it certainly is interesting," the IT guy said with a chuckle.

Greene downloaded the file. And then he sat back and watched Runa Jonsdottir give David Thornfield a blowjob in what was clearly Harrington's office.

Penelope hung her head in despair. Lily Harrington was her own worst enemy. And now somebody was going to have to clean up the mess.

Greene drummed his fingers on the desk. What did this have to do with the Harrington case? Had Thornfield romanced Runa to get access to Harrington's house? No code was used the night of the murder, but it could just have been pure luck that the alarm was disabled. Thornfield had been paid to copy Harrington's manuscript; procuring the alarm code would have been a logical step in delivering the goods. But what was the hacker's motive in sending the video? What else did he know about the murder? And would there be more surprises?

Greene sent an email to the chief: "New evidence re: Thornfield. Urgent request to meet Monday before questioning."

Greene watched a few more minutes of the video before shutting down his computer. And then he headed home in search of Ellie.

David Thornfield rolled onto his back and welcomed the breeze that floated in through Runa's open window. She was in the bathroom taking a shower, like she always did after sex. Except when they did it at Harrington's, or any of the other houses that Runa cleaned in The Point; then she would have to wait until the end of her day to go home and wash away the stench of her lover. It was not that Runa disliked sex—on the contrary, she was fond of the act—it was the men who disappointed her. Somehow they never quite lived up to her expectations or desires, lacked the personality and *savoir faire* of the men in the romantic suspense novels that fulfilled Runa in ways reality never could.

His cellphone rang. Thornfield rolled over to Runa's side of the bed and fished the phone out of his uniform on the floor. It was Terry from IT. "Hey, Dave, you're not going to believe this, but someone by the name of Lily Harrington sent Detective Greene in Homicide a video of you getting sucked by some blond. Just thought you might like a heads up, so to speak."

Thornfield went cold. *What the hell?* "Terry, where was the video taken?" Thornfield calmly asked.

"Looks like somebody's home office. There's white custom-built cabinets to the left and you're leaning against a red couch."

The deputy's eyes narrowed into thin slits of pure hatred. "Thanks, Terry, I owe you one."

Thornfield leapt out of bed and got dressed. Some smartass was impersonating Lily Harrington and sending sex videos of him to the cops. And he had a pretty good idea of who might be behind it. He stormed out of the trailer, not bothering to say goodbye to Runa.

Moments later he strode up to Richard Owen's front door and banged a fist against the wood. "Richard, it's David Thornfield. Open the door."

Owen opened the door a crack and peered out. "What do you want?"

"Open the door, Richard. I need to talk to you."

"What about?"

"OPEN THE FUCKING DOOR OR I WILL BREAK IT DOWN!"

Owen's buggy eyes opened wide in terror. He tried to close the door but Thornfield kicked it hard, tearing the security latch off the door frame and sending splinters of wood onto the floor. The door slammed against the foyer wall with a heavy, ominous thud.

Richard ran for the kitchen phone but Thornfield was right behind him. He grabbed Richard by the shirt, spun him around and slammed him against the wall, lifting his feet off the ground. "Did you send a video of me and Runa to Detective Greene?"

"N-no," Richard stammered. "W-why would I do that? Please put me down."

Thornfield slammed Richard against the wall again. "Somebody claiming to be Harrington sent a video of me having sex with Runa.

I know you were spying on Harrington, Richard. Murrelets, my ass. You knew I was doing Runa and you snuck up to the window and took a video for your own sick pleasure. Didn't you?"

"It wasn't like that, I swear," Owen whined. "Please put me down. You're hurting me."

"How was it, then? Huh, Richard? How was it?"

"I was spying on her through her webcam," he spurted out. "I didn't expect to see you and Runa. Honestly I didn't."

Thornfield's eyes darkened. When he spoke again his voice was eerily calm. "What else did you see through the webcam, Richard?"

Owen swallowed hard. His head hurt and his throat was aching now, his heart threatening to explode in his chest. "N-nothing. I swear. Y-you should go. Or-or else."

"Or else what?" Thornfield asked with contempt.

"I-I'll call them. You can't hurt me. I'm protected. If you hurt me they'll come after you."

"Who's they, Richard? Your imaginary friends?"

"The FBI. I-I'm important. Real important."

"Then let me ask you again, Mr. Real Important, what else did you see through the webcam?"

"N-Nothing."

"You're lying."

Thornfield's expression had become strangely blank, and it frightened Richard Owen into action. He kicked the deputy hard against the shin, and in his surprise Thornfield lost his grip. Richard wriggled free and bolted for the door.

Thornfield reacted quickly, slamming Richard in the back and sending him crashing to the floor. He cried out as his face hit the porcelain tiles, blood spurting from his nose and a broken tooth, his bent eyeglass frames sliding across the room. Thornfield reached down and flipped the hermit onto his back, then dropped down to straddle his prey. He wrapped his hands around Richard's neck and pressed. "What else did you see, Richard?"

Owen's eyes bulged and his legs kicked involuntarily as he struggled to breathe. He clawed at Thornfield's arms but the deputy didn't flinch, just kept the pressure on the recluse's throat until his hyoid bone snapped and Richard Owen gurgled his last breath.

His spirit left his body and watched as his killer rose to his feet, his breath heavy. "Jesus, man, what have you done?" Thornfield whispered as he came to his senses. He pushed the rising panic down into his belly and sprung into action. He washed his hands in the sink then left the tap running while he sprinted to his cruiser and took out a pair of latex gloves from the trunk. He went back inside the house, found a kitchen towel and wiped down the taps. He pulled Richard's shirt off and wiped down his neck, hard and deep, trying to alter the finger-shaped bruises he knew were forming beneath the skin. Then Thornfield wrapped Richard's shirt in the towel and made his way to the office.

What else had Owen seen? What had he recorded? Thornfield unplugged the computers from the wall sockets and tried to pry open the tower cases with his hands. It was pointless: six small screws held each case firmly in place. An angry panic flooded Thornfield and he began pulling drawers open and spilling their contents until he found the screwdriver he needed. One by one he opened each computer tower and tore out the hard drives. He collected six drives in all, found a bag to put them in, threw in the kitchen towel and bloody shirt, then fled the house.

He drove away, too absorbed in the moment to notice that less than ninety yards away a security guard was standing on Lily Harrington's porch and wondering why a Whatcom County deputy had thrown a heavy bag in the trunk of his cruiser, snapped off latex gloves, and took off, wheels spinning dust and gravel in the wind.

Greene drove down Alabama Street, headed for home. Penelope sat beside him, wondering what he was thinking about the video. She was undecided. On the one hand she was intensely annoyed with Lily for disregarding the advice to leave well enough alone for now; on the other hand Penelope was begrudgingly impressed by the obvious progress in Lily's poltergeist skills.

The rest of the drive home consisted of ten minutes of Greene squirming uncomfortably in the driver's seat like he had an itch he could not scratch. He parked the car in the driveway and hurried inside, his gait awkward, pausing only momentarily to pull on his trousers where they pressed against his genitals. Greene went straight to Ellie and began kissing her, priming her for sex. Penelope scowled in disgust and disappeared: this she did not want to witness.

She willed herself into the living room at Lily's Point Roberts house. She found Lily asleep on the sofa, her body curled around another sleeping woman. The two bore a striking resemblance, and Penelope rightly assumed the other woman was Amanda Clarins.

Penelope reached down and shook Lily. "Wake up."

Lily stirred but did not awaken. Penelope smacked her on the back of the head. "Damn it, Lily, wake up."

"Ow," she cried out as she opened her eyes to the sting. She looked up to find Penelope staring down and tapping her foot on the floor, arms folded across her chest. Lily sat up, rubbing her head as she shook herself awake. "What was that for?"

"I told you *not* to send the video to Greene. But you didn't listen, did you?" Penelope said angrily. In the time it took her to leave Greene and arrive here, Penelope had decided she was more angry than she was impressed, and Lily needed to answer for her indiscretion.

"Clearly that is a rhetorical question or you wouldn't be standing here in a huff," Lily retorted. "And so what? He deserved it."

Penelope threw her hands up, exasperated. "I know he deserved it, but these things have to be done with intelligence, with careful thought and intention, not irrationally and out of spite. That video was an ace up our sleeve, a card we could have played at the right moment. *Today was not the right moment.*"

"Why not?"

"Because the chief won't bring Thornfield in for questioning until Monday. What if he finds out about it before then? Greene won't be able to surprise him with it. He'll have time to prepare. And what about Runa? What do you think will happen if news of the video leaks? Everyone will assume she did the same thing in their homes and fire her. Then what will she do?" Penelope sighed and rubbed the hole in her forehead. It was at moments like these that she wondered why she stayed in the job.

"Runa will be okay," Lily declared, but her voice lacked conviction. "We can see to it. We can use that mind meld trick that Marcus is so fond of to keep people from firing her. Can't we?" Lily was starting to feel immensely guilty for her impetuous act of revenge.

"Is that *really* the point?" Penelope asked, her face and arms raised, begging for relief from the heavens.

Lily realized her best shot at calming the detective down was contrition. "I'm sorry, Penelope. I really am. I know I can be obstinate sometimes. But ever since I died, it's like one minute I have everything under control and the next I'm on the war path." She paused, then suggested, "Maybe it's the menopause."

"Really?" Penelope said, incredulous. "You seriously want to blame your stupidity on menopause?"

"Well, it is well documented that menopause can cause mood swings and brain fog," Lily said defensively. "And I *am* in withdrawal from the estrogen gel and paroxetine."

"I am *not* having this ridiculous conversation with you!" Penelope shouted, pacing the room to keep herself from smacking Lily into the next dimension.

She watched fearfully as Penelope continued to pace, her hand on her head. After what felt like an eternity, the detective finally stopped and looked at Lily. "I need a break from you. I'm going to see my mother in Kansas City. The one in Missouri," Penelope said and was gone.

Lily was wondering what to do next when she heard the security guard stomp down the porch stairs. She rushed outside and saw him walking briskly across the lawn toward Richard Owen's house. She ran after the guard, curious to know what the fuss was about.

She saw the broken door and her stomach leapt into her throat. She ran straight through the security guard and beat him to the kitchen. Richard Owen was lying on the floor, his face covered in blood. "Richard!" Lily cried out in horror. "No!" The guard passed through her and checked Owen for a pulse. There was none. Lily bent over and retched, her stomach void of anything to vomit. She collapsed onto her knees beside Richard, desperately willing him back to life as the guard pulled out his cellphone and called the emergency line.

"It was that horrible Thornfield," said a high-pitched voice from behind her. Lily spun around to find Richard standing in the doorway. "Broke my neck. And my nose. I know this was your doing, and now it had better be your undoing. Or else."

"Or else what?" she asked, puzzled.

"I'll call them. I'm protected. They'll come after you."

"Who's they, Richard?"

"The FBI. I'm important. Real important." His lips quivered as he spoke, and tears began to flow down his cheeks.

Lily stood up and walked over to him. "I'm so sorry, Richard. I really am." She reached out and gave him a tentative hug. He found no comfort in her touch, just stood there impassively, his wet eyes vacant and dark. Lily's heart broke.

"Wesley," a warm female voice was heard from the direction of the living room. Lily and Richard looked over to find his mother standing in the hallway, her arms outstretched.

"Mother?" he whispered earnestly, his eyes sparking back to life.

"Come here, baby," she said gently. "This is not the place for you."

"Wesley?" Lily said, confused. Then suddenly it hit her. "My God, it's true! You're in witness protection. Oh, please tell me why, Richard, Wesley, whatever. Please don't leave me with another mystery."

But Wesley could not hear Lily; all he could hear and see was his beautiful mother with her arms outstretched. He smiled weakly and nodded. He pushed Lily aside and walked slowly toward his mom. She kissed and hugged her boy, then took his hand and led him away. Lily watched, guilty and despondent, as mother and son walked hand in hand through the west windows, out into the garden, and disappeared into the bright white light dancing off the Strait of Georgia.

Greene was lying beside Ellie in their bed when the call came in. He ignored it at first, but then the house phone also rang, and Ellie answered, and there was no more pretending he could not be reached.

He listened for a moment, his expression at first shock then resignation. "Call the Canadians," he said when he finally spoke, head in hand. "Close the border. And the marina and airstrip. No one leaves Point Roberts until we find Thornfield. I'm on my way. And somebody call the chief."

It was too late. David Thornfield was already in Canada, his motorbike speeding up Highway 17A, headed for the 99 and the Vancouver International Airport.

GREENE HAD ONLY MANAGED TO GET DRESSED and start his car when the second call came in. Thornfield was gone, had already passed through the border on his motorbike. "Fuck!" Greene shouted and slammed the palm of his hand against the steering wheel. He pulled out of his driveway and turned on his siren, headed for the border.

The chief was on his way to the station. Thornfield's picture, date of birth, and vehicle plate number had been emailed to the Canada Border Services Agency and the Royal Canadian Mounted Police, and to the Transportation Security Administration and its Canadian equivalent, the Canadian Air Transport Security Authority. The CBSA, RCMP, TSA, and CATSA had each in turn broadcast the details to their members—the Canadians in both official languages—and to every other acronym they could think of. The exception was the CFSEU, the Combined Forces Special Enforcement Unit, because Thornfield was not in a criminal gang and no one ever got the unit's name right anyway. The details were also forwarded to British Columbia's new Real Time Intelligence Centre; with the push of a button, Thornfield's details were disseminated to every police force in the province. It was only a matter of time before he would be caught.

But Thornfield would know how closely the U.S. and Canadian authorities worked these days, how quickly his information would be broadcast, Greene contemplated as he sped up the highway. The airport would be a trap, as would the ferries. Thornfield's only hope would be to go north or maybe east, get lost in the wilderness. The forests were full of empty cabins, often stocked with food and water;

he could last for weeks just by going from one cabin to the next. But his actions would also be dictated by what he did not know, and what he did not know was that Richard Owen's body had already been found.

The deputy sped up Highway 99. As he crossed the small Deas Slough Bridge, he reached into the bag nestled between his thighs and threw the first of Richard Owen's six hard drives into the murky water. Two more drives were deposited in the watery ditch between the road and the farms that lined the three-mile stretch between the Fraser River and the East–West Connector. After turning off the highway and onto Bridgeport Road in Richmond, Thornfield stopped to dump another drive in a city trash bin beside an empty bus stop, and another in the commercial waste bin at a construction site. The last three drives were thrown into the Fraser River as Thornfield crossed the Airport Connector Bridge onto Sea Island.

He stopped at the gas station just before the airport and stuffed the bag with the bloody shirt and towel in the station's dumpster. He moved on quickly, abandoning his motorbike in the parking lot at the airport and sprinting into the international terminal. Thornfield scanned the departures board. There was an Air Canada flight to Mexico City in two hours; that would do until he worked out a longer-term plan. He headed for the ticket counter.

Which is where David Thornfield was when Lily Harrington caught up with him.

She surveyed the scene while the deputy bought his ticket. What to do? She had to stop him, had to keep him from getting on a plane. She owed Richard that.

But how?

The universe answered her when, just as Thornfield was headed for the check-in counter, a large RCMP officer approached Thornfield from behind, taking hold of one arm. "David Thornfield, you need to come with me please," the officer whispered. "Let's not make a scene, okay?"

Thornfield snorted. Fucking Canadians, they were polite even when they were arresting you. *To hell with them and their please and thank yous.* He hit the cop square in the face with the back of a fist, then spun around and kick-boxed him in the groin. The officer went down, gasping to breathe through the pain. Thornfield kicked him again, this time landing a nasty uppercut to the jaw. The officer was no match for the deputy's strength and combat skills, and it only took the three blows to silence the opposition. Thornfield grabbed the backpack he had dropped and took flight—but he only got a few feet away when Lily pushed a loaded luggage cart into his path, sending him head over heels onto the floor. Then, before the RCMP officer was able to react, she grabbed his Taser. People screamed as the instrument rose and hung in the air, seemingly of its own accord, then everybody ducked when its electrified prongs shot out. Lily's aim was good, the prongs digging into Thornfield's back just as he scrambled to his feet. He went down again, writhing like a snake.

Lily threw the Taser to the ground. The officer looked over, his eyes frozen wide. *Ah hell,* he thought, *there's going to be an inquiry.*

When Thornfield finally regained use of his faculties, all he managed to say was, "I want a lawyer."

"You're going to need one," Lily replied, standing over him. "And Donald, too."

Greene arrived at the Owen residence. Deputy Collins was standing guard at the door, visibly shaken by events. "I can't believe he did this," he said in lieu of a greeting. "He's one of us. We're the good guys."

He said this as if asking for reassurance, but Greene had none to offer. "Where's the body?" was all he said in return.

"In the kitchen."

He stood in the kitchen doorway and surveyed the damage. Owen was lying in the middle of the room; a blood smear marked the path his face took when Thornfield had flipped the recluse onto his back. His broken tooth would later be found five feet away in the toe kick beneath the cupboards.

Greene carefully walked over to the body and bent down to study it. Heavy bruising on Owen's neck was already visible. Greene lifted his head momentarily when the slamming of a car door was heard. Forensics had arrived.

"Looks like he strangled him," a somber Greene greeted Kerry Reeds when she entered the house and took her own look into the kitchen.

"This is one weird week," she replied, shaking her head.

Greene sighed and rose to his feet. "You have no idea of the half of it."

"Collins said the office has been trashed."

Greene scowled. He left the kitchen and headed for the office. The place was a mess. Cables dangled over the desk, disconnected. Owen's three computers were lying open on the floor, their cases flung aside. Greene kneeled down and peered inside one. He was no tech genius but even he could see the hard drives were gone.

Another vehicle door was heard closing and moments later Mick Sheraton peered into the office. "This is seriously messed up," he said.

"The room or the situation?" Greene asked, looking up.

"Both."

"He took the hard drives."

"Shortsighted plan. Owen has cloud storage."

"How do you know that?" Greene asked, surprised.

Mick smiled mischievously. "He told me. We had lots of time to chat while I was copying his surveillance video."

"Do you know where?" Greene asked, hopeful for a quick break in the case.

"Yes, and the password. Sad bastard used *Mother* for everything."

Greene smiled. "I love you right now."

"You just say that so I'll sleep with you," Sheraton joked back. "But will you love me tomorrow?"

"Get me something useful and I'll marry you."

Sheraton laughed. "I never had you pegged for a bigamist. But I can deal with that. Iverson's on his way into Olympia. I've already given him the details."

"Where did you get this money?" an RCMP corporal asked, gesturing to the stack of American hundred dollar bills on the table between him and Thornfield.

"Blow me," the deputy replied and raised his chin in defiance. He had been taken from the airport to hospital to be checked out, then onward to the RCMP headquarters in Richmond, just north of the Fraser River—where Lily now wanted to drown him. He was sitting in one of the detachment's interrogation rooms, handcuffed to the table, another officer behind him.

"So is it your submission that you earned this through prostitution?" the corporal batted back.

"You could call it that," Lily said, taking in the proceedings from a spot against the wall.

Thornfield did not reply, just gave the officer another arrogant sneer.

"Well," the corporal said with a self-satisfied smile, "it's over ten thousand Canadian and you failed to declare it when you crossed the border earlier. As such the money is subject to seizure. We'll be keeping it until you can prove it's not the proceeds of crime."

Thornfield's face fell. There went his legal retainer. "Assholes."

There was a knock at the door, then in walked Greene and Chief Babbitt. "Afternoon, Deputy," Babbitt said, his tone unfriendly. "Seems we've got ourselves a situation here."

Thornfield smiled. "Don't see why. I was just taking a holiday to Mexico when these baboons tasered me. Man's entitled to a little R&R once in a while, wouldn't you agree, Chief?"

"We found Richard Owen," Greene hissed. "And a witness puts you at the scene. You'll get the chair for it." His eyes swept across the table to the contents of Thornfield's backpack: his passport, a few toiletries, a change of clothes, the stack of bills that were likely part of the ten grand Donald Martin had paid, the Air Canada ticket to Mexico, and … a FastBack USB flash drive. Greene smiled. *Gotcha!*

Thornfield laughed derisively. "Then you'll have to wait a long, long time. These pussy Canadians won't extradite me unless you take the death penalty off the table."

"No problem," Babbitt said, rocking back on his heels, his hands in his pockets. "We'll take it off the table for this Owen homicide, get you home, then later charge you *separately* for the murder of Lily Harrington. You'll get the chair one way or another. Or maybe we'll ask them to hang you instead."

Thornfield's face fell. "You can't pin that on me! I didn't kill Harrington."

"Then who did?" Greene asked.

"That stupid bitch Runa Jonsdottir did," Thornfield replied with an angry wave of his hands, the handcuffs cutting into his wrists.

Lily gasped. *What?*

"That's nonsense," Greene argued. "We know Donald Martin paid you ten grand to copy Harrington's manuscript. You did it the night she was killed; that USB drive is going to prove it. She caught you and you killed her. Runa told us all about it." That last part was a lie, but all's fair in love and interrogations.

"That's bullshit!" Thornfield shouted, banging his fist against the table. "That bitch is lying. I paid Runa to copy the book. That was it. Only that stupid girl drugged and killed her. Called me from her cellphone to tell me she'd killed Harrington and didn't know what to do. So I go to the house and she's standing there holding the rope like an idiot. She was trying to make it look like a suicide but she hadn't thought it through, couldn't secure the rope without dropping the body. So I wrapped the rope around the post. And turned on the air-conditioning to mess you guys up. That's all I did. Then I got the hell out of there. But when I checked the file she'd copied it was the wrong one! I had to go back. Crazy bitch couldn't do anything right."

Greene was starting to believe the man. "Did she say *why* she killed her?"

"No. Do crazy people *need* a reason?"

Greene looked over at his boss. "Can I leave him to you? I need to get back to The Point."

Babbitt nodded. Greene fled the station, Lily at his side.

AS GREENE RACED BACK TO POINT ROBERTS, Lily sat in the back of the cruiser and tried to contact Penelope. Lily had no concrete idea how to, didn't know where Penelope was in Kansas City, and was unable to pick up the detective's energy trail. All Lily could do was focus her thoughts and repeat "Lily to Penelope, Lily to Penelope" over and over as if there were some sort of cosmic ham radio out there in the void.

And just when the whole exercise was making Lily feel ridiculous and ineffective, Penelope appeared on the seat beside her. "You called?"

"Holy cow, you mean that really works?"

"Not exactly. But I've been keeping an ear out. So, what did I miss?"

Lily brought Penelope up to speed on recent events. "Runa did this?" Penelope asked, stunned. "I never saw that coming. I must be losing my touch." She paused, then added, "But why? What motive could she possibly have had to kill you?"

"I don't know," Lily replied, her eyes downcast. "I'm still trying to wrap my head around it. Thornfield said crazy people don't need a reason; maybe he's right."

They reached the border. Greene flashed his lights to indicate an emergency and was quickly processed through. Collins had been contacted earlier and was waiting for Greene at Runa's trailer when the detective pulled up.

She was seated on the couch, murmuring under her breath. Her eyes were vacant and unfocused, at least that is how they appeared to the men staring down at her. What they could not see, but Lily and Penelope could, was Marcus Mantova kneeling at Runa's side, stroking her hand and offering comfort.

"What the hell, Joseph?!" Penelope shouted.

"It's not what you think!" he shouted back, jumping to his feet. "That dreadful Thornfield has wrongfully accused Runa of murdering Lily. And now they've come to arrest her. It's a ghastly miscarriage of justice. She's terrified. Look at her; she catatonic with fear. *And stop calling me Joseph!*"

Greene pulled a chair up in front of the sofa. "Runa, look at me." She raised her eyes. "Concentrate," Greene ordered her.

Runa frowned, puzzled. "Why?"

"David Thornfield is under arrest for the murder of Richard Owen. And he claims you killed Lily Harrington. Is it true?"

"Yes," Runa answered dispassionately. She licked her finger and began rubbing the head of her serpent tattoo.

Greene's eyes flickered with surprise: he had expected her to deny it. "How?"

"I went to her house after Arni left. She was takin' a bath. I spiked the wine she'd opened. She always did that; said it had to breathe, whatever that means. I had some sleeping pills I stole from David; crushed 'em up 'n put 'em in the bottle. Then I hid in the powder room. Heard her come downstairs 'n get herself some wine as I was hopin'. She went to her office. I waited till I heard her fall, knew it was time."

"And then what?" Greene quietly asked.

"I dragged her into the livin' room 'n hung her over the rafter."

"With what?"

"Sailing rope."

"Why?" Greene asked, his face a question mark.

"'Cause I love him."

"You mean David Thornfield," Greene said, trying to trick her into naming her accomplice. "Because I don't think David loves you," Greene added, looking kindly into Runa's eyes. "So if he put you up to it, you need to tell me."

"Why you talkin' 'bout David? I don't care 'bout David. I did it for Marcus." Runa looked over at him. "I love you."

Lily and Penelope turned on Marcus. "What is she talking about?" Lily furiously demanded.

"I-I don't know," he lied, waving his hands in the air. "She's confused." He pointed at Runa. "Look at her."

Greene sat back, mystified. "Marcus who?"

"Mantova," Runa shrugged as if it should be obvious.

Greene looked over at Collins. "Isn't he the detective from Harrington's novels?" the deputy asked. Greene nodded and his face said it all: *Ah crap, she's nuts.*

"Why did you have to kill Lily Harrington for Marcus Mantova?" Greene asked, going with the flow—for now.

"I had to save him!" Runa exclaimed, an earnest hand to her heart. "I only did to her what she was goin' to do to him." She looked to Marcus again. "I did everythin' you asked. I killed her 'n I lied like you told me to. Please don't leave me."

Lily's eyes went cold. She took a threatening step toward Marcus. "You! You did this! You're the cop boyfriend, not Thornfield. It was you on the surveillance video leading Runa to the house. It was you who told her to say I was depressed and drinking too much. It was you she begged to say I love you." Lily took another threatening step toward Marcus. "You slimy"—step—"sneaky"—step—"poor excuse for a man—"

"It was self-defense!" Marcus raised his arms in front of his body as if to protect himself from an expected blow. "You were going to kill me off!" When the strike did not come, Marcus went on the offensive. "I knew it the moment you starting adding in new clues. Your writing is so predictable. This is all your fault, Lily. I wouldn't have done what I did if you hadn't been so obstinate."

Marcus was so focused on Lily he never saw Penelope's fist sail through the air and land a sucker punch to his temple. He crumpled to the ground with a thud. "You used this poor creature," Penelope spit down at him. "You put voices in her head and now she's going to prison or the loony bin for the rest of her life. And for what? Just so you could continue to live out your fantasy life in Lily's novels? Christ, Joseph, I would kill you if you weren't already dead!" Penelope punctuated her fury with a swift kick to his stomach.

Marcus curled into a ball. "Ow. Stop hitting me, Penelope. You seriously need anger management counseling."

Penelope kicked him hard in the hip. "Keep it up, Joseph, and I'll find a way to kill you in your next life—if you ever get one."

She turned to address Lily, but Lily was gone.

Greene handcuffed Runa and recited her Miranda rights. The Coast Guard had already been notified of the need to transport a prisoner to the mainland and would meet Greene at the Point Roberts marina.

With a heavy heart he walked her from the trailer to his cruiser. It always pained him to arrest the mentally ill; there was something particularly unjust about the whole mess that never sat well with the detective. But at least, Greene thought as the dust swirled around his ankles, there would be some satisfaction in knowing that David Thornfield would get his due for involving Runa in his schemes. And for the death of Richard Owen.

As he unlocked the rear door, Greene did not see the child racing across the withered grass toward him. He did not hear her frantic pleas nor feel her blows when she reached him and began pounding her fists on his back. "Let her go! Let her go! Runa! Runa! Please don't leave me."

Penelope grabbed Ripley and pulled her away. She screamed and wriggled like a wild animal, fists pounding against her captor's arms, pink and white sneakers flailing frantically in the air, her golden plait slapping against Penelope's face. "Runa! Runa! Please! Runaaaaaaa!"

"I'm sorry, Pinks," Runa whispered, then she let Greene hold her head down so she would not hit it on the door frame, and settled into the back seat. She said nothing more as Greene started the engine and headed down Park Lane. Runa turned around and watched, tears in her eyes, until Greene rounded the corner onto Julius Drive, and Ripley fell from view.

Marcus slowly uncurled himself and rose from the floor of Runa's trailer. His body ached from the blows Penelope had delivered. He stumbled to the bathroom to check on the damage. A large purple welt had formed on his left cheek and temple. "Witch," he muttered to himself. It would take weeks for the bruise to heal, weeks before he could appear in public again and present himself to the ladies. As for Runa, only a small part of Marcus felt any remorse. After all, for a while she had felt loved by him; that alone would be worth some time behind bars. Women were always remarking how they would kill for a man like Marcus; that Runa had literally done so was just proof of his desirability. And he could always visit her in prison, if the mood struck.

Penelope found Lily at home, sitting on a lounger beneath the back patio and staring at her sister. Amanda was on the other lounger, nursing a cigarette and gazing at the darkening waters, the outline of the Southern Gulf Islands black against the setting sun. "She's smoking," Lily said when she sensed Penelope's presence behind her. "She smokes when she can't cope."

"And what about you?" Penelope asked as she sat down beside Lily.

"I'm trying that mind meld thing; I want her to release the manuscript to Sellinger. And then I'm going to convince Jarod Ross to kill off Marcus. They can't continue the series, anyway, now that I'm dead. My readers might be disappointed, and it will likely hurt sales, but I won't allow Marcus to get away with this." Her eyes welled up with tears. "I had other books in me, Penelope. I still had other books."

Penelope nodded and raised an arm to rub Lily's back. "I know. But you need to move on. You leave Joe to me; I'll see to it that he gets what's coming."

Lily smiled and wiped her face. "Thanks. But what about you? I guess now that this case is solved you'll be moving on to the next."

"Actually, no."

Lily looked over, surprised.

"Seeing my mom today," Penelope explained, "seeing how frail she's become ... she hasn't been well for a while now. I've been away too long, always putting my career first. It's time to go home and keep an eye on her."

Lily wondered how Penelope could really expect to take care of her aging mother, but then decided that if anyone could do it from the grave, it was Penelope.

From the corner of her eye, Lily saw a child sitting in one of the chestnut chairs in the living room, her legs nervously kicking against the leather. "Penelope, why is Ripley here?"

"I'm taking her with me. Thought I would try my hand at motherhood. She witnessed Runa's arrest and I can't just leave her here alone. And she also needs to move on. I'm hoping to help her with that. If not, at least a change of scenery will do her good."

Might do you both some good, Lily thought but said nothing. She caught Ripley's attention, smiled wanly, then waved her fingers in a gentle goodbye.

26

LILY WAS SITTING ON A BENCH in her garden overlooking the Strait of Georgia, trying to make sense of everything that had happened, when an older gentleman approached. He looked to be in his late sixties, with thick gray hair, age spots dotting his cheeks and hands, and bushy eyebrows that cast shadows over electric green eyes. He was wearing a yellow cardigan over a beige plaid shirt, brown wool pants, and brown suede loafers. He sat down beside Lily but kept his eyes glued to the sea. "Morning, Lily," he said in a low, mysterious voice. "We have to make this quick. I think I'm being followed."

"Do I know you?" she said, looking around for anyone skulking in the bushes.

"Not personally. I was a fan of your work. Read them all until *Death's Door*. That one was published shortly after I died. Kinda ironic."

"Who are you?" she asked, thoroughly mystified.

"Pat O'Grady. Vital Records Division." He looked anxiously about then slipped a manila folder from beneath his cardigan and handed the file to Lily. "There's an opening available. I thought you might want it. Beats lurking around here for eternity."

"How long have you been 'lurking'?"

"Ages, I think. Hard to tell. Time gets kinda screwed up here."

"I noticed. And why *are* you lurking?"

"Not ready yet, I guess. I was doing real well until I died: enjoying retirement, had six great kids and fifteen grandkids. Was planning a big anniversary cruise with my wife of forty years—a real good woman, Siobhan is—when I just keeled over one morning after breakfast. Massive coronary. Siobhan and me, we both took it real hard. They let me mope around for a while before ordering me to pull up my bootstraps and get to work. Put me in Vital Records on account I spent thirty years clerking in City Hall. Guess they figured my skills were transferable."

Lily opened the folder. Looking up at her with large blue eyes was an adorable newborn, the picture attached to a dossier. Name: Gwendolyn O'Grady. Born: March 15, 2016. Parents: Mark O'Grady and Sally McManus. "Gwendolyn O'Grady, huh. Any relation?"

"Yeah, my next grandkid. It'd be an honor to have your talent in the family."

"Marcus said my talent doesn't belong to me."

"Marcus is an arrogant ass. Maybe the stories weren't *all* yours but the telling of them was. The words you chose, the structure, crackin' good dialogue, hell even some of the characters and plot points you added of your own accord. It's not so cut and dried as Marcus makes it."

Lily thought about that as she read the dossier. "It says here she grows up to be a bank clerk. Married with two children. President of the PTA. Lobbies for school sports funding." It all sounded excruciatingly dull. "Are you sure I'm cut out for this?"

"Absolutely. You'll write excellent corporate query letters."

Pat saw the furrow creeping across Lily's brow as anxiety widened her eyes, and she saw a glimmer of panic form in his own. "Look, Lily, nothing's written in stone," he said, his voice just shy of pleading. "That's just what we figure will happen. If you really can't bear it you can always do something radical, something unexpected. Change your course, as they say. But after all the excitement of this life I thought you might appreciate a little peace and quiet."

"Oh, I don't know," she sighed, not quite believing him.

"Well, think about it quick," he ordered her, looking around nervously. "I'm in big trouble if they find out about this. There was this guy once who fiddled with the waiting list—put himself at the top of it when he heard the next available birth was the son of a Texas oil baron. Man, that's just asking for bad karma, don't you think? Word on the street is that the baron lost all his dough and now the kid's in public school. God only knows what they'll do to me if I get caught. And your behavior these past few days ... well, let's just say it's raised a few eyebrows."

"Then why *are* you doing this?"

A guilty look flashed across Pat's face. "'Cause it's either you or a stripper who overdosed on crack," he confessed and began picking lint off his pants.

"I see your dilemma," Lily deadpanned. "But I still don't understand. None of this makes any sense to me."

Pat snickered. "Try thirty years in government. You get used to stuff not making sense."

Lily fell silent, thinking about the offer as Pat fiddled with the buttons on his cardigan. She wondered if Gwendolyn would have *any* adventures at all or if she, too, would just spend forty years planning for an anniversary cruise that never happens. It seemed risky.

Moments passed before Pat finally lost his patience. "Look," he said through a clenched jaw, Lily's reticence clearly annoying him, "are you gonna go for it or just wander about here for God knows how long?"

"Fine," she grumbled. "All right. I suppose I'll take it."

"No," Pat pronounced. "No 'I suppose I'll take it.' It has to be a definitive yes or there's risk of a miscarriage. I'd rather have a stripper for them than *that*."

"Okay, okay," Lily agreed, raising her hands in defeat. "Yes. Yes, I'll do it."

"Good," Pat smiled at her, taking a pen from his pocket. "The next page is a consent form. You need to sign the bottom."

"Consent form?"

"Yeah, just the usual 'we're not liable if you don't like your next life' sort of thing. Never used to have to worry before but this country's become so litigious people think they can sue even after they're dead. No one takes responsibility anymore for their own choices."

"True enough," she sighed as she signed the form.

And then Lily wasn't on the bench anymore.

About M. A. Demers

M. A. Demers is a writer, editor and self-publishing consultant with a diverse clientele as far away as Australia and Columbia. In 2011 she self-published her first novel, *Baby Jane*, followed by *The Global Indie Author: Your Guide to the World of Self-Publishing*, now in its third edition, and the concise *To Kindle in Ten Steps: The Easy Way to Format, Create and Self-Publish an eBook on Amazon's Kindle Direct Publishing*. *The Point Between* is her second novel.

Demers is also a fine art photographer. Her work can be viewed at www.mademers.com.

You can connect with the author on her website, Facebook, Twitter, Goodreads, and Wattpad.

Also by M. A. Demers

THERE'S MORE TO GOOD AND EVIL THAN MEETS THE EYE...

When human remains are found in her pre-war fixer-upper in an east
Vancouver neighbourhood, Claire Dawson's grand plans to fix the
house—and her life—take a disturbing turn. Suspicious there might exist
a relationship between the discovery and her own tragic past, Claire
insinuates herself into the investigation, unknowingly placing herself
in harm's way and Homicide's Detective Dylan Lewis in an impossible
conflict of interest. And when Dylan's grandmother, a Coast Salish
medicine woman, wades into the mystery, challenging the demon whose
earthly form is behind the murder, the three find themselves embroiled in
a high-stakes battle where lines are blurred and worlds collide—but souls
are ultimately freed.

Praise for *Baby Jane*:

"*Baby Jane* by M. A. Demers is a can't put down, page-turning mystery thriller that will have you up late at night, a little afraid to go to sleep and wishing it were tomorrow so you could pick it up and keep reading."
– T. T. Thomas, Amazon review

"*Baby Jane* ... twists expectations ... A tight marriage of police procedural and supernatural thriller ... [woven] in with a compelling First Nations magic-realistic tapestry ... exploring both the best and worst of human desires."
– Scott Fitzgerald Gray, Amazon review

"A compulsive page turner ... well-paced, the main characters are well drawn and have a range of issues that make them flawed and human, and the plot has something to separate it from the crowd. I thought it was a great read and would happily recommend it!"
– Booked Up

"Wow! That was a roller coaster of a ride. Truly, truly blew me away with the thick content of the story and the beautiful way you wrote it. I simply could not stop and devoured it over two days. I loved the ending, but in all honesty I loved everything about the book, from start to finish."
– bookaddict1133, Wattpad

"Well written and suspenseful ... a tightly written character study with elements of the supernatural woven throughout. Emotional and tense."
– Meghan, Kobo review

"Unusual in that it incorporates several genres and does so in the sure hand of an obviously experienced writer."
– Julie Curtis, Kobo review

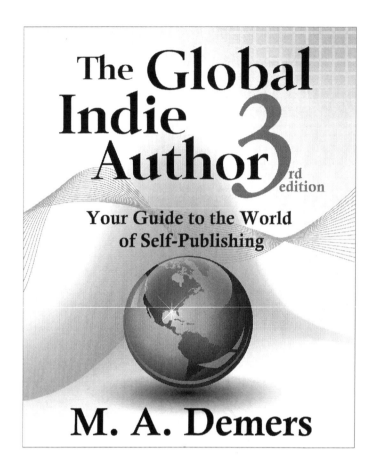

The Global
Indie
Author 3rd edition

Your Guide to the World
of Self-Publishing

M. A. Demers

Self-publishing has truly come into its own. Indie titles have captured up
to 25% of the U.S. market, and the phenomenon has expanded globally,
with success stories now found in Europe and as far away as India. But as
the business has grown so too have the potential landmines, and authors
who are best equipped to avoid the traps are those who are best informed.
The Global Indie Author, 3rd Edition is the definitive guide to this growth
industry, exposing its secrets, separating fact from fiction, and providing
clear advice for implementing a successful self-publishing project.

This edition has been completely updated to reflect developments in
ebook technology and includes illustrated step-by-step instructions for
building ePubs and Kindle books from your manuscript. Readers will also
find tips for designing a print book in a word processor, and how to deal
with quality issues with print on demand. *The Global Indie Author* covers
all aspects of self-publishing including:

* Book Structure * Manuscript Editing * Copyright and Registration * Copyright and Trademark Infringement * Libel, Obscenity, Hate Literature, Civil Liability * The ISBN System * Software * Manuscript Formatting for eBooks * HTML Editing * Cover and Interior Images * Building and Testing Kindle Books and ePubs * Print Production * Marketing * Distribution and Royalties * Payments and Withholding Tax * The Vanity Press Machine

Praise for *The Global Indie Author*:

"I have read many books about self-publishing and have to say how impressed I am with the incredible detail and research that went into putting this book together. Demers goes through virtually everything an author who wants to understand this world would need to know in order to make informed decisions. This tops my recommended list for anybody considering learning more about self-publishing in either print or ebook or both."
— Mark Lefebvre, Director, Self-Publishing and Author Relations, Kobo Writing Life

"If you are self-publishing, buy *The Global Indie Author* and read it cover to cover. It is quite possibly the best resource book available for independent authors. It combines overall strategies with step-by-step instructions and expertly guides authors through the complex maze of self-publishing both print and e-books."
— Mark Hanen, Words: *I Know What I Want To Say - I Just Don't Know How To Say It*

"*The Global Indie Author* is an excellent book for anyone who wants a comprehensive guide through the indie publishing journey, whether you are living in the U.S. or living in Denmark. What I loved best is that I know each chapter was extensively researched. I put a lot of work into finding answers on the Internet. This book saves you all that trouble. Buy this book and spend your precious time writing!"
— Kate Tremills, *Messenger* and *Queen Isabel*

Made in the USA
San Bernardino, CA
31 March 2018